THE MINISTRY
OF CULTURE

THE MINISTRY
OF CULTURE

James P. Mullaney

THOMAS DUNNE BOOKS
ST. MARTIN'S PRESS ✇ NEW YORK

This is a work of fiction. All of the characters, organizations, and events portrayed in this novel are either products of the author's imagination or are used fictitiously.

THOMAS DUNNE BOOKS.
An imprint of St. Martin's Press.

www.thomasdunnebooks.com
www.stmartins.com

ISBN-13: 978-0-312-35446-6
ISBN-10: 0-312-35446-0

First Edition: May 2007

10 9 8 7 6 5 4 3 2 1

To my parents, James and Paula,
for their undeniable love and support

THE MINISTRY OF CULTURE

She calls me around ten fifteen on the second night. I am still jet-lagged and worn-out from my excursion to the southern front earlier in the day when the telephone rings.

"Michael," she asks, "did I wake you?"

Her voice is familiar right away. It is as if I had been dreaming of her. In fact, whenever I am here, it is always like a dream—a bad one, except for Daniella. Before I can answer her she says, "Surprise, surprise. You're staying at the al-Rashid again."

"Yes," I reply calmly, "as usual."

"Are you alone?"

For the moment I am not so sure and look quickly around the room. There are elusive patterns that shift across this desert; shapes that float like sand within the wind, whispers as cool as a dry rain. "Is it possible to be alone in this place?" I think to myself. Beads of sweat line the outsides of the vents along the bottom of the walls.

"Michael," she says, "tell me you're alone."

"Yes, I'm alone."

And the familiarity of her voice is suddenly gone and I am left listening to the nervous sound of a broken line.

I open one of the complimentary bottles of wine the concierge had sent up with my dinner. The consumption of alcohol is prohibited under the Moslem faith, and many restaurants and several hotels do not offer any on their menus, but I am a foreign journalist and a Christian. I do not adhere to such policies nor am I expected to. A lavished guest, the regime believes, is apt to report positively, if not pleasantly, on their stay and in the al-Rashid a free bottle is sent with each meal ordered up to your room with the exception of breakfast. It is a South African table red and I am unable to translate the writing on the label. I am unshaven and tired and the wine seduces me like a subtle kiss. I don't feel like leaving my room. Outside these walls exists another world, a very dangerous one, and I do not have all my strength to face it again just yet.

I pour myself a second glass and then open the shades to the clear crescent sky. The sound of light gunfire plays in the distance past the outskirts of the city and lost within the bordering hills. I have heard it and much worse many times before and I am not frightened. I do not fear for Daniella either. She has told me that she has been through a lot worse.

"The early years were the worst," she'd say. "They would rape the women in front of their husbands. Then they would skin the men alive while their women stared dispossessed and violated, only to be raped and beaten again. They would leave these women behind like hollowed-out animal carcasses with only the mutilated bodies of their husbands. This is a place of barbarians."

This morning three former military policemen were executed in the town square on suspicion of spying. A large crowd of approximately twenty thousand, mostly unemployed men, watched as dark sacks were individually placed over each of the policemen's heads. One at a time, they were led to stand in front of a wooden table facing the crowd, and with a deliberate swipe of a large blade, an almost imperceptible sliver of silence borne within that small puff of motioned air, were beheaded. The separated dark sacks thumped heavily to the ground below them. With each death, the crowd roared approvingly in unison.

This, I tell myself, is not only a city of barbarians but of fault lines never to be crossed. It shakes with horror like a breeze. My way of life is as unfamiliar to these people as vanilla ice cream, and to them I am a dissident, not a journalist.

I pour the last of the wine and slowly feel my resolve weaken. I close my eyes and fall asleep like a tired child. Soon I shudder within a dream, spilling the rest of my glass on myself, and awaken to a soft knocking at my door. I look at the clock–barely an hour has passed– and now I am groggy from both sleep and the bottle of wine as I get up to answer the door and let Daniella in.

In the night her face is lost within the shadows and I kiss the bareness of light on her lips. Although we haven't seen each other for almost six months, she has brought a familiar sense of the past with her, and in this strange, torn place, it is welcome.

"Have you taken care of yourself, Dee?" I ask her.

But she is not ready for my questions yet. Her mouth is quickly on mine and I embrace her in the darkness. She reaches down to grab me and feels the wetness of the spilled wine and laughs.

"Oh no," she whispers.

Outside the room the gunfire has erupted into small explosions. The night has lifted into a state of heightened activity, the fears accompanying war much more severe in the dark. Sirens soon follow and fill the streets of this ancient place. This is the sixth night in a row. There is a shutdown and curfew in effect that comes with the wailing sirens and lasts until late morning. She will have to sneak out like a Gypsy, a reference she despises, if she decides not to stay the night.

But I am far away and safe. I am inside Daniella and am lost in the aroma of perfume off her bare neck. Its scent is like opium and triggers *a familiarity I am now playing out along the edges of her dark lips with my fingers. Bombs go off close to the city's limits and their flickering light falls like drops of rain across her body.*

It is Iraq. The year is 1984.

1

OCTOBER 5, 1984

THE SANDSTORMS COME IN pairs. Not delicately, but to those who have felt the beginnings hitting their faces and hands with small pellets fine enough to break the surface of skin, they are daunting.

At noon the sun rises to its peak high above our camp on the desert plains northwest of the ancient holy city of Najaf, bronzing everything under its steady gold rain. We are set up as close to Damascus as we are to the capital city of Baghdad in the area of the continuing Syrian Desert known as Al-Hamad, careful of the watchful and beckoning eyes from the east and not yet willing to let go of the west. When the heat is strongest, we seek cover in our tents or convene at the makeshift kitchen station drinking green tea or soda. Some members of the party even indulge in small snifters of Scotch to help pass the time when the winds outside begin to pick up and the whirls start to form intimately, like a slow, close dance.

It has been only three nights in the open desert and still it is too many. We are still far away from the southern borders lining the Shatt al Arab, the River of the Arabs, and currently home to some of the bloodiest fighting this world has known. I swelter in this heat, covered from head to toe in a thin cloth to hide myself from the harmful rays of the sun, and I am constantly worrying about the allocation of our diminishing water supply. My tongue sticks like flypaper to the roof of my mouth and I subconsciously take another mental inventory. I promised myself this would be the last assignment I would accept in this region. My profession has afforded me the opportunity to see a lot of this world, but each time I leave these parts it robs a small portion of what little faith I have left.

Mahwi, the encampment cook and mechanic, stirs the beginnings of our lunch over a large spitfire grill protected from the elements by a thin, transparent enclosure of metal netting. He slices chunks of wild boar from off the bone with a quick flick of his wrist, the knife dropping the meat into a sizzling pan, which he then sprinkles with an excess of cumin and other autumnal-colored powders. He is a small, wiry man resembling a marionette at times with his long, dangling limbs and the seemingly deliberate clumsiness of his movements. His pointy elbows move in coordination with his narrow shoulders as though fascinated by their motion. Behind the crackling of an intense orange and blue flame, his face is barely visible. His dark hand cradles a wooden spoon, stirring with a gesture of monotony a watery mixture of vegetables and stock of which I am not entirely sure of the ingredients. Nor do I wish to know.

Mahwi is a quiet man. The others, I am told, used to make fun of his high-pitched voice. The derisions grew so bad that he soon retreated within himself, and now he doesn't generally speak with anyone unless he is confronted by a government official or if he happens to be at ease, which, I am also told, is rare. His silence lends an element of mystery to the detached and distracted man, and over a short span of time those derisions have turned to suspicions. In fact, there is a pervasive suspiciousness of everything and everyone in this country, running through the land like a powerful electric current. Mahwi has worked out here on the perimeter between countries with many outlaw groups as well as several journalistic expeditions, and it can be considered a good thing, I think, that he does not talk. His eyes have witnessed too much during these years, and in his tongue he holds a potential sword.

The ruling Baath regime is permitting Western journalists entrance into certain designated areas of their country with the sole purpose of increasing international support for their cause against the "brutal and incendiary Persians." As a result, this group of foreign journalists—one American, three British, one German, one Soviet, and two French—is being permitted diplomatic entrance into the country with those very intentions implicit. The president will use us to somehow influence the Western powers to send military aid and, more importantly, to send money. The once promising economy is now ravished by war. Before the fighting, Iraq exported close to 3.3 million barrels of oil per day. Currently, the total barely reaches seven hundred thousand barrels. We will see what the president wants us to see. We will witness the lines of battered orange and white taxicabs bouncing over the hills of these ancient dirt highways as they carry home the dead and injured of battle. We will watch as women for the first time in this culture take up a visible and increasing role in public life, their delicate voices growing stronger and more independent with each day spent alone and without their husbands or fathers or sons. The boundaries of this male-dominated culture are beginning to fade as the numbers of war casualties mount. We will see the economic hardships, the steely black flames rising from the destruction of this country's great oil refineries. We will see the results only, not their causes. And we will not see the other side. Our assignments have already been outlined for us, all except this one.

Minders or official government escorts are assigned to accompany all foreigners accessing the country. Mahwi is one of three men in this camp unofficially helping us travel from Amman, Jordan, through these desolate stretches across western Iraq and over the twin rivers into Baghdad. His group has made contact with a rising political figure with whom we hope to conduct a secret interview without any knowledge of or approval from Baghdad. A formal briefing by the Ministry of Information is scheduled together with our arrival for tomorrow evening. We are to make the cannonball run the next morning at the first sign of daylight so as not to be late. The regime does not know we are out here early.

Last night Jonathon Feinrich, a German journalist that I have worked with before, and I talked with Mahwi while the rest of our group was asleep. Mahwi brewed each of us a cup of a dark, richly flavored coffee drink sweetened with the juice of dates. After grinding the beans with a ceramic mortar, he packed them into the side metal filter of a large steel pot. Then he alternately heated and cooled the liquid several times before finally serving it.

"To remove all impurities," he whispered when I asked him why he repeated the boiling process.

He politely refused when Feinrich offered him a pull from his flask.

"More for us then," Feinrich said, and split the remaining difference between our two cups.

The night was cool and still, and I drank heartily from my mug. The locals may openly reject the foreign spirits, yet I have seen them drinking their arak in secret, preferring the lesser sentence imposed on the consumption of local beer than on imported Western poison.

After a few moments, when the alcohol began to settle, I let myself relax and the three of us made simple, pleasant conversation. The sky is different in the East, filled with a darkness that almost radiates at night. The stars shine like drops of glimmering ice illuminating the landscape against a backdrop of black velvet. Although the night seems to provide cover from the eyes of the Mukhabarat and from Baghdad, when one sense weakens, another sense compensates and increases in sensitivity. We talked between us in low whispers.

Momentarily removed from his daily concerns, Mahwi suddenly became friendly. He asked us questions about our individual countries and what he had been taught about the West. As he spoke, I was amazed at how good his English was, and when he was done, I asked him where he had learned to speak so fluently.

"We are taught the language at an early age in our schooling. To be able to speak the dialect of the evil empire will help us to destroy it," he recited prophetically.

Now I watch him as he prepares the food and his slender fingers sprinkle a sharp, orange powder over the pot as the stirrings of the second storm begin. Outside, the threatening sound of twin helicopters speeding toward us causes a panic, and for a split second I fear the local rebels will turn on us. I watch Mahwi lower the flame and then immediately shoulder an AK-47. But with the propelling uproar come only the winds and the sand shaking our tents. The canvas walls shudder around us as if we are about to be swept away by a series of high-cresting waves. Around the perimeter, the binocular posts are knocked to the ground and their ocular lenses shatter, and then they are swept by invisible forces out of sight. Mahwi puts down his weapon and maneuvers the donkeys and camels underneath a tarp canopy where he ties them up behind a group of large rocks to provide shelter from the force of the wind and the moving wall of sediment. The rest of us begin the race to secure everything else in the camp. Food and clothing containers are sealed; windows and doors are zippered and then taped shut. Even our eye-wear is worn with hoods drawn tight around our tanned and goggled faces. Grains of sand manifest everywhere, and the less of this place you have to take with you the better.

Only Sabawi, our radio dispatcher, remains unmoved and seated under a thick burlap cover in the mess tent. Shots of red lights flip across the box he cradles in his lap, and he persistently ignores our pleas to pack up the communication equipment. Years earlier the president was surrounded in the small village of al-Dujayl by a group of villagers who held him and his party hostage for almost two hours until the Republican Army finally came to his rescue. Such embarrassment does not bode well for anyone, and the natives' fear in our camp is evident in the way they talk and in the way they watch. Not even the sandstorms can be trusted. Sabawi forgoes the safety of the radio equipment for his own safety, and he remains fixated on the flashings.

Al-Hakim is making hard-nosed recorded proclamations over the transmitter calling for historical change and pressing for a united Iraqi Front. He is not as radical or as anti-West as one would expect, and as a result he is a rising political figure in the international presses. These kinds of power plays are an ordinary way of life, and it is that way of life that al-Hakim is mainly disputing. He is a young and intelligent man, schooled in London, and he is seeking the influence of democracy to help unite his country. But he is also considered an infidel, and if the government knew we were camped out here, directed with the help of its own citizens, to interview him, we would surely be captured, and al-Hakim, upon his arrival, would be taken and executed.

But al-Hakim has not yet arrived, expected two days ago with his small contingent of militia supposedly traveling east from Syria. With the coming of the sandstorms our only hope is that he is not even close to our camp or even in the triangle region west of the rivers. Men and their caravans have been known to drown out here in these storms, submerged under the tides as if lost in an hourglass. Our hope is that he has taken the foreign press's request lightly and silently changed his mind.

We are usually unable to listen to our own radios during these storms. Every piece of equipment must be packed, and all we can do is cover up within ourselves and let the fury of the land pass. During these suspended moments we don't know what is going on in the world around us. But this time, the words Sabawi hears from the radio have kept him stoically in his place.

"It is not good," Sabawi proclaims, although I can barely hear him and let the comment pass with the winds that have only grown stronger outside. Only when he yells, "Al-Hakim is dead," does the solitude of the desert break and its pieces fall within our mouths as I spit phlegmy grains of sand into a tin cup and wonder who will be next to follow in his footsteps.

2

OCTOBER 6, 1984

WE TRAVERSE THE AL ANBAR district toward Baghdad in under ten hours, a triumvirate of white Chevrolets bouncing over the long dirt roads that emerge out of the distance like a mirage. It seems like days since I have seen any natural colors. The weathered landscape offers no appeal in its worn-out stretches of parched earth and desolation, and in a way I am looking forward to our arrival in Baghdad. Out here there is a sense of irony to what the desert can do to the beauty of a sunrise. The area known as Mesopotamia is ancient and it looks it.

Mahwi inspected our cars one last time before we left, showing mild concern for our safety. He checked the temperature and water gauges and then he examined underneath the hoods, measuring out the proper oil levels and generously filling our reserves. He even pulled back the rug from inside one of the trunks and inspected the pressure of the spare tires. Once he was satisfied, he distributed a plastic container of food expected to sustain each of us for the half-day journey. Water, as I have noticed, is another story.

"We part ways and must forget our reasons for meeting," Mahwi said to me. "May Allah be with you."

His serious tone reminds me that despite the conversation we had the other night and the adolescent curiosity he exhibited when we talked of music and Western movies, he is still a native. It is our caravan that is leaving this camp behind. Mahwi will silently continue to do what he needs to survive, the end of our engagement another swathe to wipe down the sword. I can only pray for his silence.

We set off at the first sign of light, the sun growing in intolerable increments across the rolling, parched lands receding and rising within itself like smooth, white waves in the distance. As we hit the first minor bend in the road, the remnants of the camp vanish out of sight, and with them all signs of life are gone. We are all aware now that Mahwi, Sabawi, and Anil would turn us in if pressed to do so by the authorities. They would tell the police how we have come into the country illegally from Syria, and they would shake their heads and hands, not wanting to describe the terrible things we had said or planned to do. In minutes we have gone from semi-friendly journalists to enemies or infidels, and our driver presses his foot down on the gas until the needle breaks forty and we coast along like a sole ship on a barren sea.

This cannonball run, as it is called, is to be made only during the day. Cars and pickup trucks sporadically line dust clouds in the distance, blazing their own paths with a sense of lawlessness that hovers above the ground like a vulture circling over the sick. Although we are attempting to keep our tracks quiet and hidden from the border patrols and from the Republican Guard, once the sun drops, the dangers will only increase. With the darkness of night, these frigid hills and roadways quickly fill up with armed bandits: army deserters, vagrants, and outlaws who hide their faces in the hollowed-out spaces of the rocks and off to the sides of the Amman road well out of sight. Others are more brazen, blocking the roadways well in advance with their beaten-down German- and French-made vehicles, their guns already drawn in the distance. If you are unfortunate enough to see a blockage ahead, chances are one is also forming behind you, closing you in. Across these same stretches several weeks ago a Jordanian diplomat sped along in a small caravan of black Mercedes-Benzes, making the mistake of assuming safer travel under the night sky. This story never made it to the press, and the bodies and automobiles of the entourage were never found. And as night begins to fall, so does the temperature. At times in the Syrian Desert, I am unable to sleep due to the cold and shiver within my blankets, trying to recall the cruel heat that was so unbearable only hours earlier.

Our guide points out the few historical remains we pass, careful not to make any markings on our maps for to do so is a crime. Half-collapsed ziggurats rise forth in the distance, their stepped walls at one time rising proudly out of the ground, now shrinking back from the heavens. We pass small mosques and burial grounds, large empty stretches distinguishable only by makeshift headstones and plot markers that have not yet been stolen or destroyed. As we get closer to the city, cement picnic tables covered by fiberglass umbrellas are set up as rest stops. They are all empty. A resurgence of greens finally appears as we approach and then pass through the city of Ramadi on the banks of the Euphrates. Lush fields thick with vegetation and rectangular patches of small trees and produce are being irrigated by the river. There are networks of canals receiving water from the Tigris outlined in perfect squares as we pass a small caviar plant, its large industrial pumps pushing fish eggs out into the cool pools to be fertilized.

"A curious crop to be producing in this country," I say, although I understand it is a recent attempt by the government to compete with the Iranian caviar exports.

And then I can see the tops of buildings poking through the cover of palm leaves and we enter the capital. To see Baghdad now is to see two cities, one the once grandiose masterpiece that flourished under the rule of the Abbasids: the Madinat as-Salam, or City of Peace, once the richest and most beautiful city in the world. Now the capital is a burnt-out, decaying slum of poverty and bitterness struggling to hold on to the hem of its once beautiful memory: an elderly woman struggling to remember the good old days while living in a present she refuses to see.

We cross a low stone bridge over the Tigris and pass over the long, lazy barges sliding fruits and vegetables and other European goods along the river below us. Palm groves cover the outskirts in a shroud of secrecy with only the occasional minaret or gilded mosque dome poking through the leaves. We have arrived quite inauspiciously, and I am surprised as our caravan passes rather leisurely through twin government sentry posts. Later I am told our passing was made smoother by a payment of $150 per passenger.

Our international press cards rule like the queen of spades in a game of hearts, only trumped by cash. But as we reach the main terminal posts of the city, heavily armed soldiers of the Republican Guard are stopping every car, and they order us to pull off to the side of the road. The elite army, founded first as bodyguards to President Hussein, is the heart of the Iraqi military and is currently being trained by the Soviets. No bribe is offered. Two olive-skinned men dressed in white uniforms striped with gold regalia and draped with a red sash question the driver, suspicious of our route into Baghdad. I understand only a small amount of Arabic, but by their expressions and hand gestures they seem to be asking why we have arrived from the west and not from the direction of either airport within the city's vicinity. But their suspicions are momentarily pushed aside when a small revolt in the eastern district of Rusafa breaks out and over their radios the soldiers are immediately ordered to the area. As a result of recent circumstances, the military has been spread so thin it is sometimes transparent.

We are ushered into the large stone building housing the Ministry of Information, where we show the attendant our press cards again, and after careful inspection the mood seems to lighten a bit.

"You have been to Iraq before?" the short, heavyset man asks us. His face is topped with thick, bushy eyebrows and he wears the drab green attire of the regular army.

"It is nice to see you again," he says to each of us individually as we pass, shaking our hands as if he were an old friend. But if I have ever met him before, I do not remember. Below his brow, a glass eye floats distractingly behind his glasses. It is a faint blue, the color of a sparrow, and stands in contrast with his other dark features. On his wrist he wears a large gold watch with the president's smiling profile adorning the gold-plated face.

"How are things in London?" he asks the British journalists in front of me, shaking their hands again and presenting each of them with a small folder containing passes to restaurants and clubs, a listing of closed VIP parties, and also their hotel room keys.

An elegantly dressed boy in black, knee-high pants and a crisp, white shirt buttoned up to the collar and covered by a green-and-gold vest offers us tulip-shaped cups of a warm, spicy tea. Caviar and French crackers, dates and olives are then brought around and we eat heartily, the appetizers a welcome change to the meals of Mahwi's limited resources.

When I receive my folder, I am not surprised to see the president's face on the cover. In fact, he is everywhere.

It has been several years since I have been in Baghdad, and the Ministry of Information building has been built during the interim. The marble floors are exquisite as is the frieze artwork decorating the tiled walls. Gold-lace trails emanate from every corner, and a magnificent portrait of the president covers the entire wall behind the lobby desks. The customs agents check our bags thoroughly, while our host, a high-ranking officer, reminds us of the strict regulations and laws of the country, which at times may seem brutal, but–he adds–we must remember that this is a time of war.

"We all do for the republic what is necessary for its survival," he proclaims.

After our bags have been checked and all questionable items claimed or confiscated, we are told to enjoy our stay in Iraq. We are then introduced to our first minder, Barzani al-Bakr, whom we follow outside to a white BMW, its interior laced in white curtains and green-bobbed trim.

There has been a small explosion of culture and art in this city since I was last here. Multilevel scaffolding and construction sites line Mansur and Tammuz streets leading up to our hotel. New buildings and shops have replaced the old, although many of the projects appear to be only half-finished. We pass the Abbasid Palace and al-Khadhimain Mosque, its gold-capped dome restored by the administration in an attempt to bind the current with the past. New mosques have been built for both the Shia and Sunni Muslim sects. A state-of-the-art hospital and a handful of modern schools have been built by the government as well. An influx of Western commercialism is also evident as we drive past a stretch of retail stores including a Gap, a Banana Republic, and even a McDonald's. The thoroughfare is immaculate and the storefronts have all been swept clean. But this is a small cross section of Baghdad. If you were to walk over only two streets, you would see lines of garbage piled waist high and houses without electricity or even basic plumbing. Outside the car, I can hear the rumblings of the loudspeaker as it calls the majority of citizens to daily prayer, and I am reminded that I am in Baghdad and not Boston or London.

We arrive at the al-Rashid and the hotel is overcrowded with foreign relations diplomats, United Nations ambassadors, and foreign businessmen. Although I am enlightened by the cultural revolution that seems to have taken place, I can not help but wonder if it, like the excesses of graciousness of our host, is only a mirage; or a front.

In the hotel lobby vendors sell everything from jewelry and small swatches of rugs and silk to cigarettes and handheld transistor radios. It has already been a long day and I could use a drink. Although I have already been given my key, I must still wait in line to check into my room, and as I do, I try to remember back to my first time in Baghdad and the changes it has undergone since. But my thoughts soon turn to Daniella and her eyes as blue as the Caspian Sea.

3

FEBRUARY 14, 1984

IBRAHIM GALEB AL-MANSUR IS enthralled. Past his feet at the edge of the bed, his fiancée, Shalira, dances seductively in the pale moonlit shadows. Her face veil and abaya, the customary black robe worn by Muslim women, are both removed, revealing shoulder-length hair as black as Indian cypress ink and falling in radiant curls across her bare golden skin. Her fingers move smoothly through its dark recesses, and Ibrahim can smell the pleasant aroma of gardenias filling the tiny space of his apartment.

Unhindered, her coquettish smiles have taken Ibrahim by surprise. The only such flirtations he has ever seen from a woman were those performed by the Indian or American actresses he watched on the big screen at the Sinbad Theatre or the one time he was invited to the exclusive Hunt Club in downtown Baghdad. Originally, he felt such displays were vulgar, but as he watches Shalira, he finds no indecency—just desire and what he believes to be love. Nothing is contrived about her or her world and within her honesty Ibrahim finds an abundance of beauty.

With each article of clothing she removes, Shalira seems to be loosening centuries of inhibitions as well. She was glad to get rid of the veil–it irritated her skin as well as her constitution. "If my parents could only see me now," she whispers to Ibrahim. According to Shalira's descriptions, he was surprised they ever approved of her going away to school in Paris.

While abroad as a student she had kissed the same European boy on several occasions, even going so far as to let him run his hands up underneath her shirt. But she politely refused his advances to go any further, and the relationship abruptly ended after a night spent tussling when he was too quick with his tongue and had called her a prude. Shalira felt he was disrespectful and refused to see him again. Eventually she went out on several other meaningless dates while in Paris. She even went further than her previous limits with an Italian boy she had gone out with only once but whose dark complexion stirred something deep inside her. When had she gotten so assertive? It was a question that often disarmed Ibrahim. Surely she wasn't taught such things from her mother, a woman whose only displays of passion consisted of slapping her only child when she misspoke or sulking in the corners of her orange patch while she patiently waited for her husband to come home after one of his frequent absences. And it wasn't learned in Europe, though granted there were more freedoms and opportunities for experimentation, especially for women. It wasn't something new so much as it felt unleashed. It was deeper and truer; something, Shalira confided in him, she had been born with. Since she was so comfortable with the soft-spoken and respectful Ibrahim, she felt able to explore these other parts of herself. And it was a welcome relief.

"You are my welcome relief," she would tease him.

Through the thin mud-cake walls of his apartment echo the sounds of another world–Ibrahim's neighbors fighting. Jaffar Kamza, obviously drunk again, is yelling and cursing incoherently at his wife. Ibrahim can hear the shuffling of wooden chairs across the bare floor. For a moment, he fights the urge to go next door to calm things down, but Shalira turns the volume of the handheld radio up, and the waltzing cadence of a slow ballroom number does its best to drown out the Kamzas.

Then she reveals herself to him for the first time. As she steps into the candlelight, Ibrahim is speechless at her beauty. Her shadow performs elegant dances on the walls around him. He is amazed at her creativity and openness, never realizing there was so much more to this person beyond her refined physical beauty and her stifled intelligence and curiosity. In fact, it was her pensive nature that had matched Ibrahim's almost perfectly and initially drew them together.

They had met for the first time one afternoon in the Baghdad Museum, each of them studying the paintings of Ibn-Haradi, an Iraqi artist. Shalira looked the part of a middle-class student with her backpack strung low across her shoulder and with her deep, energetic eyes. She had just recently come back to Iraq after graduating from the University of Paris the previous spring. Ibrahim was slightly unkempt, no vanity in his appearance, nor was he expecting to meet anyone at the museum. Shalira would later recall that her first impression of him was that he was too thin. Ibrahim joked she had spent too much time analyzing each picture. They both had come to the museum alone, Shalira just two days back in Al-Kazmiya, and Ibrahim the bohemian son of the museum's curator, Hassan Jaffa Galeb. Ibrahim frequented the museum so often he knew the entire staff, often dining with his father and one of his colleagues after his mother's passing, and occasionally getting caught up in conversations with the security guards. He was also familiar with many of the usual patrons and university professors conducting research. But he had never seen her before, and unexpectedly he asked her a question.

"The beauty is in the complexity of the colors. Such non-homogenous mixtures that he makes work so well," Ibrahim proclaimed, trying to impress her with his knowledge of style without taking his eyes off the work. "Don't you think so?"

It was the first time she had been asked for her opinion since coming home, and the gesture caught her off guard.

"*The Artist's Garden at Giverny* by Monet is my favorite," she responded, mouthing the words under the black canvas of her abaya. "Some colors are supposed to go together. There is beauty in what is intended."

And then she moved abruptly past him, leaving Ibrahim stunned at her knowledge and answer as she walked over to the next exhibit hiding a smile.

In the following months they would sit for hours under the date trees in his father's backyard while the sun lowered below a clear lilac sky. They talked about Massei bin Massei and the works of Petran al Hosseini. To Shalira, Ibrahim pointed out the beauty in their homeland, in the large historical stretches of broken land and in the illuminated night sky buzzing with life. They debated the logic of Eastern philosophers and the policies of Europe and America toward their own country. Shalira opened doors to the West that Ibrahim soon regretted not finding for himself, and Ibrahim became everything Shalira was forced to restrain upon coming home. In the shade of dusk, they would hold hands when they were sure no one was looking.

Earlier in the evening Ibrahim had entertained the thought of going to his studio instead. But after thinking practically, he realized they would be safer in the outskirts of the city. The Karkh district was flooded with police and military personnel since the shooting of three students outside Baghdad University. They simply wanted to forget, for the night, that they lived in a country at war.

Their evening had started at the Babeesh Grill on Arasat al-Hindiyyah Street. Ibrahim nervously ordered the braised lamb while Shalira pointed out the shrimp salad on her menu. The two of them sat amongst the wealthy businessmen and politicians of Baghdad, a state-sponsored artist and his Western-educated girlfriend, like two misplaced locket pieces. Several times during dinner Ibrahim caught the wandering eyes of oil executives and foreign-policy makers fall upon Shalira, and he instantly felt proud and then slightly angered. But he would not let anything spoil his mood tonight.

Jazeri, a high-ranking official in the Ministry of Culture, had made the reservation for him. It took Ibrahim ten days to paint a chorus of detailed frieze-work around the living room and hallways in Jazeri's house, and the deputy minister was more than happy to offer his influence in return. Without knowing the correct people, the only contact one would make with the Babeesh Grill was limited to staring into its large green-tinted windows from outside on the street, the glass thoroughly fogged over from the streams of cold air blown from air conditioners as large as Ibrahim's studio.

Ibrahim hardly ate, he was so nervous. He pushed the greens and olives of his salad back and forth, unable to concentrate. Shalira asked him if he was sick. He responded by saying he didn't feel well and felt as if he might be coming down with something. When she leaned across the table and put her palm to his forehead, he delicately grabbed her hand to stop her, fearful for the both of them at being touched by a woman in a public place, but also to caress the skin of her slender hand. He knew he loved Shalira and Ibrahim wanted to surprise her and make the night perfect for her. He hoped she would say yes when later he dropped to one knee in the brief alleyway next to the entrance to the Zawra Zoo.

"Be my wife?" he asked, beaming up at her, the shape of her eyes exquisite, like large diamonds, as they reflected the light of the stars overhead.

She had been so nervous herself that she couldn't help but let out a stifled giggle when he asked her. Ibrahim knew she was self-conscious that he, as an artist, could find a depth of physical beauty in things other than herself. She feared losing her charms in old age. He took inspiration from so many different directions Shalira could only wonder what would happen if one day she failed in her attempts to inspire him. Then when she noticed Ibrahim get discouraged, she reached for his wrists and pulled him up toward her.

"I would be honored," she said, and although she hadn't cried since her mother passed, tears laden with joy fell as Ibrahim slipped the ring cautiously onto her finger.

They both stared at its luster, and after a moment Shalira took the ring off and put it in the pocket of her jacket. She would never know that Ibrahim had spent the previous two weeks franticly running about the library trying to research how a European man is supposed to properly propose to a woman. Shalira unexpectedly pulled her scarf from her face, and they kissed quickly. Before she wrapped the chador back around her head, Ibrahim noticed that her cheeks had blossomed like garden roses beneath the silk covering.

But when they first got back to his apartment, Shalira quickly ran into the bathroom, and Ibrahim feared that all the excitement might have made *her* nauseous. When she emerged shortly thereafter, the makeup she had applied illuminated her face.

"My God, you are beautiful," Ibrahim exclaimed.

Now, she leans over the edge of the bed toward Ibrahim, the small protuberance of her bosom lightly brushing against his feet. Then in rhythm with the music on the handheld radio, she stands straight back, gyrating her hips slowly until Ibrahim feels a desire that momentarily robs him of breath. Her lips glisten a dark, unnatural red as though aflame, and she lightly runs her tongue over them for moisture. He has never seen a more desirous gesture. She turns slowly on her heels, quite graceful in the limited space.

As she arches her back, Ibrahim extends his hands and touches the edges of her bare hips. It has slipped his mind, the world outside the shuttered doors and windows of his apartment. On the radio, the ballroom dance has shifted in tempo. Mrs. Kamza begins to sob loudly to herself in the room next door while the troubled breathing of Mr. Kamza turns to contemplative snoring. To Ibrahim, it is a familiar scene. But for now he does not hear it, refusing to bring any outside distractions into this night. And besides, his attention has been captured.

Back in his apartment Shalira sways in the candlelit shadows. The flickering light catches off the small diamond she has placed back on her finger, and when she turns toward him, Ibrahim can't help but feel that her gaze is electric.

"I am the wife of Ibrahim Galeb," she teases, and stretches a green sari high above her head, completely exposing a darkened birthmark under her arm that he knows her to be self-conscious of. She twists the sari within her hands and playfully shies away from the bed, leaning her small body back against the golden-framed mirror on the far wall. Ibrahim stares at her reflection, at her skin the color of honey, and then at her live image moving in front of him.

"If only two of you," he wishes, "I should be so lucky."

Suddenly there is a scuffle of footsteps and the barking of orders outside the doorway. Through the walls, Mr. Kamza's snoring has stopped and the heavy butcher again begins to yell and swear incoherently, but this time without the same condescending tone usually reserved for his wife. There is the explosive sound of wood splitting open, and then a group of uniformed men quickly jump into Ibrahim's room through the broken door.

Three of the soldiers immediately rush over and grab Shalira's arms, and when Ibrahim rises to protect her, he is hit with the handle of a Russian Kalashnikov and knocked unconscious.

Later, he will wake up in Al-Wia, a semi-private hospital in uptown Baghdad. His nose has been reset while he was asleep, but he can still taste the blood dripping in the back of his throat. A short, stocky man with a deep tan and the thick, common eyebrows of the Iraqi male is staring at him the moment Ibrahim opens his eyes. He is dressed in a dark blue Pierre Cardin suit with gold rings on most of his fingers, and Ibrahim can only guess why the man has been watching him; or for how long.

"The Republican Army has made a mistake," the man says, and pulls an envelope out of his suit containing an official note for $10,000 and drops it on the hospital bed.

"I hope this will not interfere with your commission," he asks Ibrahim rather persuasively, though he is not expecting an answer. "We must learn to forget the mistakes of others."

The man nods without affection and steps away from the bed. Ibrahim listens to his shoes squeaking against the tiled floor as the man leaves the room and takes off down the outer hallway.

But Ibrahim will not be able to forget the faces of the soldiers. How the first intimate setting between Shalira and himself played out to the culmination of the five men. The split second when they burst into the room and witnessed Shalira revealing herself and the face of the soldier who hit him glaring at her midriff, a lasciviousness that will haunt Ibrahim in his dreams. He does not know what happened after he was knocked unconscious; Shalira will maintain her silence. But he has the mind of an artist. He can only imagine.

4

MARCH 27, 1984

THE TOWN BELL HOLLOWLY sounds out over the open markets and residential courtyards, piercing the mundane disposition of business life in the office towers and flowing like a reverential wind through the closed alleyways of the slums while rustling the leaves of the orange groves. High noon crests above the mullah, his worn and sour expression unchanging with the repetition of his faith, as the holy man momentarily halts the secular needs of life and calls all followers to their daily prayer.

Hassan Jaffa, Ibrahim's father, is home again; on leave from work for the entire week while recovering from a leg wound. Days earlier on Haifa Street a beaten-down Volkswagen sped uncontrollably through rush-hour traffic. When its driver swerved to avoid a mule-driven carriage slowly inching its way from the curb, the car hopped up onto the crowded sidewalk, sending a refreshment booth and fruit stand flying into the air and numerous men scattering before hitting Ibrahim's father and cracking the lower portion of his leg.

As the head curator of the Baghdad Museum, Hassan Jaffa

was used to being on his feet all day. He trusted the security guards and the cameras posted in alternating corners throughout the main floors. But it was the storage facilities down below that worried him. The items on display were just that, on display, and more eyes were fixated on the public exhibits so that to Hassan Jaffa they were safer being out in the open. It was the corridors of the underground storage facilities that he paced nervously throughout the workday. It was in those hallways and rooms, buzzing with the opposing motors of humidifiers and dehumidifiers, where the museum housed the fragile wooden planks that once supported the Ark of Noah and a pair of Florentine paintings stolen by Hitler's men during World War II. Instead, as a result of the accident, Hassan Jaffa clumsily paces about his house talking to his plants, rearranging pictures, and feeling generally unimportant.

Large crates were arriving in the museum daily from Vienna, copies of eighteenth-century Austrian sculptures and paintings scheduled for the next showing in three weeks. Due to his absence, Hassan Jaffa felt obliged to call the museum several times a day. Afterward, when his staff was finally able to get him off the telephone, he would methodically catalog the shipments received onto a series of ordered index cards. He restudied a Viennese textbook translated into English that he had ordered from the library, stopping intermittently between chapters to jot down notes on the numerous legal pads he kept scattered about the house.

Besides the upcoming exhibit, Yusuf kept calling on him, and his presence was beginning to make Hassan Jaffa nervous. Yusuf was creating quite a name for himself, and Hassan Jaffa didn't want him to come around anymore. It didn't matter that Ibrahim was married to Yusuf's daughter, the foolish old man should have known better–for all their safety. The opinions and positions he took with such a boisterous condescendence toward anything to the contrary were extremely dangerous, the arc of their severity touching those even mildly associated with the old shopkeeper. But that is not what bothered Hassan Jaffa most. It was the fact that Yusuf had been right when he had sensed disenchantment in Hassan Jaffa.

"That is how it begins, old man," Yusuf told him, and Hassan Jaffa was quick to anger because Yusuf had close to fifteen years on him.

And it was this recognition into his own stolid nature, something he had worked his entire life to suppress and keep hidden from others, that Yusuf saw easily betrayed, and for that he was jealous of the man and also ashamed of himself. Hassan Jaffa declined when Yusuf offered his services to help him rehabilitate his leg or do some of his shopping. He noted that the presence of the other visitors in the hospital had made Yusuf nervous, and now that he was home alone he didn't want to give him any reasons to visit.

Hassan Jaffa frantically searches the courtyard in back of the house, hobbling unsteadily over the cracked cement while trying to steady his crutches on level ground. He had already yelled throughout the house twice and searched each room but still couldn't find his son. The effort had taken most of his energy. Lately Hassan Jaffa was quick to grow impatient, especially with Ibrahim. To Hassan Jaffa the matters of the republic were of a serious nature and also not without serious consequences. He acted the part himself to perfection. Yusuf had picked up on it and used that angle to open him, like driving a wedge behind a hard-to-open door. His son, he feared, took these concerns rather nonchalantly, and Hassan Jaffa wasn't sure what kind of life that would leave for Ibrahim.

"It is not good to be naïve here, Ibrahim," he often warned him. "There is just reward for everything. Good and bad."

Ibrahim would halfheartedly listen to the same speech over

and over again, each time rolling his eyes toward his father, and before the old man was finished Ibrahim would hop out the front door and head off into town to the heart of Tahrir Square. But after he mysteriously broke his nose, Hassan Jaffa began to see even less of his son. He was encouraged when Ibrahim asked him if he could use the courtyard this morning. Yet he still noticed a growing reservation, however slight, in his son's manner.

Hassan Jaffa adjusts his weight deliberately. Rows of calloused skin were beginning to harden across his palms, and he had taken to folding small cloth towels over the crutch handles to ease the sensation. Overhead, several small groups of Mi-24 helicopter gunships fly past and head toward the war front in the south.

"Ibrahim," Hassan Jaffa calls out, but there is no resonance in the spare yard, "it is time for prayer."

Across a thin patch of parched road beyond the far wall of the courtyard Ibrahim sits upon a folded chair like a king on a makeshift throne surrounded by the spilt colors of gardens and sunsets, the indigo of deep oceans and the dark stains of blood. His back is to his father and with the faintest of brushstrokes he quickly adds the flying gunships to his scene of the gold-domed top of the Al-Khadhimain Mosque. The contrast of the helicopters heading toward Basra, the faint military decorations on their sides, caught in the same frame as the reverent and historical mosque is both magnificent and unsettling to Hassan Jaffa.

"It is time to pray, Son," he calls out again to Ibrahim.

But Ibrahim can't hear him nor can he hear any other sounds happening outside the boundaries of his concentration. To him there is nothing to answer to, and soon Hassan Jaffa becomes mesmerized as he watches his son's deliberate fingers capture a world that is more vibrant and alive than the one it is modeled after. Steel-gray lines escape from behind his pressed fingers hugging tightly the rising orange of flames, and when he is done, Ibrahim slowly gets up and stretches, his bare feet falling over the small rainbow-colored puddles.

Hassan Jaffa limps over to shake his son back to reality and back to a faith he himself would be lost without, forgetting for a brief moment his handicap. But he stumbles under his own weight and one of the crutches remains planted in between a cracked step. He falls forward over his bad leg and drops to the ground like a sack of farmer's grain. From the ground he watches as Ibrahim strides backward to the middle of the courtyard, a bit closer to Hassan Jaffa, and kneels in the dirt toward the ancient city of Mecca, slowly removing his hat from his head and lowering his eyes to the ground. The bell rings hollow one last time, and Hassan Jaffa lets out a small sigh of relief when Ibrahim begins to silently move his lips in repetition.

The pain in his leg burns through the limb like an electric filament and Hassan Jaffa forcefully rubs the muscle until it grows numb. It is the first time he can remember not feeling the need for prayer nor the anxiety associated with it, instead his faith replaced by the simple love of a father for his son. He understood Ibrahim held the rare distinction of knowing what he wanted to do with his life, a trait Hassan Jaffa knew he had not passed on from his lines. Even as a young boy, Ibrahim entertained no uncertainties. It made Hassan Jaffa proud that his son could hold more conviction than he ever imagined for himself. And the fact that he could state it so clearly—well, he truly is his mother's son, Hassan Jaffa thought proudly to himself. He massages the muscle below his knee more gently, and from this vantage point upon the ground he looks up toward Ibrahim and is impressed with his stature against the open desert sky.

5

NOVEMBER 16, 1972–EVEN A CHILD CAN SET EXPECTATIONS FOR HIMSELF . . .

THE SUN HINTED BEHIND the Zagros Mountains when Ibrahim suddenly awoke to the sound of running car engines. An early-morning mist clung in eternal hope to the tops of the palm fronds and grove leaves, and the animals were still and quiet. A long line of white Toyota pickup trucks arrived from the distance and mysteriously bounded their way into the tiny village of al-Diwaniya under first light, kicking up tawny dust clouds from off the eastern road. Although he was only a young boy at the time, Ibrahim felt a sense of apprehension as he watched the serious faces of the men riding in the trucks as they passed in succession underneath his window.

To Ibrahim, their town underwent a transformation as the trucks circled several times around the village's main square and then parked in columns aligning next to the rice fields. As the men got out of their vehicles, the slamming of the car doors broke the tranquility of the peaceful sunrise. Ibrahim didn't understand the importance of such official matters at the time. But he recognized a change taking place from the shift in his father's behavior when two officers called him by his full name from outside their front door.

"Hassan Jaffa Galeb al-Mansur," the taller one read off his checklist, and Ibrahim noticed a slight tremble take over his father's hand as he reached to open the door.

For the next two hours, Ibrahim watched as the sun fully ascended and the soldiers thoroughly investigated the level plains of their village. The squadrons began out past the angular cornfields, canvassing along the perimeter in a large circle that completely enclosed the village. They continued inward using a succession of smaller, decreasing circles, covering every square foot of land until they were satisfied and eventually met at the town's center, a disused well pump surrounded by patches of beetroot.

The men swept up dirt piles and pulled apart branches and leaves from the poplar and palm trees. They searched garbage bins and the flower beds, crushing delicate blossoms underneath their heavy black boots. They examined laundry hanging innocently from tied wash lines. They left hollow footprints in the muddy silt of the rice paddies, and some of the men picked dates off the trees, holding them to their nostrils before chewing them of their juices. What they were looking for Ibrahim had no idea, but from the fervency of their activity he knew it must have been important.

"They are not looking for anything in particular," his father commented. He stood in restrained defiance beside Ibrahim on the front steps. "They think we cannot be trusted."

"Why?" Ibrahim had asked, and Hassan Jaffa couldn't offer an answer in words. It was that rare thing that had to be lived in order to be understood.

Ibrahim watched as a tan, fair-haired man dressed neatly in the official dark olive slacks of the presidential guard entered the barn. Ibrahim had never seen such pale blue eyes, and the complement of the man's hair, the color of sandstone, was also foreign to him. He was used to the sun-darkened skin and swarthy features of the men in his village. Ibrahim followed the man and watched as he unbuttoned the cuffs of his shirt and rolled his sleeves up over his forearms. Then the man buried his bare hands in the animal feed bags and groped about the mealy grains. The soldier searched all five of the bags hanging by the entrances to the stalls the same way. When he was finished, a thin film of grain stained his forearms all the way up to his elbows. During his examination, several mules had tentatively made their way over, curious of the activity taking place at the spot where they took their food. An auburn-coated mule lowered its head and began to lick the residue off the man's skin. Ibrahim noticed the man smile, the glint of steel from off his shouldered rifle reflecting in his cool blue eyes. Then the soldier extended the other arm and with his free hand stroked the animal gently across the top of its head.

The rest of the town woke up rather quickly and in muted conversations. Firas Bawi and his wife, Souham, silently brought out a tray of tea and porcelain cups for the men, placing it at the foot of the soldier who had read their names from off the list. One by one the rest of Ibrahim's neighbors pulled back their shades to stare at the men in their streets and anxiously awaited their own calling.

"What is going on?" several people cried, but upon seeing the soldiers conducting their surveillance they fell silent with fear and even grew distant with one another, a neighborly suspicion extending like smoke from one house to the next.

Two at a time, the men walked up to each house and were admitted without question or hesitation. No one offered any resistance except Abhad al-Sharistani, the town schoolmaster and Ibrahim's neighbor across the cart pathway. He opened his door yelling and cursing such words as Ibrahim had never heard. Only after the soldiers had entered his house was he abruptly quieted.

Al-Sharistani was Ibrahim's favorite, always telling him colorful stories of his journeys abroad and describing the landscapes and grandiose metropolises of Paris, Cairo, and London. He often brought Ibrahim back books of experimental and abstract art the Baghdad Museum was not authorized to carry. It would be years later when Ibrahim finally wondered how these items ever passed through customs. Hassan Jaffa and al-Sharistani were close too. The museum curator opened his door at any time to the colorful al-Sharistani and they had quickly become friends. Persistent rumors claimed al-Sharistani possessed the aristocratic blood of the wealthy landowners whose property had been lost to the ruling Baath Party. It was also rumored that the same man who played his *atarak* and sang tales of mice and of trains with the children during the last light of summer was Persian.

As Ibrahim and his father opened their door to two well-built soldiers, Ibrahim saw al-Sharistani sitting Indian-style within the bushes next to his house, his back to the street. Ibrahim noticed the blood from his bound wrists. Hassan Jaffa let go of his hand and had to place his own hands inside his pockets to keep them steady.

"Please be courteous," Hassan Jaffa pleaded. Without acknowledgment, the two men whisked him aside and proceeded with their inspection.

"You're lucky your mother isn't alive to experience this," Hassan Jaffa told his son as they waited outside on the front steps, the sense of parental authority alighting back into his voice.

"Praise Allah," Hassan Jaffa said sarcastically when he heard a heavy thud overhead and then glass being broken. He smiled for the sake of his son.

"Remember this, Ibrahim," he instructed. "Remember all of this that takes place."

By noon the searches were complete. Out of sight of the villagers, a group of soldiers had quietly gone about constructing a perimeter of barbed wire approximately two hundred yards from the closest house and encircling the main area of al-Diwaniya. Throughout the morning a short, mustachioed man had been idling around the town's center carrying a large bullhorn. When the soldiers finally joined him, he slowly made his way to the middle of the main street. He dragged his right foot behind him, unable to raise the lower part of his leg or to keep it in cadence with the rest of his stride. In order to cross a cement walkway, the man stopped stubbornly and, balancing himself on his left foot, raised his right leg up with the help of two hands cupped behind the knee and pulled the damaged portion over the small curb. When he reached the center, he lifted his pant leg, and the villagers' suspicions were confirmed when a pair of soldiers came over and grabbed hold of each side of the general. The short man bent and began to grotesquely twist his lower leg until Ibrahim, his father, and the rest of the residents gasped in horror and the lower portion of the leg suddenly fell to the ground. Then he positioned himself upright on his one good leg and pushed the other men away. He stared defiantly at the crowd while they stared back at the open space beneath his knee.

"This is the inhumanity of the snake," he barked through the bullhorn. "This is the result of the brutality employed by the enemies of Arab nationalism. An explosion too close to the human waves of their own children they send out like cowards to die," Tariq Hamza, a general in the Iraqi army, explained loudly, a chatter-like sound following his speech in echo.

He studied the frightened villagers staring back at him. Ibrahim noticed his teeth were the largest he had ever seen, big white squares resembling the domino tiles his father and Ab-had al-Sharistani used to play with in the coffeehouse.

"Do not be afraid," Tariq Hamza bellowed, the clicking of his teeth amplifying through the bullhorn. "Today we are here to celebrate and instill a national pride. Know that our enemies will continue to be defeated."

Across the rice fields, the soldiers formed into two short lines across from each other and in front of the Toyotas arranged in parallel columns. One by one, they began to salute, starting with the men closest to the town line, and eventually all held the pose as a caravan of black Mercedes-Benzes pulled through the makeshift corridor of trucks and steered around the main square into town.

"Today the people of al-Diwaniya are honored to be visited by the vice president."

As he spoke, his words emanated in a descending haze over the crowd, and Ibrahim felt as though he were suddenly lost in a dream. Years later he would remark to his wife that at the time the entire village of al-Diwaniya seemed dispossessed of both spirit and soul.

When the vice president emerged, Ibrahim felt his father's hand squeeze his more forcefully. Dressed in a farmer's baggy pants and a loose vest, the man smiled without expression be-hind his wide dark eyes. He perfunctorily waved his hand while an entourage surrounded him as a safety precaution. But he soon pushed them aside and began to make his way with ease through the crowd.

"How many boys do they have?" Ibrahim heard him ask Tariq Hamza.

Behind the Bawis' rose garden, a plywood stage had been erected sometime during the morning, and two chairs were placed on its platform. Saddam Hussein al-Tikriti made his way up the steps and sat regally in one of the seats. Ibrahim and his father joined the others surrounding the stage like spectators at an outdoor concert. Tariq Hamza marched over to the vice president with an officious air of respect. He saluted once and then bowed at the waist—unable to drop to one knee—and handed the bullhorn as if passing a newborn to the vice president. His voice suddenly washed over Ibrahim and it came forth with such authority that the fear gripping the villagers was immediately gone. The people of al-Diwaniya became transfixed.

"We are blessed to be the historical and cultural redeemers of the Arab world," Vice President Hussein al-Tikriti began.

"Once again it is our responsibility to assume its leadership. We are the sons of the area known as Mesopotamia, the birthplace of civilization. With a cultural heritage rich in victory and achievements, we are the holy warriors of Hammurabi and Ashurbanipal. In their names, we shall rise up and crush the head of the snake with our boot tips."

Ibrahim appeared to listen attentively, but his mind soon drifted elsewhere. Abhad al-Sharistani was nowhere in sight. Souham Bawi was on her front patio picking up the teacups left behind by the soldiers at her front door. Ibrahim wished he could escape to the other side of the village to the base of the cornfields. From there, he would be able to see the entire spectacle and, undisturbed, try to lend it a type of permanence. But he was just starting out with his paints, and Hassan Jaffa was still mad at him for changing the colors of the kitchen walls while he was at work.

His daydream broke when he was tapped on the shoulder by a man reeking of onions and with pockmarks large enough to stick your fingers through. Ibrahim and the other boys in the village were being singled out and were directed to form a line leading up the small ramp to see the vice president. They went up one at a time, and once each was onstage, Hussein al-Tikriti placed his arm around the boy's waist and smiled paternally for the series of cameras clicking away since his arrival. Ibrahim would remember that the photographers always waited until the man smiled at them and then frantically took the pictures before his expression faded or he turned his head. A total of twelve boys waited on line, and when Ibrahim was next, a soldier leaned down and offered him his hand. Ibrahim, unsure how to act, took the man's hand and was led to the open seat next to the vice president.

"Such a strong boy," Hussein al-Tikriti said, beaming, and to Ibrahim he looked more handsome in person than he did in the newspapers or on television. It was like the awe one might experience upon meeting a movie star. "And what is your name?"

"Ibrahim Galeb al-Mansur," Ibrahim responded in full, and the vice president broke out in subtle laughter. Ibrahim could smell the expensive aroma of pine and ginger from the man's cologne. It was a smell he would forever associate with power.

"Is that your full name?" Hussein asked, inquisitively placing his chin on his hand. The same man who would, upon seizing control of the Republic of Iraq, shorten his own name to obscure any tribal affiliations to his own village.

His hair was dark as charcoal, his eyes like onyx pools and almost hypnotic. He was a fit and athletic man, his shoulders broadened from years of swimming.

"Someday you will make a good soldier. Yes, a proud soldier."

Ibrahim embarrassedly caught the eyes of Hassan Jaffa, who tried to smile back at his son, but the lack of color in his expression only disheartened Ibrahim.

"A proud soldier. Yes?" The vice president repeated with a hint of persuasion.

His smile widened and Ibrahim felt momentarily at ease. The photojournalists continued to snap away with their cameras, and the entire village was watching Ibrahim nervously. He didn't understand why they feared this man so much. To Ibrahim, it was as if the man were magnetic, there was such a powerful presence that seemed to pull in everything around him. Just as young children are drawn to those they feel comfortable or at ease with, Ibrahim felt the man's energy and began to draw from it. Although only a young boy, he felt comfort in the man's smile and a sense of security in his accessibility. Up on that stage, Ibrahim was only eleven years old, too young to understand the purpose of the vice president's visit to increase morale and support for the Republican Army and the Baath's newly enacted conscription laws. All he knew at that exact moment was that the presence of the man they would soon call the Butcher put him at ease. And as he looked out upon his neighbors, he could tell it was a feeling that wasn't shared. He didn't know it would be only three weeks later when the soldiers came back into the village. This time not to recruit support for the draft but instead to purge the country of all Persian blood. Ibrahim would then watch as the soldiers set Abhad al-Sharistani's beard on fire. His favorite schoolmaster would scream in blood-curdling defiance, the same man who let Ibrahim sit in his classroom when Hassan Jaffa was at work after Ibrahim's mother died, and who had taught him along with the older children of the village. Ibrahim would watch as the man had eight inch-long spikes hammered into his head, the horror momentarily broken by the crisp blue stare of the same soldier he had witnessed searching the feed bags only weeks earlier. Ibrahim would recognize the man's smile as the lifeless body of Abhad al-Sharistani collapsed in pools of blood and smoke around him.

"I want to be a painter, sir," he responded with a renewed enthusiasm. Only when the vice president's smile slackened did Ibrahim feel the energy slipping away. "A painter, sir, I am to be a painter."

6

OCTOBER 8, 1984

TWO MORNINGS LATER, FEINRICH and I ate our parting breakfast in an outdoor café on the Cornice, the paved walkway of shops and restaurants lining the banks of the Tigris. The currents of the infamous river swept strongly past us, thick with silt and debris as if carrying away the remains of its long and often tumultuous history.

Feinrich ordered his coffee–"black as molasses," he called it– with a side of Glenlivet served quite inconspicuously in a small Styrofoam cup. I found it hard to think of him without a drink either in his hand or already in his stomach, a slight paunch settling comfortably off his slender frame. I drank the customary green tea, which was so bitter that the addition of multiple lemon wedges ironically helped to stabilize its taste, and a western omelet consisting of a thin, gray meat and a series of rainbow-colored squares, almost too crisp and tasteless to be considered vegetables. Iraq is not known for its cuisine, but watching Feinrich empty the Styrofoam cup into his thick black coffee I am reminded of what this country is known for–oil.

41

We silently read separate copies of the London *Times*, both of us enjoying the sounds of the flowing river as we began to collect our thoughts for the long day ahead. A series of gondolas are out on the water ferrying tourists and workers across the river's width. An assortment of vibrantly colored pennants hang lazily from their edge posts, motionless in the dead air. It is hard to believe there is a war going on.

When the check came, Feinrich and I started to argue over it, but when I noticed the total was equivalent to only $2.65, I decided to humor him and let him pay. In return, he wanted my company to briefly shop the local culture before we headed back to our hotel and our respective assignments.

"For flavor," he added, nodding toward my half-eaten breakfast, and we started out browsing along the promenade heading in the direction of the square.

Rush hour in Baghdad can only be experienced and not described. There is no reason or logic behind the shifts and movements of businessmen, carts, automobiles, and bicycles. One must stay alert to avoid getting nipped by a wheel cart or run over by a foreign automobile or mule. There are a multitude of conflicting street signs and all of them are routinely disobeyed. *One way* means the way one happened to be going, and any etiquette of commute must have died long ago with the ancient caliphs. A rotary pops up at almost every major intersection, and unlike the comedic scenes in London where cars slowly inch their way forward while trying to gain entry into the circle, cars instead dart straight across or even counterclockwise. Horns blare forth from every direction like obscene mating calls. I wonder if there is a Department of Motor Vehicles in Baghdad, considering there is a ministry office for everything else, and what its waiting lines must be like.

We push past fruit stands selling dates and figs and too ripe papayas. We brush off the satin merchants displaying their elegant fabrics seductively from the overhead rafters. Farther into the business sector, we bump shoulders with oil executives dressed in Parisian suits as we stride past the high, gilded arches of the Abbasid Palace, restored rather magnificently by the current administration. It is one of the oldest monuments left behind from Baghdad's glorious past, built during the thirteenth century toward the end of the Abbasid reign when the capital was moved from Damascus to Baghdad. The blue of its brocade is placid and clear like the summer waters off Narragansett Bay. A small group of foreigners have gathered outside its doorways, only adding to an already crowded sidewalk.

Feinrich turns into the Sarava Bookstore located on the corner of Al Junub Street. In front of the shop a wall of heavily wrinkled men hawk jewelry—sterling rings and necklaces and stones so devoid of color as to be almost humorous. They grab at our shirtsleeves as we pass them. There is not enough air to even stir a slight breeze.

Inside the Sarava Bookstore the wood-paneled walls are lined with high mahogany bookcases reminiscent of the libraries at Columbia University. Cool air streams forth from the opened vents in the floor, and it is a relief to be off the hectic streets and away from the growing, layered heat. The store's proprietress greets us as soon as we step through the door and well before the tin bell over our head signals out our arrival.

"Good morning, good morning," she repeats in broken English, guessing at our language from our appearance, and comes running over to us reaching out for our hands.

Feinrich, a bit tipsy from his morning Scotch, stumbles backward into an umbrella rack while trying to safely get out of the woman's way. I don't know what I find more absurd, that Feinrich is running away from a woman or that there is a need for an umbrella rack in a place that averages less than six inches of rainfall a year.

"Don't you be shy," the women exclaims.

She bends to straighten the rack and then pulls Feinrich and me into an open area in the middle of the store. Prior to the war, it was not common for native women to be found in the work-place. But as more men and boys are being sent to the fronts, a need has developed back home to maintain a sense of stability and for the overall sake of routine. Unlike their neighbors, Iraqi women are being integrated into the daily lives of the cities and, as a result, are gaining a sense of freedom and independence at one time considered radical and improper.

I notice the image of the Iraqi flag underfoot. My feet cross its triumvirate of stars. I am also aware of something missing, al-though I am not sure what it may be. I have never been in this store before.

"You are Westerners?" the proprietress asks with the dally-ing graciousness of a forgotten maiden. "Yes, all Westerners are always welcome. We are a friendly establishment. You are friends of ours and are always welcome."

She is a vibrant woman, but very small, and her posture is extremely bent. I wasn't watching her closely when she bent down to pick up the umbrella rack, but it appears she never straightened herself out. Her height is hard to determine be-cause her back is curled so much. When she walks, her balance causes her to lunge forward and she has to shuffle her feet in order to keep pace with her upper body. She could easily be the Middle Eastern poster child for scoliosis, a reminder of the tests American children are required to take during grammar school, if not for the years that have left thin trails of colorless lines branching out from the corners of her nocturnal eyes.

"How do you like our most beautiful and advanced coun-try?" she asks with such enthusiasm I can only wonder if she is serious.

"It is truly an amazing place," I offer, and try to turn my attention back to the books, intending to purchase several for the sake of international goodwill.

"President Hussein has led us back to the peak of the Arab world. We are truly grateful for him."

Feinrich stands directly and almost blasphemously on the lettering of *Allahu Akbar,* Arabic for "God is great." I know he does it on purpose. I like Feinrich, but only on the surface. At times he is comical, but he also carries a belittling arrogance toward anything non-European within his heart. A provincial indifference he feels is his birthright.

"What do you think of the president?" Feinrich asks the woman, dangerously turning the tables. "What do *his* people think of him?"

And I almost expect to hear intimate details from this exotic and bent woman about conjugal trysts between her and the self-appointed ruler.

"Saddam is wonderful. Yes, a good man. He is a true leader of the people."

It is true, he is a leader of people, but I do not like the direction of the conversation and intend to alter its course. To talk of the state is dangerous enough; to speak specifically of the president borders on suicidal.

"There have been many changes since I was last here," I tell her, implying this is not my first time in Baghdad. "You have made many improvements."

"The international press doesn't do this place any justice," Feinrich adds sarcastically.

The woman cowers half-erect at his side and her eyes search the store for any other shoppers. There are none.

"Do you believe in the Zionist lies of the West?" she asks us rather secretly, and I know I can't help but be a bit discouraged considering her earlier proclamation that all Westerners were welcome in her store.

"Well, if they are lies . . . ," I begin, but quickly remember where I am and who may be listening. "I don't believe in any lies," I continue, which is partly true.

"Well, I suggest you read this for the truth," she tells us and then begins to thrust several books from a box by her feet into our arms. I then realize what it is that has been missing.

Only when she heeds our advances to stop and several copies fall to the floor do I notice what the books are—hardbound editions of *The Historical Life of Saddam Hussein.* On its cover the president is dressed in a white suit and sitting in a straw highback chair set against a series of palm trees. It is his autobiography. He has not been missing, I correct myself, only his picture was absent.

I motion to Feinrich and then to my watch. If he wanted flavor, then he was getting a solid dose of the rampant ambiguity mixed within the local culture.

"How much?" he asks the woman, reaching for his wallet.

In Baghdad, imports of books and literature have recently slowed to a halt. Instead, varying historical perspectives on Iraq and its link to Arab nationalism and the ancestral lineage of its president to the holy prophet Muhammad are being massproduced. The state has undergone a huge propaganda program to instill national and Arabic pride in its people, and on the surface it is not necessarily a bad thing. This country *has* been disjointed since its inception. But regardless of the truth, a new history is being written by its leaders, and it has taken the place of Western literature and its imported textbooks and journals, setting the learning curve, especially for Iraqi doctors and scientists, back decades.

The woman takes Feinrich's hand in hers before he can reach into his pocket.

"Such light hair and eyes. You have blood from the north, no."

"As far north as Berlin," he replies dryly.

"For you," she answers with a hint of flirtation aimed at the German journalist, "for you they are free."

The woman presses several copies of *The Historical Life of Saddam Hussein* into his hands.

"A gift. You must take it." And the intonation of an order in her voice disarms Feinrich, and I am glad that we will soon be parting ways. We are not on vacation. We are journalists, and although all countries are inherently dangerous, this one sets an example.

"Thank you very much," Feinrich answers after regaining some of his composure. He gestures into his back pocket and pulls out several dinar notes, the Iraqi currency, with the president's face now also visible on the paper money.

"Please do not insult me," she demands, "we live very well here. Saddam, he takes care of his people.

"Now you must go." And she quickly ushers us across the floor and out the door without uttering another word.

As soon as we are outside the store, the heat falls upon us. Feinrich and I cross the street and buy two bottled waters from a vendor. We drain them quickly and then buy two more. It is nine thirty and I am due to meet an official from the Ministry of Information back at my hotel with orders to depart to the front by ten o'clock.

We take a shortcut off Tammuz Street and cut through the Salem Bazaar. Animal carcasses hang from the metal hooks at the entranceway, and I look at the possible origins for the colorless meat I had ingested earlier. Luckily, I do not see anything remotely close. We make our way rather easily to the far end of the bazaar. Most of the shoppers are browsing outside and we exit into a small, vacant alleyway behind the last booth.

We cross over a sparse, marbled garden in the rear of a private landing and begin heading back to the hotel when I hear several metallic whistles coming up from behind us. Two policemen are running up quickly in our direction. They must be after Feinrich and me because no one else is around. A fire erupts in my stomach, not from nervousness but rather an awakened sense of frustration. We stop and I instinctively reach into my vest pocket to pull out my papers.

"Halt–do not move!"

The policemen are close to ten yards away from us and they are aiming their pistols at our heads. I raise both my hands in the air and hope Feinrich is doing the same next to me. One of the officers waves his gun purposely in Feinrich's direction.

"Drop the bag," he yells, and mimics the gesture several times.

Feinrich releases the paper bag and the several hardbound copies of *The Historical Life of Saddam Hussein* drop with a heavy thump to the ground. As the books spread out, I can't help but think the proprietress of the Sarava Bookstore might have something to do with this spectacle. I find out soon enough while sitting under the shade of a linoleum awning and watch as Feinrich is arrested for shoplifting.

The woman had phoned the local police as soon as we left her store to report a theft. She was angry over the pilfered books but was also in hysterics and scared the man might come back to hurt her. The entire episode was ridiculous. I am almost certain his German complexion, to the uninformed, may have aroused suspicion and helped in his being targeted.

It is later that morning on the road to the southern front when I am warned, a bit too late, of the practice. Store owners and shopkeepers commonly offer their goods free of charge to Westerners with the intention of having them arrested immediately afterward for stealing those same items. The detainee naturally will plead his innocence but will eventually end up paying both the owner for the goods in full and also a stipend to the local police for their trouble. Both amounts currently inflated because it is a time of war. The intricacies of the Baghdad economy; nothing is free in this place, and nothing is without consequence.

7

OCTOBER 8, 1984

"HOW NAÏVE IS THE thought that Iraq could be the prize or bloodlust of the imperialistic tendencies of others throughout the last seven hundred years and not itself be affected by it? After being the submissive, how could it not want to taste the advances of expansion with its own tongue?"

This statement from Qadro, my government-appointed minder and escort. He is a tall, well-built, and strikingly handsome man more like a Hollywood version of a minder than an actual one appointed by the Iraqi Ministry of Information. He is a sharp contrast to the disheveled and quietly humble nature of our desert guide in Al-Hamad, Mahwi. His clothes are neatly pressed into high, crisp arches creasing his olive green shirt and tan pants and giving one the impression that he has just been unfolded. On his tanned face rests the customary short-lipped mustache common, if not obligatory, among the country's men. His hair is slicked back into tight black ribbons, and the obvious conscious care he takes with his appearance is a reminder of his country's secular leadership as opposed to the religious authority of the army they are fighting against. Islamic rule frowns upon appearances, evidenced by the shaggy, unkempt beards of the ayatollahs and their modest wardrobes. A difference that is confirmed by the images of the country's president, Saddam Hussein, which are everywhere–posted on billboards, televisions, dishes, pens and watches, even toilet seats.

I left Feinrich earlier in the small police precinct located in the heart of the capital. He remained locked up while the authorities waited for the owner of the Sarava Bookstore to close her shop and come down to sign off on his charges and receive her payment. To pass the time, Feinrich played backgammon with his cellmate, a winemaker from the north accused of inflating the price of his grapes. His possessions were filed in a metal basket next to the copies of the book he was accused of stealing. A young officer had even taken to reading one before I left the building. Earlier this morning three military policemen were executed on charges of spying, and as a result the holding cell was one of the safest places in the country. When the German ambassador arrived shortly afterward carrying a suitcase of money, I wished Feinrich luck and departed. I was not charged with any absurd accusations nor did the police care who I was or why I was with Feinrich. They were more concerned with the military police and any suspicious behavior detected within their own ranks. When I arrived back at the al-Rashid hotel after a light jog, Qadro was already there waiting for me.

"It is a good thing we are not running to the fronts," he said without sarcasm, a calming friendliness offered upon our shaking hands. He helped me with my bags and we soon set off.

Qadro lacks the predictable Iraqi accent, and it is a good thing he is well-spoken because he talks incessantly and without any noticeable conscious effort. He was educated at George Washington University in Washington, D.C., and journeyed back to Baghdad once Iraqi MiG-23s began to drop bombs and artillery from the sky in an attempt to destroy the Iranian air forces at Mehrabad and Tabriz. All of this information he offered to me freely within our first hour of meeting.

"You Americans—how can you think what is good for the goose is not good for the gander?" he adds with a sly smile curling the edges of his lips.

He is a likable man with an affinity toward opinion. Yet his persuasive tone is not intended as condemnation or argumentation but simply for the sake of dialogue and with the primary intention of keeping the doors of conversation open.

"How many people know what a gander actually is?" he asks me and then presses the horn several times as the car swerves over a wooden plank bridge and heads out in the direction of the southern war fronts.

We cross several dispatch areas in Al Hillah and Nasiriyah, southern cities affected heavily by the war. We speed past lines of high reeds standing proud and protective in the bordering eastward marshes. There is a sense of detachment to the country that only increases the farther away from Baghdad we travel. Small villages appear like distended bellies past the wetlands as the ground rises in patches of smooth green velvet and the offspring of the rivers lends to the secret lives of the roving tribes. We speed past small wooden shacks temporarily stationed to house injured and dying soldiers. Although we have driven out of the Baghdad traffic over two hours ago, Qadro still honks the car horn repetitively as we pass.

"It serves to make the car go faster," he informs me.

An extreme shortage of doctors and medical facilities has created the need for these posts. Small buses and ambulettes circle nonstop along their semidesignated routes picking up and transporting the needy and hauling off the dead in a measure of efficiency normally uncharacteristic of the region.

When we come to the outskirts of Qurna, the sky up ahead is ashen and I can't help thinking that we are venturing into a large netted area, the heavens a patchwork void of color. I am reminded what my late colleague Mayer had once written while stationed in Beirut: "War is gray." A sentiment I am sure he was not the first to express.

I watch long, thin trails of smoke rise from the ground ahead like ancient spires blowing off heat. The earth is scorched. Fields previously lush with irrigation provided by the rivers have been burnt by napalm, and the green velvet rise of the marshes and backwater villages smolder with a solitude reserved only for the mourning.

Our Toyota pickup whirls past an outpost where a lone man waits in tattered clothes. His neck is slightly bent like a curious pigeon's and his head is raised defiantly toward the sound of mortar fire ringing out from the east. As we drive past, I notice one of his arms is missing, as is his right ear. He stands motionless like a statue unaffected by the observer.

"Is he alive or dead?" I mutter thoughtlessly to myself.

"Does it make a difference?" Qadro answers me abruptly, and I am a bit shocked at his lack of compassion.

"Did it ever *make* a difference?"

"Have your eyes been open, man? Look around you, Mikhail—there is nothing of compassion here."

The outposts increase in number the farther south we drive as do the number of soldiers and tattered bodies waiting in them for pickup. Traffic has begun to accumulate rather quickly and dozens of taxicabs are waiting in lines to make the trip back north. The blaring of their car horns has no effect on their velocity as they slowly inch along bumper to bumper. Coffins are secured on roof racks, the weight of the caskets bowing the frame of the metal ceilings, and are draped across in the red, white, and black stripes of the Iraqi flag. The bodies will be afforded a hero's funeral and a "death" payment from the government will be paid to members of the immediate family.

Qadro is telling me a story about a Russian businessman he escorted weeks earlier, but I am not listening. His words register only in periodic phrases broken by the bumps along the dirt road and the intermittent blaring of the car horn. We ride straight into Basra and are greeted by a huge mural of President Saddam Hussein. Its colors are electric, and in his banana-cream suit he looks as if he should be cultivating cigars in South America instead of invading foreign countries. He is accepting a palm tree from a figure representing the Babylonian sun god, Shamash. Under a pale sky filled with soot and gunpowder, the implication of sunshine seems rather absurd, yet the colors, I notice, are striking.

"Who paints such things?" I ask above the explosion of combat fire miles away and over the rising hills toward the east.

"Oh, he is good. He is a friend of mine," Qadro answers quite proudly. "He's very good, my friend. The best. It is unfortunate that his skills cannot be better utilized here."

We are forced to stop at the sentry gates leading into a large gated Iraqi military station. It is the end of the road for our travels south. Beyond this military outpost, Iranian forces of the Basij, a volunteer army consisting of men and boys ranging in ages from nine to forty-five, along with members of the Iranian Revolutionary Guards known as the Pasdaran, have pushed close to the city limits. The Iranian forces are successfully clearing a pathway for their oncoming tanks to charge through and reclaim parcels of land. We pass the checkpoint rather easily after flashing our government-issued passes, and Qadro speaks briefly to the guards in Arabic, showing them his Ministry of Information badge and my authorization signed by Saddam Hussein himself.

"This is as far south as we are permitted to go," Qadro states, and pulls the truck alongside a large, gated enclosure. We park next to several buses and walk over toward the open lands where the armies fought not too long ago. Long coils of barbed wire cover the ground in a series of bushlike hedges demarking the war zone and partitioning the ever-changing territorial claims.

"Over there." Qadro points past the makeshift boundary and over to the east. The sun overhead is at its peak, the color of burning charcoal behind the soot. Pieces of shrapnel, bare tires, and the hollowed-out frames of automobiles and tanks litter the entire landscape. The area looks like a junkyard, except for the bodies scattered about in grotesque poses. A man lies completely bent forward at the waist, the fleshy portion of his lower back gone and a vacant cavity left behind where his kidneys have been removed. Two boys sit cross-legged and facing each other, both of them leaning forward so that their foreheads touch. I am told that the heat of a nearby explosion caused their skin to solder together like two Siamese twins joined in death.

"Approximately fifteen thousand to twenty thousand dead Iranians lay past this outpost," Qadro informs me.

I offer him a cigarette and he inhales the smoke deeply as if quenching a thirst. He takes my elbow and leads me past the gate, and I follow him up a small, dirt hill close to a hundred yards from the station house. Due to the pollution in the area, shadows are cast about in disproportionate patterns, but farther south a break in the sky has created a small river of sunshine that flows down and illuminates several patches of fields in a subtle bronze. Qadro points toward an area once covered in dark green fields with abundant marshlands thick in palm trees and reed thickets. Now it is a caustic and burnt stretch of dead earth.

"Over there is your mythical Garden of Eden," he says with a hint of sentiment.

There are other civilian trucks in the barracks, and several journalists are already out in the field taking pictures and interviewing soldiers. There are other government-appointed minders as well; nothing takes place without the watchful eyes of Baghdad present. We are not permitted to the actual front where the fighting is going on. We are authorized only to the zones where an Iraqi victory has already been secured. When it comes to foreign presses and correspondents, the government poses the most calculated and lamentable circumstances in Iraqi favor. The Baath Party, in its attempts to gain favor from the international powers, supervises and directs all the activity in its country and eliminates from it all public and private displays of disloyalty or anti-Baath sentiment. It is a contrived existence, something I am reminded of constantly during my stay.

Several Iraqi soldiers fire their guns into the air in a victorious cheer, but it is also a waste of needed ammunition. Several hours ago in the same area, the Persian army had finally retreated after relinquishing a five-hundred-square-mile tract of Iraqi land. One Iraqi soldier removes his helmet and replaces it with an Iranian one taken off the open fields. He pokes his index finger humorously through the bullet hole puncturing its side. A faint smell like that of burning almonds lingers in from over the hills.

An enclosed medical station sits opposite the parking field with men laid out on a series of cots and tables made of folded metal and ripped sheets. Chaotic orders are shouted from every direction to help the new arrivals, but I am unable to notice anyone resembling a doctor or nurse. A group of soldiers lean outside against the gate. On the ground in front of them is a tattered black-and-white picture of the Ayatollah Khomeini.

"Die, Khomeini," they chant murderously in unison. "Die, Khomeini."

"To bring this picture on our soil is blasphemous," Qadro says.

The ayatollah is considered the top enemy of Saddam Hussein

and a threat to his regime and overall control of the Shia majority population. The Iranian revolution of 1979 resulted in the Shah's forced withdrawal from his own country after his family's fifty-three-year reign and the subsequent return of the ayatollah out of exile from France. The fear was that the revolution would spread from Tehran into Iraq. The Baath regime swiftly responded with the expulsion of fifteen thousand of its own citizens considered Iranian nationalists.

One of the soldiers crudely unbuttons his trousers and begins to urinate on the picture of the revolutionary Iranian leader. The others cheer and start clapping their hands in encouragement. Some of the wounded men actually sit up in their cots to watch the spectacle. Another gun discharges in the air.

"Do you think there are men on the other side doing the same to your leader?" I ask Qadro.

"Damn that," he says pointedly, "these men will piss on him too."

Suddenly my hearing cracks and then it is completely gone, replaced by a hollow drone that filters out sounds as though I were underwater. Droplets of crimson splatter through the air. Small fragments of skin and tendon cross my lips. Qadro is writhing on the ground in front of me, his rigid body shaking in electric spasms. The end of his ankle is frayed out like the end of a thick rope, and blood flows freely from the stump, staining the ground around him. I am deliberately pushed aside by a group of men, who quickly wrap the bottom of Qadro's leg in a bandage of towels and gauze and then carry him off into the tarpaulin-covered medical station. The whirling sound of being sucked through an underground tunnel comes and goes as I sit back upon the dirt, unable to balance myself. A young soldier kneels down next to me and pours water from his canteen over a spare cloth. He gently wipes my face and I notice the stains I leave behind.

"I am sorry," I mouth weakly, not really sure what it is I am apologizing for.

"It is not your fault," he responds, and dabs my lower lip and chin.

I look past him and notice a dark, leathery package hanging off a string of barbed wire overhead, its seams burst at one end. When I realize it is Qadro's foot, blown apart by the impact of an amateur mine, I feel myself begin to get nauseous.

"Your friend will be fine," I am told, and then I close my eyes to the hot, gray sun.

8

OCTOBER 8, 1984

"YOU ARE NOT MARRIED yet?" Qadro asks me incredulously, still looking for conversation despite his recent trauma.

It is a common theme I am growing accustomed to after my several visits to Iraq–that when its people are comfortable with you, they will talk for hours. They become extremely hospitable and courteous. It also helps to take their minds off the oppression and constraints they suffer during their everyday lives.

The sun has receded in the west across vast stretches of savanna and then the open desert plains, the sky the color of a fine red wine. The siren of the ambulette rotates in silence on the cracked dash, illuminating the inside of the vehicle in momentary flashes and adding to the impression that we are draped under surveillance infrared.

"No," I answer, cracking the shell of a betel nut between my teeth. "We're just two eligible bachelors out here beyond the gates of hell."

I am relieved he is going to be alright and that he is once

again talking. I notice a series of small, faint patches beginning to outline themselves through the base of his bandage.

"Twelve years," Qadro replies, a smile forcing his eyes to crinkle at their edges, and for a moment in the darkness he looks like an older child. He slowly raises his arms and stretches out all of his fingers and then flashes two more in the air for the sake of addition. "I've been married twelve wonderful years."

There is no wedding ring on any of his outstretched fingers.

"The government," he answers solemnly as if reading my mind. "For the gold. The government has collected all gold–utensils, watches, coins, even wedding rings–for the war effort."

He shamefully inspects his hands, turning them over and bringing them up to his face as if to inhale his own scent, and then he does a strange thing–he lightly presses his tongue against the skin on the back of one of them. Then he drops his arms down to his sides, his expression turning to one of deep thought, and within seconds he is sound asleep; the exertion of our short conversation exhausting his last remnants of strength. After a few moments, his snores echo loudly in the quiet of the ambulette ride back to Baghdad.

The color had found its way back into his cheeks though his skin is still several shades away from his ordinary caramel tint. I once witnessed a man being attacked by a great white shark off the Cape of Good Hope in South Africa. Over the course of several minutes, the fish tore the man's entire leg away from his body. When we were finally able to pull him back up on board, he had been so drained of blood that his veins were traceable strands of blue transparent through his skin, which had turned white as wax parchment. Within a short time the diver had bled to death. Earlier when I had found Qadro on a metal table in the medical tent, two men were working on his thigh and trying to suppress the flow of blood to prevent him from meeting the same fate. The color of the muscle was quickly receding to that of lamb's milk. Small traces of delicate indigo cracks had already begun to branch out on his upper thigh.

But the blood was soon allowed back into Qadro's thighs after the edges of the rupture were cauterized and the immediate danger had passed. It is only eight hours later and I am amazed at Qadro's resolve and ability to overcome and deal with such physical anguish and pain as well as the prospect of living his remaining days crippled. I watch him stretched out on an aluminum cot in the back of an ambulette whose cross-country purpose seemed so foreign to us only hours ago.

"All things appear distant when you are going in the opposite direction," he'd said philosophically when earlier we skirted past the bundled traffic stopped for pickup outside the first post. I praised the break in the congestion.

His left foot had been blown straight off from above the ankle by the detonation of a crudely made Soviet palm-held mine. Qadro must lie supine and keep his leg raised above the level plane of his upper body. Since he needs to get to a main hospital quickly to prevent the onset of gangrene, unofficial orders from a sergeant at the front have put me in charge of his ride back to Baghdad. As a result, we travel alone. At the first outpost, there are more dead soldiers than injured ones and a line of taxicabs has formed next to the makeshift coffins, their drivers procrastinating over their final cigarettes before bending to lift the heavy caskets onto their hoods or roofs.

"This man needs a surgeon immediately," a small man dressed in a white sanitary uniform explained to our driver before we left. He briefly opened the bandage to show the frayed stump, although the gesture was not needed since the leg abruptly ended and a foot was visibly missing. "You have a few hours. Do not stop."

The efficiency of the smaller Soviet-made mines, like most of the weaponry being used in the Iran-Iraq conflict, is questionable and characteristically unreliable. The majority of munitions deployed–guns, tanks, and missiles–are left over from World War II or more recently fought wars and are considered "fossilized." Their reaction beyond the trigger point is never guaranteed. In fact, many items have not been retested, and since they are over forty years old they are either dysfunctional or simply not functional at all. They were purchased rather cheaply on the black market from the Russians, and the Iraqi soldiers have not been properly trained and are ill-equipped when repairs are needed. If the weapons themselves are outdated, then the parts to fix them are ancient. Many soldiers on both sides have cornered the enemy or assaulted opposing groups only to have their Kalashnikovs lock up or a "dead" grenade roll hollowly into the trenches, and then retreated as the weapons of the enemy malfunctioned in retaliation as well. It should have been no surprise the war was a stalemate to date. Statistics from the International War Bureau claim the average to be nine mines out of every hundred functioning properly. Qadro had been subject to one of the nine.

The device had mistakenly fallen out of the pocket of an injured Iraqi soldier while he was being carried into the medical tents. Because of its size and reputation for impotence, soldiers in the camp had ignored it until the moment Qadro was sent flying five feet in the air and his foot catapulted into the barbed-wire mesh of the demarcation fences overhead. I was pushed backward toward the soldier pissing on the image of the ayatollah, knocking him onto the stained picture.

After several hours, the initial shock had amazingly worn off and the wound had been cleaned, wrapped, and the bleeding slowed almost to a stop. Two men, one who claimed to be a doctor and the other a gardener, worked nonstop on the leg for close to an hour with a rebirth of enthusiasm.

"They are just happy that the patient is not a dying one,"

Qadro joked with a slight slur, the painkillers taking moderate effect. "Fellas, you must save my dancing career, *salaam alaikum.*"

"*Salaam alaikum,*" the gardener responded.

Now Qadro sleeps and we drive on in silence. My Arabic is not strong enough to make conversation with the disheveled elderly man driving us. Plus, he looks as if he hasn't slept in days. Dark shoots of thick hair protrude wildly from the sides of his head in the dark. His eyes dart hurriedly from left to right like a scared squirrel and he blinks incessantly. I am drained after the day's events and don't really feel like talking anyway. Tracer fire echoes from the war zone behind us, and I also don't want to break his scurrying concentration. I lean forward and close the clear plastic partition dividing us.

The night sky in the Middle East is magnificent. The infinite stars radiate like offertory candles up to the heavens. Local legend suggests that for each soldier killed in defense of his homeland a new star emanates from the sky. Out here, past the haze and man-made constructions of any Western city, and as we leave the smoldering war front in the growing distance behind us, it is clear to see the millions of men and boys shining over these troubled lands.

I have only been in Iraq for two days, but already it feels like months. Everything here is a contradiction, from the promise of unhindered reporting to the rewritten history and the gift of free books. We had been invited to report on a war that is basically foreign to and unseen by the rest of the Western world, brought in to report on the travesty and injustice being inflicted on the Iraqi people by religious zealots. What this government doesn't seem to realize is that the Iranian leaders are also claiming their own injustices on the other side. We were invited in with open arms, but as soon as we enter this country those arms quickly close around us. We are denied permission to the active war zones and are instead shuffled to scenes of Iraqi victory

from battles fought days, even weeks, before. The episode earlier today was bizarre and unreal, like a play being rehearsed
for our benefit. Most of the bodies had already begun to decay,
and the pungent smell of rotting flesh and a lingering aroma of
almonds wafted over the entire area. The small explosion had
kicked everyone with a dose of reality, and within several
hours all the journalists and foreign reporters had been
rounded up, told to pack their belongings, and were driven
back to Baghdad in taxicabs weighted down with the packaged
bodies of men and boys we were not supposed to see. The Iraqi
government does not grant anybody the accessibility to move
freely about the country, and although we have been invited by
the foreign minister and the president, we are not allowed in
any vital areas. I am beginning to not only wonder why I am
here, but what is really taking place as these two neighboring
countries continue to fight.

I stretch my neck out the back window, the cool air without
hint of breeze and smelling like camel shit. I am tired and cantankerous, feeling a sudden sense of anger at the stupidity with
which my new friend had to lose a foot. We are approximately
twenty miles outside Baghdad, and as the lights of the capital
grow closer, narcissistic murals of Saddam Hussein begin to
sprout once again like ragweed and garnish the rising urban
landscape. He is a military man with his hand pressed flat
against the base of a Kalashnikov, one I can only bet is fully functional. He is a smiling, savvy businessman dressed in a gray, pin-
striped suit, his expression as forced as his regime's sense of
purpose and identity. As his image becomes more common the
closer to the city we get, I decide that I am going to take the time
to investigate a different approach to my reporting on the war
here and on Iraq in general. If the artist is a friend of Qadro's, as
he claims he is, I would like to meet him. I watch the marshy
fields speed away in the distance under the vigilant eyes of a

straw-hatted president smoking a six-foot-long Cohiba cigar and can't help feeling that I am being watched as well.

Qadro has awoken and shifts his lower body slightly on the cot. "The pain is only bad when I wiggle my toes," he proclaims with a short, rested laugh.

In the darkness of the ambulette his teeth and eyes glow red like bike reflectors and I can see he is smiling. I lean over and place my hand on his shoulder. I take a cigarette from the pack in his shirt pocket, place it between his lips, and light it for him.

"Like the nectar of the gods," he says after taking a long pull.

The ambulette creaks across the wooden bridge spanning the Tigris. I point to a large painting of Hussein astride a white stallion.

"Your friend," I say, nodding in the mural's direction. "I'd like to meet him if possible."

"He would like that too," he replies.

The ambulette slowly pulls into the emergency ward of the Say ad Manood Hospital, and amazingly the waiting room is close to empty. An elderly couple sits off to one side, the old man eyeing us suspiciously as soon as we pull up to the sliding entrance doors. Two young children, a boy and presumably his older sister, doze calmly underneath a television set. On the small screen is a snowy reception of a recorded speech given by Saddam Hussein proclaiming a great Iraqi victory on the battle-fields outside the Shatt al Arab, the River of Arabs, located to the southeast and bordering Iran and Iraq. I watched the exact same speech subtitled in English two nights ago on Al-Jazeera while in the hotel restaurant eating a plate of sliced apples and dates.

The hospital staff denies me permission to enter the ward with Qadro due to the late hour and my being a foreigner. I am too tired to struggle with authority. Before the attendants pull him away, we make arrangements for me to call on him tomorrow. I begin to write down my hotel number on a piece of paper in case he needs anything in the interim, but Qadro shakes his head.

"No need, Mikhail," he whispers to me out of earshot of the attendants, "I know your room number—and telephone number too—in my head." And he taps his forefinger against his brow.

Now that we are back in Baghdad, we can relax a bit and both laugh with mixed intonations of anxiety and restrained nervousness. I am not sure what Qadro means by this statement and can only assume that the painkillers must be clouding his thoughts.

"Let me know if there is anything I can do," I offer one last time.

"Thank you, Mikhail," he says, waving his hands away as the electric doors open and then swallow him and the two attendants into the mouth of the hospital.

I walk the three blocks back to the al-Rashid with my hands pressed deep into my pockets under the cautious eyes of uniformed men brandishing rifles and patrolling the eerily quiet streets. I pass by the empty rostrum where the three military policemen were executed. No signs of the lynching remain except a brisk chill scratching at the skin like uncut fingernails across a chalkboard. I seem to be the only civilian out.

The lobby of the al-Rashid hotel is overcrowded. An Arab Economic Conference is letting out, and I press myself through the corridor and into a noisy elevator full of white-turbaned men reeking of whiskey and currency. They show an uncommon restraint by holding their tongues in my presence. I take the slow ride up to my floor in silence, and after pushing my way out of the cab I can hear them start to mutter again before the doors completely close behind me.

As soon as I am in my room, I kick off my shoes and pull out the room service menu from inside the desk. It is then that I hear a faint static struggling from the side of the bed. I flick the light switch on the wall next to the closet several times, but only the light in the bathroom switches on and off. As I walk over to the bed, the static sound increases. I grab the lamp on the nightstand and rip off the dusty brown shade. Underneath, there is no light-bulb, just a three-inch-long strip of microphone screwed in its place instead. I am amazed at the brazenness of the regime's sur-veillance techniques and suddenly remember what Qadro had told me. I break the microphone free from the lamp, a series of small sparks jump excitedly from the socket, and I walk into the bathroom and flush the entire piece down the toilet.

"You can listen to the sounds of a thousand people shitting instead, you bastards."

It has been a long day, and as I lie back on the bed, I am not sure how long my eyes have been closed when the telephone begins to ring.

9

MARCH 29, 1984

"YOU ARE THE ONE who has to decide, Ibrahim."

Yusuf al-Mahoudi is sitting across the wooden table, sipping his late-afternoon tea and smiling a bit impatiently. With his eyes hidden under the shade of an Arabian tea rose tree and a hooded caftan covering his head, his expression is hauntingly incomplete.

"You have to decide if our lives are going to be mere whispers," Yusuf continues. "I have experienced and I believe I will continue to experience the consequences of my faults. And that is not something to be taken lightly."

Ibrahim has grown a little nervous with the tone and content of the conversation. But he maintains his composure and is careful to stay respectful toward his father-in-law though he is finding it harder to bite his tongue. His late-afternoon break will be over with in fifteen minutes and by then the paint should be fairly dry.

Ibrahim had found Yusuf waiting for him in the corridor next to the entranceway. This unexpected meeting was no way for him to relax. It was Yusuf the soldiers had come looking for that night months ago. A mistake had led them to Ibrahim's apartment rather than Yusuf's studio a block from the gardens. Yusuf was known to change his apartments monthly, and he often slept in the alcoves by the university or behind the shops on Arasat al-Hindiyyah Street. Eventually Yusuf will finish up his preaching and he will leave and Ibrahim will go back out into the square and cover up the painted wall to protect it from the elements and various night vandals. The following morning he will repeat the entire process all over again and continue to finish the image of the president astride a thunderous white stallion overlooking the entire town. The routine was getting to Ibrahim, the daily monotony draining away his creativity.

"Yusuf, I appreciate your concern. But, please, you must understand—"

"I understand too well, son," Yusuf interrupts. "I understand better than most, it seems. This is a way for you to make a difference."

There is the cantankerous sound of metal scraping against metal as Tapiz feebly pushes open the iron-latticed gate leading into the backyard from the outside alleyway. Too short to cast a shadow and bestowed with fingers too thick and meaty to properly cradle a paintbrush, it was bewildering to many how Tapiz had received his commission as an apprenticed painter. But it was his physical inadequacies that had helped him obtain the job, his stature combined with his innocent and trustworthy nature. He was not the aggressive or athletic type and although he lacked any innate sense of masculinity, he was certainly not in any way effeminate. He was simply a good-natured character who couldn't seem to stay out of his own way. He could not be expected to fight the Iranians and most soldiers didn't want an uncoordinated fool fighting alongside them—for their own safety's sake. But Tapiz could be expected to do exactly as he was told. He was loyal to the policies and affiliations of his employer, the government, almost to a fault. He shuffles out from under the causeway, speckled with dollops of color, and Ibrahim feels an affinity toward his helper like the feelings a teacher may hold for a trying student.

Tapiz is extremely prompt, a creature of moderate routine, and he usually arrives in the early-morning hours while the temperature is still cool. He starts his days by unfolding the canvas tarps that will be draped across the gilded dome tops or barren street corners, invoking the settings before Ibrahim would later arrive and with a seemingly effortless flick of his wrists begin to create their identity. Their current project is commissioned from seven thirty in the morning until four in the evening, a longer day than usual, with a pair of intermittent breaks and a two-hour respite when the sun hangs at its peak.

"Sir, the sky has almost fallen. Shall I start to pack our things?"

"Thank you, Tap. I forgot the time myself for a moment," Ibrahim responds with a friendly smile, recognizing the joke between them. "Hopefully it won't fall completely before we are able to finish. I will be out shortly to help you."

Tapiz and Ibrahim nod toward each other with the common subtlety of people who have worked together for a long time. The iron gate swings slackly into place behind him, and Tapiz shuffles back out into the square to begin to break down their station for the night.

"With all due respect," Ibrahim begins again, resuming an air of resolution, "I am not–nor have I ever been–concerned with matters of this nor any other government or its policies. It does not interest me, Yusuf. You politic, I paint. That's what we do. The nature of your business humbles me."

"Ibrahim, so young and so naïve, what do you think the purpose is for these–your great pieces of artwork?" Yusuf asks, and spreads his arms out toward the half-exposed surface of brick and sandstone wall outside on the street corner, carefully block-aded by three stories of scaffolding.

"For what purpose do you think this work is for?" he repeats.

Ibrahim does not like such strong discussions; in fact he used to be scared of them. But lately the fear is gone, instead replaced by a growing tolerance he was not accustomed to. He has always been able to express himself through his private work, and he knows he is fortunate because it is more than anyone else is permitted; to do so any other way is much too dangerous. In his lifetime, Ibrahim has known words to kill more people than bullets. He feels his palms moisten as Yusuf stands up and steps over beside him.

"Propaganda," Yusuf whispers into his ear. "You–and you must forgive me for saying this–are a mere instrument of their propaganda."

Outside the yard, cars have begun to honk in circular repetition, and the rising tides of rush hour have settled over the neighborhood. Food shortages brought on by the war had slowly found their way to the capital with no bread, rice, or milk deliveries received within the past two weeks. Ibrahim's stomach rumbles loudly like the hollowed-out burner in the basement of his and Shalira's apartment. Lights are sprouting up like weeds from the second-story windows as the complex's tenants return straight to their homes after a workday performed with minimal sustenance. In the waning hours of daylight, there is a void of energy, and everyone, as expected, has grown a bit irritable. Ibrahim can hear someone scolding Tapiz outside on the street corner. The man is warning Tapiz to get out of the entranceway, threatening the young apprentice under the duress of some type of hunger-induced violence.

"And who is the organizer of this great democratic party?" Ibrahim asks, and looks up at Yusuf, the old man completely shadowed within the midst of the delicate tea roses.

Across the yard, a tall office worker pushes his way through the side gate and turns to press it shut behind him, in the process locking out Tapiz, who had been following at a safe distance. Tapiz plays the knob over several times and then gives the door one final shake, but it still does not open. Denied entry, he curses back at the worker, who has already let the moment pass and is scurrying up the side steps to his apartment while stuffing a slice of olive loaf into his beckoning mouth.

"Who is their leader?" Ibrahim turns and asks again.

Yusuf drums his fingers on the wooden tabletop and has grown quite anxious himself with the fluttering movements of the late afternoon. He is a man unable to be at ease while on the streets.

"I am," he solemnly responds, abruptly stopping his fingers for a brief moment.

Suddenly the backyard is awash in radiant white lights, the timer floodlights casting their illuminating prescence over the entire patio, Ibrahim, and his father-in-law. Both men have been on edge and jump back from the table, eyeing the immediate surroundings with caution and apprehension until nothing has changed except the fading degree of sunlight, and then their heartbeats settle and the tension passes.

"Are we now scared of our own shadows?" Yusuf asks, and his expression softens.

Ibrahim knows his father is correct when he tells him to be more careful and to remain aware of the things going on around him. But Ibrahim has also grown to detest the false sense of security his father exhibits by insisting on keeping his mouth shut and suppressing his own ideas and thoughts. He is surprised Hassan Jaffa hasn't gone crazy yet, living like a skeleton. Ibrahim also knew that Hassan Jaffa did what he thought was necessary in order to survive and that his father's wisdom was not to be overlooked—he always had their best interests at heart. It was

Hassan Jaffa who encouraged Ibrahim to go study the great European artists in Florence, Rome, and Vienna, to travel and live abroad, to take in different cultures and help expand his creative spirit. But Ibrahim could never bring himself to leave Hassan Jaffa behind. Since Fazeera's death, they were all each other had.

Ibrahim focuses his eyes in thought, mindlessly contracting the muscles of his face until he can feel the small crack in the base of his nasal passage opening. Then the memory of that night floods its way back into his head like the throbbing growing steadily behind his nose, and Ibrahim is soon overcome with a murderous rage. It is a rage foreign to him until only recently, and one he is growing scared of and unsure of its projections.

He looks up at Yusuf, the father of Shalira, and for the first time that late afternoon he can see his full expression, his eyes deep black and cavernous and awash in the abundant lighting of the Samah Apartments. But there is no depth to his stare. Ibrahim recalls that same quality in the president, whom he had met many years earlier during a visit to their village when Ibrahim was still a young boy.

10

MARCH 30, 1984

THE COLORS HAVE SOULS and spirits, invisible patterns lending to their personification. The indigos, silently calm and controlled, maintain their posture for integrity's sake, always keeping up a professional demeanor. The thin whispers of maize, streaming restlessly like a concubine awaiting her release, are full of energy yet restrained and slowly grow frustrated. The splashes of red are simply murderous and all he has come to know and hate in his homeland. If he had his way, there would be no need for red, a country devoid of scarlet and vermilion.

Scholars will state the work is the manifestation of his creativity; of an inner being, a subconscious brimming over with an idea or a thought as though it were passing through the mind of someone else instead. Eventually, when complete, it will present itself intimately and without candor, beating strong with its own life so that others may feel that flutter too within their own hearts; a separate entity. If the premise holds true, then why can't these instruments be imbued with their own senses, alive as well, with and without the creator?

His mind dances like a slow waltz between the palette's rainbows, the shades flattened and dull so as not to burn his eyes. He has come to the edge and recognizes only the drops at his feet, the murderous ones staining the soles. Even pain is an emotion, and with any emotion one feels alive. Without, we are merely whispers.

In addition to his memory, he uses an old photograph from a summer day spent swimming within the cool crystal waters of the Mediterranean Sea. He trails an ethnic line from the corner of her defined cheekbones, slightly glossy and youthful with hints of faraway light, and although he knows her youth only from pictures, she is coming alive again as a young woman. He pouts the fullness of her violet lips, careful not to provoke, and in her eyes he spends the rest of the day, searching for her sensitivity in pinpoints of aqua speckled with mahogany and whits of gray, for these are the most refined of colors.

When he is done, he removes his T-shirt from his thin frame and wipes the sweat off his brow and arms. It has been close to seven hours without a break. He retreats to the sink, large and metallic, where his brushes and tins echo with the impassioned voices beckoning him further. But she is finished. Colors melt into pools of gray underneath the hot water of the faucet, and he chips a hardened piece of green with the edge of his thumbnail, wiping away the memory within his fingerprint. Only when he is finished cleaning his instruments does he go back into the room and carefully uncover the canvas sitting in silence on the wooden easel.

"I am your mother–Fazeera," she calls to him, *"awakened with the help of your touch, my beloved son, the artist. Please tell your father I have come back to see him."*

⌄

75

For the past thirteen years, it has been only the two of them, each of them relying on the other as their source of meaning and of family. The extra care and concern that often comes when losing a loved one directed, without thinking, upon the other.

His pictures talk to him. They always have. Even as a young boy painting a tree, the leaves would call out for the wind, howling for the caress of their company, or the rustic sound of a sketched car engine would cause him to stand up and peer out his windows almost expecting to see the arrival of an unannounced visitor. He doesn't know where the voices come from; he only fears that one day they may stop and with them his talent.

When his father had set up the meeting with the Ministry of Culture, Ibrahim wanted no part of it. He didn't want to work for the government. But it had become next to impossible to make a living in Baghdad, let alone in the creative arts. With the threat of war looming, opportunities were scarce. He had originally intended to go to Paris or Vienna, to some grand European city his neighbor Abhad al-Sharistani had described to him in lavish detail while Ibrahim, as a child, fingered through the black-and-white photos the old schoolmaster had taken while abroad. The images and visions he had in his mind of the world outside his own country had come from al-Sharistani, and also from his father, Hassan Jaffa.

Hassan Jaffa set up an internship for Ibrahim with the curator of the Palazzo Capponi in Florence, whom Hassan Jaffa had worked with for over twenty-five years. He wish was for Ibrahim to see the historical works of the Renaissance and the Enlightenment; to walk inside the Sistine Chapel, to tour the great amphitheater, to see what Michelangelo had seen and not bear witness through the secondhand eyes of someone else's pictures. Hassan Jaffa hoped it would transform his son, and he wanted to offer him all the inspiration, all the tools, the world could provide, although in their knowledge he himself was quite limited. He bought Ibrahim a one-way plane ticket to Italy for his eighteenth birthday, keeping the part regarding the internship a secret. But when Ibrahim refused, it should have come as no surprise. It had been only the two of them since Fazeera's death when Ibrahim was only ten years old.

Ibrahim had found her prone and struggling with her consciousness in the small garden she tended next to their house. She had found her own inspiration in the color of the irises and in the perfume of the lilies. Being a strong and even-tempered woman, she never complained or let on about the growing pain in her chest. In fact, she kept it entirely to herself. One morning she collapsed in the level dirt before Ibrahim could reach her.

"My son," she began, and Ibrahim waited patiently for her to finish her sentence.

But she never did; leaving him with those final words. Hassan Jaffa never had a chance to say good-bye.

They found out later that when she had lost her breath, her lungs were almost entirely filled with fluid and had caused her to choke to death. As was her nature, her last breaths passed without much notice of her severe internal struggle. The examining doctor commented on how much pain she must have been in. "And for a considerable amount of time, I suspect," he added.

Ibrahim and Hassan Jaffa made a pact soon afterward to keep no secrets, promising to keep everything that happened, even the mere common disturbances of sleep or the harmless rashes that broke out on Ibrahim's forearms from the cheaper oil-based paints, open and discussed between the two of them. Fazeera's stern approach had offered them no final words, and the regret hung between father and son like leaden sacks tied around their necks.

"I am to stay here with you, Father," Ibrahim had told Hassan

Jaffa, the plane ticket resting idly on the table separating them. "I made a pact and I intend to stay here with my family."

Within the next week, Jazeri, an official at the Ministry of Culture, sent a letter requesting Ibrahim to come to the building for a meeting. Ibrahim was skeptical at first. He was used to rejecting all matters concerning the government out of his own indifference. But he was growing tired of seeding and pruning the cracked soil during the growing season and working part-time in the Baghdad Museum unloading and sorting through deliveries that had already been opened for official inspections upon their arrival at the airport terminals.

"I will start immediately," he informed Jazeri upon being told of the opening.

"Excellent," Jazeri answered, and quickly stood up to shake Ibrahim's hand. "I suspect you will make the regime very proud of your appointment."

But Ibrahim wasn't listening anymore. All he understood at the time was that he was going to be able to make a living in his own country while being able to stay home with his father. He would keep what remained of their family together with the hopes of enlarging it in the near future as well. The financial benefits were generous, more than he needed to survive on, and Ibrahim quickly grew excited at the prospect that he would soon be able to propose to his *asheikety*, Shalira.

Then one night soldiers from the Republican Guard broke his nose. He would never find out the specific reasons why they smashed their way into his apartment, but deep inside he knew it had something to do with his father-in-law. They crashed through the walls of his personal world, disrupting his life and corrupting the most poignant of gestures; forcing him, by his own very nature, into their game. Shalira withdrew from him, slightly at first, and on those rare nights when they shared supper, she would often leave the room whenever Ibrahim started to talk about his workday. Ibrahim failed to recognize his own budding resentment. The same silence he had once made a pact with Hassan Jaffa to never again let into their lives settled itself into the invisible cracks of their marriage and began expanding. And with the unspoken words, the voices of his pictures also began to fade away.

11

APRIL 2, 1984

THE FINE MIST OF flour from off the biscuits and flatbread produces a harrowing fog-like aura leading down into the basement. He glances up the street one more time and then behind himself to make sure he hasn't been followed and quickly steps through the sweet clouds into the darkness under the eaves.

Ibrahim was not someone who acted out of fear because he rarely felt any fear at all. The only anxiety he did hold was regarding that day he would wake up and be unable to paint, sitting dumbfounded about how to proceed amidst the assorted colors of his oil tubes. The Republican Guard had incorrectly presumed he was involved in some underground movement, but Ibrahim had always made it his business never to get involved in much of anything and to limit his attachments. The men had come looking for Yusuf. They had found Ibrahim and Shalira instead. The address had been wrong and the soldiers acted out of their own respective fears. It was an absurd accusation to him, but with the recent murder of Anas Muttalib, the most vocal of the current anti-Baathists, all the different political activities and parties—the Iraqi Liberation Party, the Iraqi Centrist Party, the National Socialists for Iraq, and the Iraqi Democratic Party, among the most notable—immediately ran back into their separate holes to hide. Any unity Muttalib had tried to foster among the groups died just as he did. The well-educated Al-Hakim seemed to be the next in line for a more prominent role, but his views were too pro-West for many of the radical parties. The chain was temporarily broken.

The government made a quick dash to round up as many outside party members as possible while the body was still warm, taking thousands of prisoners and executing many others. Ibrahim was still curious about how they had managed to misjudge him. He was a governmental employee, though not understanding his affiliation didn't amount to much of anything. The regime rarely made mistakes, and when it did, it was rarer still for the regime to apologize for them. Ever since that night a lingering rage had begun to grow stronger inside him, eating away at his soul. He began to crave the satisfaction of retribution, the taste of which, Ibrahim assumes, must surpass tenfold the sweetness of the pastries and cakes being baked overhead whose aroma gently seeps from underneath the crack in the door, inviting him in.

Ibrahim recognizes more people, besides Yusuf, than he had originally thought he would. There was Savos Adonan, the assistant deputy minister of education, and Mohammed Baznil, owner of the Kabajesh Grill along the western bank of the Tigris. Omadan, a street sweeper in the upper-class neighborhoods of Baghdad whom he had passed on many early mornings, was talking fervently with a small, wrinkled man in the far corner of the room, mimicking the circular motion of his broom. And Ibrahim saw Korobash, a small-time arms dealer from Syria whom he recognized from his pictures in the newspapers, standing at the front of the room fingering through pamphlets and nodding as he spoke with Yusuf. Almost fifty men were packed into the basement of the Papous Bake Shop off Haifa Street. Nervous upon entering the room, Ibrahim's unease increased when he noticed the broad class and social range of the men in attendance and the familiarity of some of their faces. He pulls his head covering tighter about his face and across his cheeks, hoping to prevent his own recognition.

Rectangular pieces of balsa wood have been nailed over the windows across the upper portion of the basement walls. Outside on the street four older boys stand watch, paired together at each end of the avenue. The lights in the bakery on the main floor are on as the proprietor—a solidly built Greek named Georgi Papous—kneads large mounds of dough with his paw-like hands and heartily sings aloud his favorite native love songs.

In the basement underneath the shop, chairs have been assembled side by side to form several rows in the small room. Placards are posted on the walls advertising slogans of revolt. THE ONLY ALTERNATIVE TO THE BAATH IS REVOLUTION and FIGHT BACK & BREAK THE INSTITUTIONS OF FEAR are painted in large red and green, boldfaced letters. A few brazen men wear buttons with the Arabic acronym for the ILF on their jacket lapels, the initials for the Iraqi Liberation Front, a growing party in central Iraq promoting the ideals of capitalism and democracy. An organization comprising close to a hundred textile workers and farmers stretching from Nasiriyah to Fallujah, the ILF was gaining steam and received funding from militant groups in Syria, who had also sent the arms dealer to invoice any weapons needed by the group for the fulfillment of its purposes. Weeks earlier, the ILF had claimed responsibility for the bombing of three police cruisers outside Samarra that had also killed four civilians. The group had followed up the attack with a failed attempt to destroy the Bank of Sadou, rumored to house the majority of the regime's money, in downtown Baghdad.

Ibrahim picks a small pamphlet off the table by the back entrance. On the cover is a charred and burnt generic Iraqi city above the statement "We fight as our cities and heritage are destroyed; and yet another palace goes up on the blood of our brothers."

Ibrahim knew he had made a mistake by agreeing to come tonight. The other day while they'd sat in the courtyard, he had just wanted Yusuf to go away, and Ibrahim had only nodded his head when Yusuf insisted that he would not leave until he had committed himself.

"The youth of today lack the proper commitment towards anything," Yusuf had claimed.

The tenants coming home from work had made Ibrahim anxious. He didn't want to be seen with Yusuf. His link to the old man was what had caused the trouble in the first place. Ibrahim had previously submitted an application to the board of the Samah Apartments with a portion of the $10,000 he had received from the general as a down payment for an apartment, and he was waiting to see if he and Shalira would be accepted into the complex. He had just wanted to be left alone so he could finish his work. At the time, Ibrahim had felt like hitting him with his bare fists, cursing the old man and telling him that his principles and ideas were not for everyone and to leave him and his father alone. But Yusuf had struck a chord when he had questioned the purpose of Ibrahim's work. Then he had sensed Ibrahim's rage and acted upon it, smiling and telling Ibrahim that his anger was the manifestation of his own frustrations and that *he* had ultimately brought out such feelings. Yusuf failed to mention his own daughter's growing reticence. He didn't have to.

"But to grow angry with me," Yusuf claimed, "is to show anger towards the liberator."

"Praise be Allah," Ibrahim swore to himself, "this man is crazy."

But now as he sits with his face partially covered in the basement of the Papous Bake Shop, Ibrahim reads the same pamphlet over several times and he can't help but wonder if it is possible that all these men could be crazy as well.

"Gentlemen," Yusuf commands from the front of the room, "I applaud your safe arrival and continued discretion. We have recognized the fundamental need for self-organization. And it is upon this principle that the foundation for our struggles ahead must be built; to not only further our own ideals of a society without fear and boundary but to also monitor the movements and activities of our enemies.

"They may have murdered the liberator Muttalib but they do not understand there are a million more men waiting eagerly in line behind him."

Yusuf quickly takes hold of the room with the ferocity of his rhetoric and the rising cadence of his voice. His own words energize the old man, and for a second Ibrahim forgets he is his father-in-law.

"We will be a by-product of the state no longer. Why should all not share in the common needs and concerns of the individual? Why must we be afraid to speak our minds?"

The men begin to holler and yell in agreement. Omadan, the street sweeper, rises up from his chair and begins to applaud. Yusuf levels a small gavel against the wooden table, a thin, sweet cloud rising off its surface, and brings the room once again to silence.

"We must keep our voices low," he continues. "The ears of the enemy are everywhere."

And with this statement, he reaches into his frock and after a short moment of deliberation produces a small, wrinkled plastic bag. He places it gently on the table in front of him, and several men seated in the front gasp at the gnarled piece of folded cartilage inside purported to be a severed human ear.

"Everywhere," Yusuf repeats with a deadened stare.

A light shiver creeps its way through Ibrahim's body, and he rubs his palm over the skin of his forearm, the fine hairs standing to quiet attention.

Ibrahim had never been able to take Yusuf seriously. The old man lacked courtesy, even in the most common of conversations, like one whose purpose or aim outweighs the need for manners. He was unrefined and abrasive, and these characteristics were more irritating and harder to ignore given his advanced age. But the more he spoke, the more Ibrahim realized his appeal to the working class he was trying to ignite. He spoke like a common man, with truth and desire, about working toward the betterment of the individual and their families. He reflected on the shop he'd owned years earlier and the peace it had brought him at first. Then he evoked the theme of family.

"It is the family who should rule our hearts," Yusuf preached. "Without family there is no connection to reason."

As Yusuf stood preaching in front of the small room of men, he resembled a disheveled schoolteacher rather than a revolutionary; a teacher educating grown men on the principles of democracy and on an alternative rule whose mere discussion, once made public, was punishable by death. Yusuf was dressed in a tan and white frock secured by a black rope tied loosely around his waist. A gray beard reached into a triangular point three inches off his chin, and his eyebrows were arched high into sinister patterns. For the first time, Ibrahim realized, Yusuf could easily be mistaken for the Ayatollah Khomeini.

"They have taken our land, our identity, and our pride. They cannot succeed in taking our free will because it is something we were never allowed to possess in the first place. The time for silence is over."

A wave of apprehension shoots through Ibrahim's joints and he suddenly wishes to flee the basement meeting. He rises to leave the room, and as he turns toward the door, the white square outlined on the floor where his chair had rested catches his eye. Then Yusuf calls out to him.

"Please remain in your seat until we are all done," the old shop owner demands. "Our aims are not unjust nor are our methods. They are all that we have to work with at the moment. Our actions are not for the individual but for the common good. We must not forget that pride is a sin. Please sit, we are all"–he stretches out his arms, draped religiously in shepherd's cloth, to embrace the room–"we are all each other have."

At that precise moment, Ibrahim can understand the frustration that causes many people to act against their own will, regardless of whether Yusuf felt one possessed it or not. Ibrahim knew he was stronger than most people. He would not be led, and although he understood and agreed that pride was indeed a sin, he still intended to make it known that his sins were his own doing and free from anyone's control.

Ibrahim turns to confront the old man, but before he can utter a word of protest, a series of abrupt knocks echo off the floor overhead. Papous, the Greek baker, hammers out a measured code with his broomstick.

"Be silent," Yusuf says, and puts the back of his hand to his mouth.

Two of the boys who had been standing watch outside run through the side door and quickly make their way over to Yusuf. They struggle nervously with their breath, and their faces are drawn tight with fear. Ibrahim watches their lips move excitedly at the ear of the old man, their adolescent jawlines hardening beneath the skin. Then Yusuf sweeps them aside with his thin arms.

"Vacate the premises immediately," Yusuf orders, and the men quickly begin to storm out of the room.

As Ibrahim follows the large, meaty back of Korobash, the

arms dealer, out the back door and into the side alleyway, he turns to look back at his father-in-law and catches Yusuf still waiting at the podium and staring directly back at him. Then Ibrahim is pushed out through the fog of flour and sugar straight into the night by the arms of the men struggling to exit behind him.

12

APRIL 4, 1984

"THEY SNUCK IN WHILE I was at work here with you."

Tapiz starts to grow angrier with each word, the skin on his neck and around his ears beginning to redden. He is seated on a fragile wooden chair whose legs bow slightly underneath his formidable weight. He looks uncomfortable and his pant legs have ridden up a fair distance to reveal his pallid white calves.

"And they took my typewriter. Those bastards didn't even try to cover their tracks. Everything was tossed about and scattered. But what can I do? How am I to write my book?"

"I didn't know you were interested in writing a book," Ibrahim replies with a growing sense of concern. He hadn't told anyone that a few of his personal pieces had recently gone missing from his studio. The artwork had taken him close to six months to complete, and Ibrahim felt as though time had been stolen from him as well. To Ibrahim, Tapiz looked unharmed, there were no physical markings, and *his* nose had not been broken.

"Yes, I am interested," Tapiz answers humbly, "but it is impossible to be interested in anything here that doesn't promote the ideas of our great leader, the king. 'White are our crafts'—that is bullshit."

Ibrahim has been trying to teach him the proper way to mix colors on a palette, but all Tapiz seems capable of doing is covering his lumpy thumb over and over again from where it protrudes through the opening for support. He didn't know it had taken Ibrahim weeks to find a palette with a hole big enough to accommodate his large finger.

"I guess for once you might have to keep that finger out of your nose," Ibrahim jokes, nodding toward the nub swaying grotesquely under a thick pool of evergreen.

"Maybe the ladies will like me better," Tapiz says, and he begins to paint the length of his thick forearms, "green like the American Hulk."

Both men break into laughter. Workdays with Tapiz were always humorous, and despite the stumpy man's lack of dexterity and creativity, Ibrahim felt lucky to be working with him. Ibrahim appreciated his good-natured humor, and a bond had developed rather quickly between the two, enabling them to speak more freely with each other during the course of the day.

Silence had become common among people, even between neighbors and family members. Suspicion nestled everywhere, and the open friendliness that was once a characteristic of the capital city had been replaced by a state of distrust and fear. Cafés sat dimly quiet while the men played backgammon and dominoes without speaking. The only conversation stirred in public pledged allegiance to the state or poked fun at the athletic misgivings of the national soccer team. To Ibrahim, it was as if something had sucked all the colors out and left behind a cold, gray society. He remembers the old black-and-white photos of Vienna and Paris after World War II and can't help but think part of his job was to try to inject some color back into his country.

When Ibrahim was first assigned Tapiz, he was not looking

forward to working with someone. He had always worked alone and was spared from the worrisome behavior that afflicted everyone in public. He detested being watched. It was a small sense of freedom he enjoyed; working, usually outdoors, without guard or constraint.

The morning of their first day together Tapiz had failed to secure the locks on the scaffolding. When he pulled himself up onto the first level, the shifting of his weight caused the upper three levels of metal brackets to collapse loudly around him. Ibrahim couldn't remember the last time he had laughed so hard. He watched as the top of Tapiz's head poked above the last folded layer of the contracted landing, seemingly unharmed, and then as an arm raised itself slowly in the air and extended a middle finger from its hand.

From that day forward, Tapiz was put in charge of breaking down the scaffolding stations rather than building them up. In the mornings he would gather their paints and brushes, unfold the tarps, complete the chores deemed "undangerous" but necessary—"the prep work," they both had called it. Ibrahim accepted Tapiz's shortcomings without any reservation and was grateful for the laughter Tapiz brought back into his life.

"Could you imagine me on the front?" Tapiz asks aloud. Both of his arms are green up to the elbows. He stands up and flexes his arms across his chest in a mock bodybuilder's pose, his ample belly the only area protruding under the exertion.

Unfortunately, Ibrahim could imagine Tapiz on the front. He could imagine his fattened torso lying bare, with his uniform blown apart, and motionless on the sands outside Basra, the skin hardening like leather under the weight of the midday sun. Tapiz wouldn't have made it one day in the firing lines, Ibrahim knew as much, and he began to feel guilty that he had not been conscripted into the army as well.

Ibrahim did not fear death and would proudly have fought for his country. He was physically fit and would have been more than able to train and fight. Brandishing a Kalashnikov, he would have headed east in the direction of the Persian army just like every other Iraqi male. He knew many men his age that were sent off, many able-bodied men. Most of them never came back. But he was more concerned about leaving Hassan Jaffa. He worried about leaving him alone. He understood Hassan Jaffa would himself die if anything happened to Ibrahim. The responsibility to his father was greater than any responsibility he felt toward his country. Yusuf had proclaimed that family should rule the heart, and the old shop owner was dead-on—no civic duty could outweigh the pull of one's own blood.

Ibrahim reaches for Tapiz's elbow and gently turns it so that the palette lies flush and sturdy across the squat man's forearm.

"No more shows, Hulk, please," Ibrahim says. "We need to spare as much paint as possible."

Tapiz works the different-sized brushes, rotating them in his thick fingers, and mixes shades into the palette. He slowly becomes graceful with the repetition, the motion like the fluttering wings of a butterfly. Ibrahim leaves him to his concentration and goes to sit within the shade of a date tree. He pulls a cigarette from his pocket, and as he lights it, he watches Tapiz and is proud of the progress he has made in the six months the two of them have worked together. Frog missiles blast off in the horizon, but they have become such a common occurrence that Ibrahim does not pay any attention. Firefighting broke out earlier toward the northern district outside the city of Kadhimain. Hours later the gunfire has finally begun to diminish, and desultory shots ring out only every half hour.

"To think I could have been in Italia instead," Ibrahim whispers to himself, eyes closed to this world and focusing instead on the black-and-white world in the photos taken by the old schoolmaster al-Sharistani and in his own imagination.

It was four years ago, on his eighteenth birthday, when Hassan Jaffa had presented him with a one-way ticket to Florence. "The old man is still pretty clever," Ibrahim thought to himself at the time, "sending me abroad to avoid the draft and the war." In reality, Hassan Jaffa had wanted to give his son the world, not to shelter him from it. Ibrahim's pride would never let him avoid the responsibilities of war. But the actual fighting was taking place so many miles away that it often seemed to be going on in a different country altogether. Its ramifications eventually worked their way up to Baghdad but were only subtly felt in the occasional food shortages, the raised prices in the markets or the empty place settings at the dinner tables. Television and newspaper reports proclaimed great Iraqi victories at Mehrabad and Tabriz. Bandar Khomeini had been destroyed by French Exocet missiles, and the oil-rich areas of Kharg and the Farsi Islands were close to being fully occupied by Iraqi forces. According to the majority of reports, the Iraqis had won almost every battle to date.

Then six months ago he'd felt an itch stirring in his belly. It was an unseasonably warm November morning when he'd walked into Jazeri's office in the ministry building. The small man sat at his desk reading the newspaper *ath-Thawra* with his legs stretched out on his desktop. The tips of his black leather shoes barely reached the edge of the wood. The responsibility of love within Ibrahim had loosened its grip with the simple pull of pride.

"We have achieved another great victory," Jazeri proclaimed when Ibrahim entered the office, and he folded the newspaper neatly across his lap.

"It is amazing that this war is still going on with so many of our victories."

Behind him, a large bay window opened onto downtown Baghdad. Dispossessed minarets rose above the canopy of palm trees, and from this vantage point the streets of the capital formed simple geometric patterns down below them. Several blocks away on the far banks of the river a three-story building with its middle torn out like the body of a gazelle captured by lions stood in mild defiance. Members of the Iraqi Liberation Front, a militant terrorist group, had been charged with rolling explosives through the street in a wheelbarrow and letting go halfway to the building so the wheelbarrow could continue unattended toward its entrance. But its delivery fell short as its wheels twisted against the curb, and the explosives detonated before reaching the entrance gate to the Bank of Sadou, blowing through its gut and killing all seven people standing in the hall corridor.

Jazeri pulled a cigar out of a small wooden dresser next to his desk and insipidly bit through the bitter end with his front teeth. Bits of tobacco stained the enamel. He leaned back and puffed deeply until the end of the cigar glowed orange like a miniature sun and stared off into the city.

"The insurrectors have no brains," Jazeri said, and pulled his leather chair up to the window. "Who bombs a bank at six thirty in the morning? And on a Saturday nonetheless."

He puffed tentatively, sucking on the edges of the cigar rather than drawing its breath. An unlimited supply of Cuban cigars was one of the benefits of being a high-level government official. Iraqi president Saddam Hussein received bimonthly shipments directly from Fidel Castro pledging his support. Ibrahim, in his appointment, had never even been offered one.

"I am sorry to bother you, sir," Ibrahim began.

Jazeri turned back toward Ibrahim and grew serious for a moment. He put his feet back up on the desk. Ibrahim noticed the soles of the man's shoes were unscuffed and shiny and he could still read the maker's logo on the bottom. The rugs in these governmental buildings must not be coarse on the feet at all, he thought to himself.

"Sir, I would like to take a leave–to go fight at the front. I mean no disrespect, but I have been idle here too long. I feel I must do my part."

The deputy minister looked quizzically at Ibrahim.

"The idea is a very commendable one," Jazeri replied, "and filled with such good intention." Then he stood up and turned once again toward the city below him, biting down hard on the cigar in his mouth.

"I remember being a young boy and walking down these same streets. It was much different back then, struggling for an identity after the Turks and the Brits. My childhood existed against a background of military seizures of power. There was never any stability–I couldn't even tell you what my father did for a living, he had so many odd jobs–and a child born into a life without stability is the saddest thing in this world."

"Yes, it is a sad thing," Ibrahim agreed in appeasement.

"You are doing your share. Everyone has a part to play," Jazeri replied after a slight pause. He gestured beside himself. "Please."

Ibrahim walked around the desk and stood next to the deputy minister to look out the window. Cars were circling around the Saddam Arts Center. News trucks were parked in repose along the street across from the Bank of Sadou. Ibrahim could see the red hats of the Republican Guard soldiers moving like glowing targets in the distance.

"People do not like it when their loved ones die. Regardless of purpose or intent, that is human nature and quite understandable. We are struggling with our own stability, for the futures of our very own children. Since the gains are not immediate, we can lose morale rather quickly. Although we have achieved great victories, we have also paid a tremendous cost. We must always remember that. For this is our city we are fighting for, and for all the northern and southern territories. We cannot afford to lose our identity, and we must continue to show the greatness of our supreme leader."

They stood in silence watching taxicabs and dilapidated buses jockey back and forth. The bells of the Kadhimain Bazaar sharply rang out. Over on Mansur Street, a mule carriage had upturned and was blocking traffic from making the turn onto the thoroughfare. Cars began to honk against the animal. Distressed by fear, the mule proceeded to empty its bowels in front of the traffic jam.

"It is our great prosperity we are fighting for," Jazeri continued, "our stability. You are doing your part."

"But, sir," Ibrahim tried but was cut off immediately.

"Besides, I know how fond of your father you are. Leaving him alone, well, if anything were to happen . . ."

Ibrahim suddenly grew nauseous and for a moment he thought he was going to get sick. Jazeri had struck the right note. Ibrahim thought of Hassan Jaffa coming home at night after work, the family he had begun in hope now completely gone. All the reasons he used for his own silence performed in vain. Then Ibrahim felt an arm fall across his shoulders.

"Forgive us our transgressions. It has been decided by those in power that you are of better service here," Jazeri started, "and, you will be happy to know, you have also been assigned an apprentice. You will meet him tomorrow at sunrise. An amiable fellow who you will instruct."

The six months passed rather quickly and quite smoothly. Ibrahim had accepted the idea that he was of "better service" at his current station. He also knew that it wasn't for the same reasons as those in charge had intended. Islam forbade the depiction of human or animal forms in art, and by painting the president, Ibrahim felt slightly liberated and brazen, as though he were disobeying the laws of twelve hundred years.

Ibrahim has finished his cigarette and closes his eyes underneath the date tree when Tapiz comes over and sits down against the opposite side. Ibrahim senses the man's clumsy movements as the dirt stirs with each footstep. He can also hear his strained breathing. A pleasant, moderate breeze trembles through the leaves, and it is at these times during the day, when the noon hour has passed and a good half day's effort has already been given, that Ibrahim feels at peace.

"They have your wife's father."

Ibrahim opens his eyes to the sound of his apprentice's voice. It takes him a moment to shake the daydreams from his head and for the location of his surroundings to register.

"Tapiz?" Ibrahim cries out, shocked but futilely hoping he had not heard correctly. "Tapiz, on the souls of your children, can I trust you?"

Bewildered and a bit deflated at the level of trust he was accustomed to with Tapiz, his shoulders slacken and he reaches for the water bottle in his jacket pocket. Ibrahim takes a long sip, recognizing the general suspicion that has momentarily deprived him of saliva.

"Yes, boss," Tapiz responds, and tosses a folded-up piece of paper behind him and next to Ibrahim. "He is in Sijn Al-Tarbut."

"The casket prison?" Ibrahim asks, and opens up the paper.

Inside, written in small Arabic lettering, is the address of the Papous Bake Shop on Haifa Street, the location of the ICP meeting the night it had been raided.

"Yes, the casket prison," Tapiz replies. "They tried earlier when they came to your apartment based on information that he would be there. Boss, you must be careful."

Ibrahim pauses for a few seconds, accepting the immediate comfort of silence. Several birds sing from high up in the trees overhead, a few descending to a small concrete fountain resting empty since the war began.

"They are watching you," Tapiz warns.

13

OCTOBER 9, 1984

I RISE TO THE ethereal sounds of a harp being lightly plucked, and for a meditative moment I am in a gondola under the pale Venetian moon, our skin hues of blue. But the mood is quickly altered as a man cackles loudly in Arabic from outside my hotel room window, and I contemplate the importance of language in music, his voice and the words it bellows forth far more suitable to the revving of a twelve-cylinder tractor engine than my subliminal wanderings.

Outside, a trio of men dressed in ankle-length caftans perform an Arabian rendition of a midnight Bourbon Street corner. One of the men delicately fingers a large gilded harp whose appearance on a crowded street corner during the morning rush hour is quite mystifying. His fingertips search with the tenderness and deliberation of an artisan the stringed intestines worn pale and thin in the middle. Another, an overly enthusiastic and heavyset man, dances about on his toes and appears to be writing mathematical formulas in the air, his gestures as wild as his voice, which streams forth from a mouth wider than the ancient tomb of Hammurabi. The third man, and the smallest, is seated in the corner behind them cradling two metal brushes over the surface of a small camel-skin drum resting neatly between his legs, the fur of the animal covering its sides to provide some comfort from the wood's coarseness against his limbs.

Daniella is gone, fleeing under the stars and the threats accompanying the imposed curfew despite my attempts to persuade her to stay the night. A white terry-cloth bathrobe hangs used and slightly damp over the desk chair, a subtle reminder that she was here in person and not in one of my dreams. She had fallen asleep by mistake—and rather quickly—and soon she'd shuddered delicately under the power of her own thoughts.

"I was dreaming of a tremendous snowfall and the kissing sound of ice skates moving across glass," she told me before silently closing the door behind her.

It has been like this for close to three years; a revolving door in and out of each other's lives. Over time we have done our best to respect each other's distances for whatever personal reasons we might individually have maintained, politely abstaining from questioning the motives of the other. But deep down I knew I held no reasons of my own for the absence. I used Daniella's instead as a cushion to soften my own hard-headedness and to lend an excuse for my inability to steer her more rigidly in my direction and away from a career that has become her constant companion and obsession.

I would wait weeks for a letter in her hand addressed from the coast of an Indian city or a postcard adorned with the lush vegetation of an untamed hillside in Brazil. I would scan the London *Times* for her stories and then mindlessly run my finger over her name until the ink stained my skin.

We would possess strangers in the interval. I focused my energies on my own career, researching story lines and conjuring up ideas, distant and foreign alike, to keep her from entering my mind. I coped by the same means I had come to regret in her. I played a simple man's game—I simply waited. But last night I could smell the fragrant berries and plumeria nestled deep within her silken black hair, and all the excuses and diversions melted away like the snow left falling in the trembling of her faraway dreams.

Nineteen eighty-one. I am on my way to Cairo for my first international assignment to cover the murder of the Egyptian president Anwar Sadat. The previously assigned foreign journalist for *The New York Times,* an aged and respected veteran, had driven up to Stamford, Connecticut, to be with his wife, a cartographer, after she had begun to go insane. Her work, the complex patterns of streets and cities composing detailed maps, began to contain the danger of sharper angles, of places nonexistent or invisible to the public eye, and of subjective distances measured in arcane phrases rather than mathematical specifications, a mirror image of the thoughts that had begun to unravel in her head.

I was working hard making a name for myself in the presses. I had recently covered the murder of John Lennon for a weeklong series running in the *Times* and had received a critics' award for those efforts in conjunction with my domestic reporting on the influence the papal authority held over American businesses after the failed assassination attempt on the pope less than six months earlier. A promotion at the expense of the health of a colleague's wife wasn't the break I was waiting for, but the story was not about to wait for me to resolve my misgivings. As one primary editor told me, "It's either you, Michael, or someone else." The international front was the next logical step in my career. I stopped by Saint Patrick's Cathedral and silently said a prayer for the New England couple, lighting a votive candle before I made the drive out to JFK Airport.

I arrived by chartered plane from London along with several other foreign journalists and touched down in Cairo sometime in the early afternoon after fourteen tedious hours. All arriving flight numbers were being processed and checked for security clearance while still hovering in the sky. Once they were approved, each plane was permitted to land one at a time. A small army was stationed outside the airport blockading traffic in both directions with a contingent of jeeps and tanks. The soldiers, boys no older then sixteen, searched everyone and confiscated any objects that appeared suspicious.

In the following years, I would never encounter a more densely populated city. The streets and passageways, every crevice that at one time in history might unbelievably have stood empty, were packed with a dizzying abundance of bodies both human and animal, dead and alive. People slithered through the streets with their shoulders pressed together, the subtlest of motions permitting forced movements like the rotation of pieces in a jigsaw puzzle. Stuffed trolleys and buses moved lazily under the exertion, fearless beacons unto the city known as the center of the Arab world. Camels and donkeys poked and pitched their way along through the bustle, toting lumber and small rugs, milk crates and farmers' grain, as crabby and belligerent as tardy businessmen. Cars sat idling in scattered rows, bicycles scraping along from their bumpers, and everything baking slowly and evenly under the strong African sun. So much was taking place that I felt a sort of suspension, as though I were watching everything playing out before me like flashes passing across a movie screen. The city was awash in fever. You could taste the infection in the air, as putrid and decaying as the sliced animal carcasses hanging off the overhead hooks lining the streets. It nestled like a contagion in the crevices of folded skin, clinging to the lens of my eyeglasses.

A small group of militant Islamic fundamentalists had shot

the ambitious leader while he was paying public tribute during a holiday parade celebration. The unmarked car had rolled past Sadat's official platform while he waved to the participants and unceremoniously opened fire into the stands. The characteristic distrust and violence poked its head out of the desert sand once again, a common theme in these parts of the world. Cairo was now extremely dangerous, and with each nudge of an elbow or prolonged stare the level of suspicion only increased. Jail cells were overcrowded with detainees, people not formally charged with any crimes, and several municipal facilities had been set up in private buildings to help contain the overflow. The situation reminded me of a sentence I once read in an old history book: "In Cairo, everyone remains a target until the dust settles."

Due to the crowded fairways and streets of the city combined with the intensity of the current situation, I lingered in the mundane media rooms to find some solitude and escape from the throngs of edgy and obnoxious masses. I sat with my feet up in the back row of a University of Cairo lecture hall recently converted to a press conference room, and I studied my notes before the Egyptian ambassador was scheduled to come out for our daily briefing. Several others sat scattered about in the large room listening to their headphones or dozing under the swirling stale breeze generated by the overhead fans. I busied myself reading Sadat's biography and a truncated history of the opposition group responsible for the assassination. I took down notes to questions I halfheartedly expected the ambassador to answer. I thought for a minute about the scant differences between these types of opposition groups around the world and their aversions toward democracy and any movements toward peace. I realized those differences were as thin and transparent as a spider's web. And their struggles often as relentless as those reporting on them. Then I saw her for the first time.

She sat four rows ahead of me next to an older gentleman whose long gray hair framed a face hardened by both time and wind. A tan vest clung to his tall and lean upper body, purposely lending an air of wisdom. I immediately recognized his profile from the stoic black-and-white photo in the London *Times*. He was Johnathon Burkett, the world-renowned British journalist who had been awarded the Pulitzer Prize for his work covering the visit the slain Egyptian president had taken to Israel to meet with Israeli prime minister Menachem Begin. In doing so, Sadat became the first Arab leader to officially visit the Israeli state and, in the process, helped set forth the anger that would seal his fate some four years later. Burkett spoke quickly while the young woman at his side copiously wrote down every word on her legal pad. At times, he placed his long hands upon her forearms while she wrote and casually leaned over for a quick inspection. When he was satisfied, he nodded toward her and would only remove his hand after, I noticed, he tenderly squeezed the muscles of the women's forearm.

I was suddenly nudged on my legs by three short men dressed in unraveling clothes. Without hint of manners they moved themselves into the row and sat in the vacant seats next to mine. As I dropped my legs, other turbaned reporters flooded into the aisles, also lacking the basic courtesy needed in a crowded room. Several men tried to wedge their slim bodies into the tiny spaces between two already occupied seats, their frayed elbows out at the sides like subtle weapons. An older man cursed at a stain spreading curiously across his chest as another man set scurrying toward the aluminum chairs in the front of the room, still carelessly managing his lightened cup of coffee. I could smell the change in the air as the room quickly and surprisingly filled to capacity; a blend of sweat and garlic and mud lifted in thick bands by the lazy motion of the fans and now coursing unpleasantly throughout the room. The remaining seats were quickly filled and also all the spaces in between them. Upon entering the classroom, any additional correspondents were directed to seat themselves upon the floor against the back wall.

I closed my journal and made my way to the refreshment table in the back, sacrificing my seat, which was quickly taken over by the bony asses of three Lebanese reporters. I poured myself a cup of Turkish coffee, whose rich aroma helped to temporarily contain the wafting odor. I stirred in the last of the cream with a small white straw and then discarded the empty container in the garbage bin underneath the table. Feeling a sudden surge of confidence, I decided to introduce myself to Burkett and began to push and slide my way up and over to his row while cautiously trying not to spill any of my coffee.

"Mr. Burkett," I tried, extending my hand over a pair of Moroccan reporters who made no attempt to let me pass. "Michael Young, *New York Times.* It's a pleasure. . . ."

"Oh, a *NYT*," he shot back with the familiar foreign euphemism without turning to face me. "The pleasure is most often mine, young man. Why must you Americans assume all pleasure?"

But before I could answer him, the front doors quickly opened behind the overhead projector and out came the Egyptian ambassador toward the podium set up in the front of the room. He lowered the microphone to compensate for his height, his brooding eyes barely edging the top of the podium, and he began to arrange his documents into some semblance of order, the rustling sound soon echoing with the press of the microphone button throughout the small room. Johnathon Burkett inched his way over, creating a space with his shoulders, and slapped his hand on the empty spot created beside him. I noticed a small smile curve the edge of the woman's lips.

"Members of the foreign press corps and our own distinguished countrymen, good morning to you all," the ambassador began, and for the next two hours we were briefed once again on the events that had taken place the previous day and on the current state of the investigation and the stability of the local government. There were no new changes to report in the twenty-four-hour interval since the ambassador's last briefing.

"I must first warn all of you," he instructed, "no one's safety can be guaranteed. We are in a state of national crisis. The Egyptian government cannot promise our limited resources for the protection of anyone except our own citizenry. We have far more pressing matters than to sacrifice Egypt's most urgent interests at this time or to put our own domestic safety and our country at further risk."

I tried not to get distracted by the woman's delicate hands, red-tipped and briskly covering every important word uttered in the room. A rivulet of dark hair darted into oblivion in the space etched at the base of her neck. After several minutes, her hips swayed to the side for comfort and she adjusted her slender legs and the pad she rested on top of them.

Later that afternoon after the session was completed, I was sitting at the bar of the Bamhoudi Café going over my notes when I saw her walk in alone. She was dressed in a sand galabiya, a loose gown bordered by ancient hieroglyphics first written in these same lands hundreds of years ago. She sat down on the stool next to mine and began to take out her notes as well. The bartender brought her over a drink and placed it on a cocktail napkin in front of her while she spread her papers out around the glass and began to write in their margins.

"My name is Michael Young," I introduced myself.

"Yes, so you have told me," she replied formally. "I am Daniella Burkett." She gestured her eyes toward the entrance she had passed seconds earlier and through which her father, the award-winning journalist, now made his way. "Please tell me you didn't come to see him."

And then she tilted her head and smiled warmly. For a moment it felt like a rustic autumn night in some cozy, nameless bar in Greenwich Village, and without thought I felt myself smile too.

We would meet again in Washington, D.C., two months later, anxious with the uncertainties of a new relationship, and courting each other in the partisan restaurants of Georgetown. Then in Baghdad, as a conduit to Tehran, during the early stirrings of the Iranian Revolution when Saddam Hussein began to settle into the Iraqi presidency. We spent four months in Grenada, finding the solace and beauty lacking in the Communist state within the company of each other. In Venice, I kissed her under the early-morning sun outside St. Mark's, a flurry of pigeons taking flight in waves of ordered ascension, her lips lifted delicately toward the sky and my head drunk with the early-morning dew, breathing deeply the thick air alive with the motion of the birds. In Cairo, we began a journey that would take us to seven different cities, five countries, and span close to four years, a story neither of us realized we were covering. And our own.

14

DANIELLA BURKETT WAS FIVE years old when she found out she was of Iraqi descent. The shy and reserved little girl withdrew from her classmates when she realized that the essential fluid flowing through her veins was comprised of something foreign and distant to the rest of them. As a result, in comparison to the other children her age, she understood herself to be different. One midafternoon when the schools had all let out and the playgrounds were quickly filling up, several fair-haired girls refused to let Daniella in line to jump rope.

"Gypsies aren't supposed to jump rope," teased the taller girl, whose hands secured the rope at one end.

The others quickly followed the lead of the taller girl and blocked Daniella out, turning their bony, arched backs into a circle she could not break.

She had the remarkable strength not to let the hurt show itself on her face, and she walked with her head held high over to the birdhouses on the far reaches of the playground. Not once did she feel the urge to turn around and look back. The tiny paper dwellings hung off the tree branches from colored loops of thread and were decorated much nicer than the birdhouses her own class had made. She sat down and watched in silence as the birds fluttered into and out of the different paper homes. Only later that night in the comfort of her own home did the tears start to roll freely down her innocent cheeks, and Shahrazad, her mother, began to explain to her the blessings of her mixed heritage.

"You should be very proud, Daniella," Shahrazad commanded sternly, her own nationality the one called into question. "You are one part British and one part Iraqi. Your bloodline is a historical timeline dating back to the world's oldest civilization. You are truly a child of the world."

But to a child, the explanation had not been enough. The reasons her mother gave her existed only in her own world, the world of adults. To a child, being different meant that you were somehow cursed. Shortly thereafter, Daniella began to deny her heritage altogether. On those days when Shahrazad would come to pick her up from school, the teacher would call out to tell Daniella her mother was coming up the walkway. She would register the heat of the stares of the other children rising on her cheeks and neck while she waited with the remaining students in the lobby to avoid the English rainfall.

"No," Daniella replied harshly, "she is not my mother."

And she had to be taken away in a fit of adolescent rage, her saddle shoes kicking the air around her while Shahrazad dragged her by her arms away from the school. Daniella could see the other children pressing their faces against the glass to watch the spectacle she had created.

Over time, the pretenses changed to defiance, then to belligerence, and when Daniella was fourteen, she knocked three teeth out of a neighborhood girl's mouth with her knee. The girl had made the mistake of calling her "a darkened Arabian." Daniella wasn't quite sure what the words meant or why they made her so angry. But she heard it spoken with a hint of disgust contained in the girl's tone and inflection. Without thinking, Daniella had thrown her books at the girl's head, and when she'd doubled over in fear, Daniella had whipped her knee up solid against the underside of the girl's jaw and felt the resonance of two rocks slamming together through the muscle in her thigh.

She refused her skating sessions and no longer participated in her swimming instructions. She never stayed after school and purposely shied away from group activities and anything where the interaction with other children was a prime necessity. She immersed herself instead in books, reading voraciously the works of Jane Austen and Charles Dickens, imagining herself as an orphan running wild and free in the darkened world of Trotwood Copperfield or seeking the solace of the sisters she never had, praying for the fulfillment of her own dreams just like the character of Catherine Morland.

Daniella also developed a love of animals, and at one time it was assumed she would become a veterinarian. Sitting on a park bench, she would pull the edges of bread from her sandwich and feed them to the birds and rabbits that frequently came across the carriage path from Briermere Farms. Her quick temper would often come through on those occasions when her intended beneficiaries lingered around a bit too long, unaware of her offerings, and several stray cats or the neighbors' German shepherd would scoop in and steal the food without leaving a morsel for the others. She would then kick her feet at the bellies of the strays or flail a stick at the dog, upset with the creatures' incapacity for sharing. To Daniella, those animals were the most like humans, and it was the innocence of the others that had originally drawn her closer. Over time she would come to respect the authority and keenness of the thieves.

"All creatures must eat," Shahrazad told her, and Daniella

was soon consumed by the ferocity and purposefulness with which the animals lived; eating and defecating, sleeping and hunting, and doing so, as it appeared to her, without judgment.

It was when she was told that her affinity toward the animals was a trait shared by her grandfather and uncles who had bred Arabian horses on their own vast farms outside the northern stretches of Baghdad that a feeling like pride began to stir in her maturing limbs. Shahrazad told her stories of her own father, Daniella's grandfather, riding through the mountains surrounded by hundreds of the powerful steeds, warding off robbers and intruders with a bare rifle and the inbred loyalty of the horses.

"Your grandfather could prevent another man from stealing his property, but he could not prevent the government from taking it by decree," Shahrazad told her. "Age renders all men equal. By the time he was seventy his best horses had passed him by and all he was left with was his pride."

It was around this time of which she spoke that a war broke out between Palestine and Israel. Following the example set by the Egyptian and Syrian governments, Baghdad sent fifteen thousand of its own troops across the waters of the Jordan River, only to be met by swift defeat at the hands of the Israelis. Arab nationalism grew stronger out of the renewed anger directed toward the Jewish state, and back in Iraq people began to resent the European rule and the alleged favoritism the great powers harbored toward Israel.

Along with the stirrings of hate an unsettling fever also crept its way over the land between the two rivers. Floods rained down from melted peaks as caps warmed off the mountaintops, and a series of dramatic rainfalls submersed farmers' fields and cities under levels of water polluted with both dysentery and trachoma. Crop harvests were destroyed. An already deteriorating steadfastness beset by a lack of common social services and an economy dormant since World War II turned its pallid eyes against England and the quasi-monarch it had established. Numerous revolts erupted throughout the city, antigovernment demonstrations in the corridors of the universities and protest marches outside the bazaars set up at the river's edges. Holy leaders congregated outside their mosques calling for change divined "under the will of Allah." Localized attacks against those in power culminated in torched properties and the bombing of police stations. Dissatisfied workers marched with unemployed citizens and energetic college students, protesting loudly but nonviolently against the current conditions, through the palm-laden alcoves leading into the town square, where they were cut down by police gunfire. Others demonstrated across the Mamun Bridge, only to run into smaller groups of similar protesters on the opposite side, all of them collectively executed by the brass sophistication of the queen's army.

In the midst of this turmoil, Johnathon Burkett arrived in Iraq in 1948, absent of the imperialistic ardor of his homeland and armed with a strong desire to educate himself in the intricacies of a country both foreign and disregarded by those trying to govern it from back home. He arrived from London, shortly after the British sailed out of Jaffa, to investigate the problems concerning England's continuing sovereignty over the nation of Iraq.

Shahrazad was only a young woman of nineteen, but she would remember him as being handsome and well-mannered. His skin adjusted quickly, darkening to a healthy copper, and he wore a radiant smile made brighter by the Arabian sun. He seemed surrounded by an aura of mystery and adventure that Shahrazad had recognized in the actions and personalities of her father and uncles. Johnathon Burkett traveled lightly and his movements lent to his impression of having nothing weighing him down, even the pressures of the common daily world. He ate when he was hungry and slept when tired, and he seemed to move freely from one moment to the next as if the transition between the two were something he had planned for in advance. Shahrazad's brothers would tease her as the fair-haired adventurer drank tea with their father underneath the portico in the backyard.

"He talks as if he has no lips," they would joke, making fun of his scholarly accent by trying to mimic the language.

But deep down inside, she knew they all respected him and the tender care he brought with him to everything he encountered, not as a conqueror or a ruler but rather as a student in a foreign country, their country.

He taught them how to ride a motorcycle, laughing hard when the clutch failed to catch and the machine kicked them off to the ground, but always remaining careful not to let the heat of the exhaust pipes burn the skin on their legs. They reciprocated by showing him how to control a breathing horse, where he encountered his own similar difficulties. He brought FM transistor radios with him and introduced them to television, the static of even the snowiest reception still able to arouse their curiosity. In return they had opened their doors to him. In any other village, born into any other family, Shahrazad's friendship with the Englishman would have been forbidden. But to them he was not an Englishman; he was not part of the imperialist machine. He was an outgoing stranger filled to the brim with possibilities who happened to casually ride his motorcycle onto their property one sunny day and, after being given a formal invitation, decided to stay for what turned out to be three months.

Shahrazad's father was a liberally educated man, and on those cool evenings when he sat outside on the earthen porch and listened to the ballroom jazz of an American named Morton, he knew in his heart that his family's link with the Mesopotamian soil had finally run its course. Although he wished for the land of his youth and imagination to someday rise again to the pinnacle of civilization, he didn't want his children left shadowed under its decaying weight.

Those suspicions he held silently within his bosom were to be confirmed years later during the Iraqi revolution. By official edict, large parcels of privately owned land were broken down into smaller segments and the new lots made available for purchase by the local farmers. Soon thereafter, all the plots and parcels were broken down even further and were bought instead by the government and taken under its full ownership as collective farms, reducing the family's once grandiose property to a small parcel no bigger than ten parking spaces.

When Johnathon Burkett sped onto their property atop a loud duster seeking directions to the ancient ruins of Ur of the Chaldees, the biblical birthplace of Abraham, Nuri Effendi felt a proclivity from deep within his chest upon which he could predict a future in the stars overhead for his ambitious daughter, one taking place in a land far away.

Daniella Burkett was born almost four years later on July 23, 1952, the same date a military coup forced the last king of Egypt from his throne. She opened her eyes to this world within the same hour that a youthful King Farouk withdrew to Italy to continue his penchant for food and thievery, forced to steal from the pockets of streetwalkers rather than the world leaders that used to dine at his table.

In a balmy hospital on Andover Street located in the prosperous suburb of Berkenshire, Johnathon Burkett tenderly kissed the sweaty forehead of his wife and within twenty-four hours his feet were to touch down in Cairo and the eventual Republic of Egypt.

"You see, your father has a thing for covering the elimination of world leaders," Shahrazad whispered in Arabic to the baby kicking its tiny legs discontentedly at her bosom.

A trait, like that of the love for animals and an adventuresome spirit, already flowing like an electric pulse through Daniella's limbs and passed down through the transmittal of Iraqi and English blood.

15

PECANS. SHE WOULD FOREVER associate the sweet, syrupy aroma of pecans with her own level of professional success. To Daniella, it began as no more than a simple acquaintance. The first time happened within the confines of a wooden booth nestled inside a dark Devonshire pub while she lazily ate a slice of pie made from the extract of the nut and topped with its crumbled residue. The moment she had put her fork down, Shahrazad came barging through the bar's large oak doors looking for her. Daniella noticed the redness of excitement flushed across her mother's cheeks and the brightness of the midafternoon sun Shahrazad carried in behind her the brief moment the tavern door was open.

Shahrazad hustled directly over to where Daniella was sitting and handed her the large white packet she had been carrying under her arm. Daniella was struck by the presence of the refined woman in Shep's and then she noticed that the corners of the envelope had already been carefully sliced open.

"I am sorry," Shahrazad apologized, "but I could not wait."

Words to mark the first time Shahrazad had ever felt the need to apologize to Daniella for her maternal intrusions. The gesture still didn't make it right, but Daniella tried to practice a little bit of patience with regard to her mother. Shahrazad came from a large and close-knit family and she was used to being surrounded by many of her relatives. She had been a daughter herself at one time, and a sister and a wife, an aunt, a niece, and many other things to so many other people besides being solely a mother to Daniella. And despite the new life Shahrazad had made for herself in England, Daniella knew her mother often got lonely. She wondered if Shahrazad had ever wanted more children.

She let the envelope sit between them, refusing to reach for it even as a small river from the water pitcher meandered its way across the table and threatened the contents. For as long as Daniella could remember, if Shahrazad was happy, then Daniella would by turn be sad. If Shahrazad felt a burst of energy, it was Daniella who claimed to be tired. She contingently played opposites like blowing smoke into the wind. Shahrazad was obviously excited to the point where she couldn't even wait for Daniella to come home. Her enthusiasm was marked by her surprising arrival at Shepherd's and was met by Daniella with her own display of conflicting indifference, frustrating Shahrazad once again with her presumed lack of interest.

"Really, Dee," she began, her accent still thick and a bit ruddy despite living in London for the past twenty years, "you must take more of an interest in these types of things."

Daniella inspected the return address silently and from a table's length distance, careful not to let herself appear too eager. Although she tried to mask her own excitement, her expression must have widened, and the glimmer that Shahrazad never failed to recognize in her daughter's eyes illuminated once again when Daniella recognized the emblazoned crest of Columbia University's School of Journalism.

"Congratulations." Shahrazad could contain herself no longer. "I take it you'll be leaving this summer."

It was at Columbia University's School of Journalism a few years later, while Daniella was anxiously studying for her final exams in her small rented basement flat, when that sweet smell made its presence felt once again. Her roommates had gone to Langeri's to celebrate the end of classes, but Daniella had decided to stay behind to take advantage of the empty apartment. She didn't like wasting the short amount of time it took her to walk to the library, and she was already deep in concentration when the ringing of the telephone brought her back to reality.

"Of course I accept," she coolly informed Jules Markey, then a rising editor for the London *Times*.

Daniella, without consciously doing so, assumed the same air of indifference toward the woman's exuberance as she did with Shahrazad. It was only after she hung up the phone that she realized how blasé and unappreciative she must have sounded. She called Jules back immediately and began to explain to her that the offer had taken her quite by surprise and she apologized for not sounding too enthusiastic.

"To tell you the truth, Jules," Daniella said, "I was not expecting this. You completely shocked me."

"My gosh, Daniella," Jules Markey exclaimed, "for a moment I thought I had the wrong number."

"I am sorry," Daniella said, and they both began to laugh. "You know I have wanted this opportunity my entire life."

Daniella proudly stretched herself out on the coffee-stained couch and reveled in the good luck and fortune bestowed upon her, and she felt herself blessed. A position with the London *Times* was where her father, Johnathon, had ended his career, not begun it, and she was proud that on this respective point of their individual timelines she was already outpacing him. She sat back, contented with a future now in progress, and finished the hardened, sugar-coated pecans she had bought hours earlier, when they were still warm, from straight off the steaming charcoals of a street vendor.

To Daniella, her major accomplishments and the aroma went hand in hand. She held no doubt that on the day she intended to walk down the aisle, somehow that smell would find its way down from the rafters and seep through the sun-lightened cracks etched around the stained-glass windows to once again assume its rightful and proper position somewhere in the same room.

In the order she had mapped out in her mind, Daniella rose to the level of foreign correspondent rather quickly. Her first assignment to the United States sent her to New Orleans, where she was to report on the corruption charges brought against one of the largest British shipping magnates. As fate would continue to entwine them, no sooner did she open the French canopy doors in her hotel room than her lungs breathed in deeply the sugary hints of those dulcet nuts, the subject of a Louisiana festival held hours earlier, with children dressed as planters and elderly couples shuffling their hips to the zydeco of the accordian players' melodies.

But along with the smell of pecans, Daniella's successes were also attached to the hornet's sting of her father's reputation. Johnathon Burkett's notoriety preceded Daniella before each and every one of her personal accolades. At her pre-admission interview in New York City, the professor had been more interested in discussing her father rather than Daniella's own reasons for selecting Columbia. Prior to the telephone call from Jules Markey, her father had been granted a seat at Oxford University for the upcoming spring semester and was also offered his own television spot providing commentary for an international news bureau. As was his temperament, he politely turned both positions down. Then just two weeks before her promotion to the foreign desk, he received the Pulitzer Prize in journalism.

Daniella still seized the opportunities as they presented themselves, always grateful for their existence, and would then work diligently and without rest to prove her position was based on individual merit rather than inherited reputation. If as a young girl she sought to distance herself from the family tree rooted specifically in her mother's soil, it would be years later, during her professional career, when she sought to run away from the shadow cast by her father's well-known name.

In the years following her promotion to the foreign desk, she spent the majority of her time overseas and away from England. She easily put her family and her past behind her and focused on setting her feet firmly in new terrain, virgin to the adventures of her renowned father. She concentrated on the stories of others, not wanting to be humbled by her own, and immersed herself completely in the lives and experiences of the people she encountered. Her eye remained keen on the individuals within the context of her stories and never once did Daniella rely solely on the subject matter alone within her work. She would disappear for weeks and sometimes months at a time, no letters or telephone calls, and the only way Shahrazad knew her daughter was doing all right was by the bond she had formed over the years with Jules Markey, who faithfully kept the family informed of Daniella's whereabouts and her continued well-being.

"She's a roaming spirit, Raz," Jules would offer.

And Shahrazad would coolly reply, "She is hardheaded like her father."

It was when Daniella was reporting on the neofascist terrorist organization the Great Wolves in Turkey that Jules Markey tried to track her down to inform her Shahrazad had been diagnosed with lung cancer. The news would outlast her by four days. Daniella permanently packed up her bags, leaving Istanbul and the story behind for someone else to finish. She flew into a gray and rain-soaked Heathrow Airport not quite sure how she felt to be going home again. But more importantly she was not sure how she was supposed to feel. She prayed in silence for the benefit of her mother and was unmoved when a fight broke out several aisles ahead of her over the trivial matter of a window seat. When the plane touched down in England, no one was awaiting her arrival. Drenched to the skin, she abandoned the last of her worry in the airport taxi terminal and paged a gypsy cab for the ride home to bury her mother in the misty arches of St. Evangeline.

The days leading up to the funeral were a whirlwind. Daniella felt as though time were passing in someone else's life. She felt suspended upon a cloud, flying over the days rather than through them. The telephone calls and visits from friends and relatives consisted solely of polite and simple conversations, and it was during these encounters when she realized she had never developed any kind of lasting relationship with anyone. She would humbly remark that she knew more about a Polish man who had lived through the immense racial insensitivity of the two World Wars and later fought against those same injustices as pontiff. She had spent more time talking with a pregnant prostitute infected with a rare, human immunodeficiency virus who had fled to Amsterdam while searching for health care and wound up sitting in front of the World Health Organization describing the then relatively unknown disease. With regards to her own flesh and blood, Daniella knew almost nothing except their names.

Her mother had developed bonds as though she were consuming glasses of water; they were a daily necessity in her own life. For the first time Daniella understood she may have judged her mother—and her father—a bit too harshly. She was struck by the simple fact that people need to feel important and that they often look for that importance within each other, keeping themselves open to the possibilities of one another. This last thought stuck with her because she knew—how could she not, with the conscious effort she had made throughout her life?—that she existed like a phantom racing in and out of countries, out of people's lives, running away before even the simplest of connections could be established. She was a ghost, occupying the hollowness in the lives of her family and friends, forever stuck in the emptiness that lingers for a brief moment after the simplest of introductions.

It was never more evident than in those days preceding Shahrazad's funeral. Just as most people experience an awkwardness during times of distress, Daniella clung to the idea of trying to become remote or invisible. She also didn't want to do the wrong thing. So, at first, she did nothing, her deference motivated by selfishness and self-defense. If Johnathon Burkett needed his daughter, well, he was going to have to say as much.

Lost within the daydreams of places she had traveled to, their images rotating in her thoughts like pictures in a slide projector, Daniella would sometimes stop dead in her tracks and take a good hard look at the things surrounding her to understand where she was and why she was there. As she did as a young girl, she recoiled from the world and only crossed over the line into the realm of human relationships when she telephoned her elderly uncles still living outside Baghdad. She thought of herself as not being much of a help to her father during that difficult time, but years later she would realize that if it weren't for her presence, Johnathon, so distraught himself at the time, would have slipped further into his own grief.

It was three days after the funeral when the sun finally found its way to a clear sky and a light tap at the bedroom door awoke Daniella from her first night of restful sleep. She had stayed in her old room almost the entire visit after Johnathon had cornered her her first night back and asked if she would mind staying in the house for the remainder of the week.

"It is too noisy when it is empty," he had tried, the ever-present youthfulness of his face corrupted, despite his fortitude, by the death of a spouse.

Daniella dressed quickly and met her father downstairs where he was waiting for her with fresh coffee and warm bagels. They ate quickly, their appetites beginning to unknot themselves with the slow passage of days. When Daniella was finished, they went for a long walk together, the first time since she was a little girl, mindlessly walking over the cobblestone roads and past the storefronts of Mapplethorpe's Variety and Fenmore's Corner in shared silence.

Most of the neighborhood had changed, as is the custom of childhood towns seen years later through the eyes of an adult. The small local shops had been replaced by larger corporate entities, and Daniella felt a slight sadness when she noticed barely any children playing in the parks or prancing across the open lawns. Over the years a subway stop had inched itself closer to her home like an advancing tide, and its rumblings stirred even the quietest of mornings.

"I don't know what I would have done without you here," Johnathon broke out after they had been walking for close to an hour.

If he had been able to say so, or if he had been able to recognize it himself, a bond began to form over those sun-brightened cobblestones between father and daughter; a bond that had been waiting patiently since the day the fair-haired Englishman had flown off to Cairo while at the same moment his daughter had begun to kick her tiny legs in defiance against the world. It was a bond based on the two different types of love each of them had for Shahrazad, one grateful for the time they had shared together and the other filled more with a sense of remorse than sorrow.

Both of them soon realized they had more in common with each other than they had previously cared to admit. Johnathon Burkett saw more than himself in his daughter, he saw an independent and ambitious spirit more disciplined than he had ever been, more direct and less careless, and someone he felt would not make many of the same mistakes he himself had once made, due to the thoroughness of her preparations. Daniella began to appreciate the wisdom of years and experience in her father and the decisions he made during his life. Within a short period of time, the two began working together, both comfortable with the complementary style of the other.

By the time Daniella arrived in Baghdad in 1984, she had already succeeded in surpassing her own expectations, and her father had since retired to write a book about his travels and experiences, which, according to his account, culminated in his meeting the thin, emerald-eyed woman he would later marry. He held no regrets about retiring from journalism, and just as he always moved from one moment to the next with the ease of a swimmer gliding through water, he moved freely and contentedly from the world of action and participation to the cherished one contained in memory, where he succeeded in keeping his heart alive by putting it all down on paper.

Daniella also sought to find herself in the things that made her happy and content. But for her the problem was she didn't know what–if anything–did make her happy. She had spent so many years covering the stories of others, losing herself in her work, that a loneliness had crept its way into her soul. She began to regret all the time she spent abroad and the invisible rift she kept between her and the people she undoubtedly cared for. She had sought to outrun all that had given her life meaning, to distance herself from everything that would define her until she was able to someday define herself. She immersed herself so much in her career that she lost hold of herself, and by trying to find meaning in her work she ironically lost her identity in the world around her. She wanted a foundation for herself, regretting the foundation of family she had once denounced as a small girl.

In those days after the funeral, she grew grateful for the family she now wished she knew better. As she and Johnathon came back up the sidewalk to the house, she noticed a package had been delivered while they were out.

"Your mother insisted," Johnathon said. "I hope it is not too much, Daniella."

She felt the last strength of her resolve evaporate and the emotion she had kept inside set loose. But with the tears came an exasperated laugh, finding immediate humor in the absurdity of the gift while a warmth gently began to lift itself over her heart. It felt good to laugh again, as if a lever had been released.

"She adored you," Johnathon said, himself overcome with emotion. "Your happiness was all your mother ever wanted."

On the front stoop sat a small potted tree about the size of a grocer's brown bag with a series of tiny, delicate branches stretching out in the subtlest of directions. She bent down to pick it up and read from off the plastic instruction tag wrapped around its small trunk: AN AMLING PECAN TREE CULTIVATED IN GEORGIA, USA. She would never be able to recall ever mentioning the tree's significance.

And although the cool and damp English climate is not considered suitable for the warmth and sunshine needed by the tree, she would plant it in her backyard anyway as a testament to the life of her mother, and she was not surprised months later to see the tree flourishing, its branches reaching out in all directions like legs kicking defiantly against the wind.

16

THE VILLAGERS CLAIM THE eyes of the mural follow them; that those suspicious black circles are alive and watching everything that happens with staunch vigilance. One day, the villagers claim, the eyes will veer off to the left out toward the open markets. On other days one eye has mysteriously closed to intently focus the other, following them through the streets and into their private gardens, fearlessly seeing right through the walls and into their apartments. At night, the sanctity of their homes has eroded with the image that watches from outside their doors. There is no privacy, many say, since those eyes came to watch over them, and not only are they scared, but they have grown tired of their trepidations as well.

Ibrahim shrugs off the idea because he knows better than anyone. He knows those eyes and he knows they do not move. His paintbrushes produced the mural, creating an image where there had been nothing except cement and plaster, just as he has done almost a hundred times since the start of the war. The picture is a bust shot of President Hussein topped with a white, flowing head cloth tied around and secured by a thick, black cord. He is dressed in a white suit and a white shirt with a thin black tie knotted sharply at his throat and falling down over his formidable stature. At the time of its commission, Ibrahim had been bored with its lack of colors. Now, less than three weeks later, he is back to touch up the president's skin, suddenly pock-marked and sprayed a shade close to ash from an abundance of artillery fire. The villagers silently hold a small amount of hope that Ibrahim has come to remove the image, and they cautiously watch over him working just as they believe the image he created watches over them.

Ranking administrators at the Ministry of Information have attached great significance to the painting. Its ominous presence resides on the far wall of a recently abandoned schoolhouse overlooking a large and once bustling intersection in Al-Kazmiya. Just weeks earlier, uniformed schoolchildren were a common sight in the area, kissed a healthy bronze by the unhindered sun and scattered about singing "Al-Salam Al-Jumhuri," the Iraqi national anthem, or reciting passages of the Koran, their adolescent voices lending a wholesome beauty to its passages. Before the war began, Al-Kazmiya had been a prosperous middle-class suburb branching out with the distribution of wealth into smaller prosperous arteries flowing throughout the surrounding districts. It housed a private hospital, newly constructed mosques, and even one of the republic's first private schools. New settlements had begun to sprout up all throughout the capital city and in the outlying territories as a result of the economic boom of the 1970s. National oil money was being funneled into Baghdad faster than it could be counted. Baathist policies achieved a boost in public opinion when the government finally seized control of the country's overall oil production and with it all the facilities in the north and south. The Iraqi National Oil Company was formed, a crucial step toward finally granting Iraq ownership of all the oil reserves stirring underneath its own feet.

But since the outbreak of aggression against neighboring Persia, many of the shops and the school have been closed. Now only the mosques and the hospital are still open, although most of the holy men and medical workers have since left. Al-Kazmiya remains occupied by the few villagers who have not fled under the threat of war or by those people possessing no safer haven. Like many of the buildings in the smaller bordering towns, the school was converted into a prison camp. Insurgents from the city and revolting Kurds captured in the north were transported in and temporarily detained in the abandoned classrooms. Days earlier, the last of these prisoners were marched along the same path the students once took, down the dull brown steps past the double chalkboards and three-foot-high lockers straight out into the playground, where their blindfolds were removed to allow them to see the faces of their captors. Under the solemn stare of the large mural of Iraqi president Saddam Hussein each of them was executed amid a series of bullets echoing over the cracked cement like a chorus. The school has stood empty since.

Ibrahim operates on that same mural like a surgeon, removing bullet fragments from the president's cheekbones with pliers and smoothing the creases in his forehead with thin lines of plaster. He touches up the lower portion of the chin with a shade of light peach and removes speckles of blood off the neck with a wet towel. He doesn't spend too much time wondering about the men who have been murdered while standing in front of this picture. But if someone were to ask him, he is confident he could provide a fairly accurate count. Yesterday, Ibrahim received the assignment from the deputy minister of information, Jazeri.

"The president's image must not be corrupted in any way," Jazeri religiously warned, "or else our image as Iraqi nationals is corrupted as well."

The personal visit had surprised Ibrahim. Jazeri arrived in the late afternoon with a small contingent of police officers, cordial yet authoritative, and he politely refused any attempts at hospitality Ibrahim made by claiming the lack of time.

"But, Jazeri," Ibrahim offered, "please, stay for tea."

"It is important the enemy see our proud and supreme leader intact and without these abrasions," Jazeri explained. "All images of our great Saddam are to be flawless, and they are intended to remain that way forever. This building will not be used again until you are finished. So time is essential."

"You can still sit for a cup of tea."

"I am afraid I cannot. I am running late. It is not so easy to move about the suburbs with the war coming closer to Baghdad."

"It is getting closer, Jazeri, isn't it?" Ibrahim asked.

"Yes, unfortunately it is. You can almost smell the foulness of the Persian army." At this, Jazeri gave a cold, dignified sniff at the air in front of him. "Or maybe that is only our own sewage systems. Maybe we should have had you paint a proper drainage facility instead."

"I am sure that is something Tapiz would be able to handle on his own," Ibrahim replied. If I could only find him, he thought to himself.

Tapiz had not been at work for the past two weeks. Although Ibrahim did not want to say anything that might get his apprentice in trouble with his superiors, he had grown more than a little nervous with his extended absence. Ibrahim naïvely hoped Tapiz was just taking the time to begin working on his book.

At first, the presence of the police with Jazeri made Ibrahim wonder if they brought word of Tapiz. Usually the man came alone or sat by himself in his office whenever Ibrahim visited him. The accompaniment often meant trouble.

"Your work looked good," Jazeri said while eyeing the length of Ibrahim's apartment, "and it will look good once again. Just like the rest of the country."

The leaders of the Baath were in the midst of a tremendous propaganda program. The idea was to promote a sense of Iraqi nationalism among all of its people–Shia, Sunni, and Kurd. Prosperity from Baath economic policies had led to close to $85 million spent on mosques and shrines in the hope of appeasing a Shia majority lacking proper representation in a Sunni-dominated government. Kurdish representation in Baghdad was also proposed with one eye fixated on the rich oil fields found in the northern highlands. The Baath recognized the historical association of both Arab and Kurd comprising Iraq and revisited the topic of Kurdish autonomy in the northern region. Literature and poetry described the unity of the once great land. Sculptures and paintings, which Ibrahim was commissioned to produce, decorated the landscape, depicting curious common themes among the country's brethren and a history recently rewritten to be all-inclusive. The once grandiose ancient city of Babylon felt the revival as well, knee-deep in the midst of its own tremendous restoration. It was with this contrived sense of history that the president attempted to unite the disparate groups of the country by tracing the lineage and legitimacy of its leader back to the prophet Muhammad himself, and by making it a priority to stress a national identity in Mesopotamia fostering Iraq's place in history as the first civilization. Where ideals and ultimately control were once historically based on religion, the Baath purposely pushed for a silent conversion to the secularization of a unique and separate state. A state promoting, for the first time, Iraqi nationalism and one with Saddam Hussein as its supreme leader.

Jazeri handed Ibrahim a small card with the address and a stack of five-thousand-dinar notes.

"Thank you as usual for your kindness, but I must attend to other urgent matters," Jazeri repeated.

Ibrahim did not insist further. The fiber of their friendship had already been broken with Jazeri's subtle mentioning of Ibrahim's father, Hassan Jaffa, months earlier in the ministry office. The two men had spoken only twice since that meeting: once when Jazeri telephoned Ibrahim to ask how the new apprentice, Tapiz, was doing, and the second time to congratulate Ibrahim on his marriage. Jazeri had missed the celebration while on a two-week leave of absence in Syria.

Almost a month had passed since the wedding day, and Ibrahim was relieved Shalira was not at home in the apartment when the four men arrived. She had gone with her cousins to the bazaar to buy groceries for Ibrahim's twenty-third birthday celebration later that evening. He sensed her unease around government officials and soldiers and was upset when she refused to talk to him about it, closing herself like a fist whenever he asked her questions. It was common knowledge her father, Yusuf, was holed up in the casket prison of Sijn Al-Tarbut, detained like an animal in a steel box. Her silence was her protection, and Ibrahim had recognized the same trait in himself upon witnessing the murder of his neighbor, the old schoolmaster, when he was a young boy. Something had broken, besides his nose, during that night several months ago, and Ibrahim continued to pray for the healing powers contained in time. He understood he could not force such things.

Ibrahim noticed the line of sweat creasing Jazeri's brow. Despite the deputy minister's visible warmth, he still wore the full green uniform of the elite Republican Army. Ibrahim wondered about the reasons behind the formal dress. And why the three-policemen escort?

Jazeri took a crisp white handkerchief with a picture of the Iraqi president embroidered in the silk from out of his front

pocket and wiped down his forehead. He quickly motioned the
other men out of the apartment and abruptly closed the door
behind them. Then Jazeri turned to Ibrahim with a disarmingly
paternal smile, and after an intentional pause he began to
yell abusively at him, spewing forth a stream of curses and de-
meaning phrases in Arabic. The deputy minister of information
walked over to where Ibrahim was sitting and placed his hands
affectionately on his shoulders. His face had grown bright red
with his continuous ranting, and for a moment Ibrahim thought
the man might pass out for lack of breath. Jazeri motioned his
eyes toward the closed door and the soldiers waiting behind it,
and Ibrahim understood that there was some underlying purpose behind Jazeri's manipulations; something in Jazeri's smile
that contrasted with the man's tone and language. He continued
to curse at Ibrahim, and at one point he furiously slammed his
fist down upon the dresser top. Jazeri then produced a thick
manila packet from inside his khaki jacket and tossed it onto
the floor in front of him. Ibrahim stared at the package on the
floor and noticed the inch-long scuff marks stretched across
Jazeri's leather shoes. With his foot, Jazeri pushed the manila
packet underneath the table next to Ibrahim. He paused for a
moment to catch his breath, an awkward silence now taking
place of the abuse. After a few moments when his breathing
had settled, Jazeri's face hardened and he regained his sense of
composure.

"The president is very proud of your work," he said softly, his
thin hand resting firmly on the doorknob. The man looked sick.
His skin was drained of color and his eyes were sunk deeply
into the bluish welts of sleeplessness beneath them. He nodded
once toward Ibrahim as though the simple movement of his
head would explain the reasoning behind his actions. With a
turn of the knob he joined the police officers outside in the hallway, and then they were all quickly gone.

Ibrahim buried the manila folder at the bottom of his paint-brush case. Shalira and her cousins arrived home shortly after Jazeri and the officers had left, barely missing each other by a few minutes in the courtyard below, and although Ibrahim was relieved, he did not have a free moment to examine the enve-lope's contents.

He breaks about ten thirty, rinses the paint from his brushes, and then cleans the plaster mixture out of its tray before it hard-ens. When he is done, he sits in a shaded corner on the second floor of the abandoned school. A small group of villagers are standing on the outside stairway across the street smoking ciga-rettes and watching the mural with the fading hope that Ibrahim had come to take it away with him. They seem to have grown mildly disheartened with the resurgence of color radiating once again in the president's skin.

Ibrahim strikes a match and lights a small Sterno canister on which to make his late-morning tea. He closes the classroom door and places a piece of rubber tire firmly underneath as a jam. He sits back and listens to the peaceful sound of heat rising from inside the metal tin. Thick iron chains with shackles hang down from the ceiling in pairs, and the wood floors below them are stained as though having been burnt. Piles of ropes rest in the far corner next to the windows, and empty syringes are scattered about the floor. Ibrahim stands up and kicks the nee-dles away from him and toward the shade of the far corner. From the window he watches for a moment as one of the vil-lagers throws a rock at the president and then as all the men run fearfully down the stairs and into the alleyway across the street to hide. It takes only a few minutes and then the teakettle begins to sing.

Ibrahim removes the rubber bands from around the manila

folder. On top are communication papers between high-ranking Baath officials stamped with the red-and-black Presidential Palace logo across their heading. He fingers through letters and memos all alerting the leadership of underground revolutionary activity taking place in and around Baghdad and of the consequences of such continued activity.

Not only the abolition of such groups but all who do not oppose or make known their existence . . . , Ibrahim reads.

As he continues through the papers, Ibrahim has seen the names of most of the major groups before–the PUK, KDP, IUGM, INSF, and the ICP. There are memos detailing the increased activity of these groups in recent months, even linking them to the destruction of the Bank of Sadou in downtown Baghdad, and the credible suspicion that Iran was backing many of them through an underground network of bankers, businessmen, and religious scholars coming in from the north. One folder contains lists ranging in number from five to several hundred names beneath each acronym heading, and Ibrahim is not surprised to find Yusuf's name listed tenth under the Iraqi Nationalist & Socialist Front and first under the Iraqi Centrist Party. Typed next to each high-ranking name are also the details of their occupation–farmers, teachers, and businessmen– their dates of birth, cities of origin, and the bloodlines of their respective mothers and fathers along with a small family tree regarding marriages.

Ibrahim finds a memo addressed to Saddam Hussein from an officer in the Mukhabarrat, the secret state police, warning of the possibility of members of the Communist Party of Iraq potentially joining forces with Iraqi Nationalist Party members to form a larger and more dangerous group. The officer also warns of the union of all Kurdish groups under one heading in the north, and of the disparate revolutionary, socialist, and democratic groups around the capital doing the same.

... the threats are increasing every day ...

A memo is attached mentioning an operation called Hidden Fist calling for the clandestine eradication of all members of such groups. The dotted line for the president's signature is blank. What was Jazeri thinking of, giving him such dangerous and extremely sensitive information? Ibrahim resolves to burn each paper in the abandoned classroom as soon as he is finished with them.

... these transgressors, Ibrahim continues to read, *must be wiped out without prejudice or concern so as to preserve the great state of our leader, the Great Saddam ...*

Underneath, Ibrahim finds a thin pad of information on his father-in-law, Yusuf al-Mahoudi. He reads through the data, still unsure of Jazeri's reasons for giving him the folder, with the hope of finding some good news to report to Shalira about her father.

Educated at Baghdad University and then the Holy College at Najaf; former wealthy shopkeeper on Arasat al-Hindiyyah Street; recent acquaintance of Mahm Korobash, Syrian arms dealer, creating the potential for obtaining mass weaponry used for assault and/or revolution; can be found sucking on his nargileh pipe like a serpent in the tea shops by the university.

Ibrahim does not find Shalira's name in the details nor her mother's, but he finds an example of the regime's propensity for deceit and lies when he comes to the next line:

Mother, Su'ad, born of the poisoned blood of Persia.

And Ibrahim is aghast, considering Yusuf's open disdain toward the Iranians and his proud recognition of his strict Arabian heritage. He finds nothing concerning Yusuf's imprisonment and continues scanning the names, not recognizing anyone else, until he stops his finger at one underlined in thick red ink:

Tapiz Mahmud.

"My God," Ibrahim whispers as he brings his fingers up to his lips, "Tapiz. I am being surrounded."

There are no details next to Tapiz's name, the next-to-last name under both the headings for the Iraqi Centrist Party and the Iraqi Underground Guerrilla Movement. For the next half hour Ibrahim continues through the documents searching for more facts about his apprentice. His heart momentarily skips a beat when he gets to the last piece of material, a close-up picture of a stout-headed man, his face scarred by a series of small circles burnt into the flesh of his cheeks and neck. Brutal purplish mounds swell from around the forehead and ears and there are thin, dark cracks projecting out from the corners of the lips like tributaries. But it is the eyes that dominate the picture, the hauntingly dark, narrow eyes peering vacantly through circular holes cut out of the skin of the man's eyelids. Around the neck hangs a metal plate with the name of Qurtiyya, a prison located in the General Security compound of the Saddam City district in Baghdad. The listing of twelve numbers on the bottom of the plate matches the numbers written in black marker across the skin of the man's upper chest.

Ibrahim stares in unbroken awe at the brutal photo, at the perfect circles of skin cut out to reveal the eyes even in closure. He can taste the rising disgust in his mouth like gasoline. After a few moments he regains some sense of composure and place, but his feeling of horror only increases when he accidentally turns the picture over to shield himself from its image and finds Tapiz's name, date of birth, and address written neatly across the back and stamped with the official seal of the Republican Guard.

"My God, Tapiz, everything is falling," Ibrahim cries out, and feels the ominous presence of someone watching over him.

He rises and through the window he can see the villagers still hiding from the painting in the alleyway across the street.

The man who earlier threw the rock is bent at the waist and searching about for something else to throw among the trash cans. Then Ibrahim notices the stare of Saddam Hussein watching him from the adjacent street corner, and for a brief second he thinks he sees the president's eyes, those same dark, cavernous eyes he had touched up earlier, blink at him. He quickly returns to the folders Jazeri had given him and begins to burn each paper one at a time. When they are all reduced to ash, the hiss of the dying flame in the metal canister is like an alarm signaling him back to his work.

17

APRIL 28, 1984

THE MUSCLES IN YUSUF AL-MAHOUDI'S legs are mostly gone, stripped off the femur bones due to the lack of nourishment and movement. His thighs have eroded to resemble thick ropes, the hamstrings withered to nothing more than scar tissue. Even the simple pleasure of stretching one's limbs is deprived him as he spends his hours squatting inside the confines of a one-meter-high steel cage, impossible to stand or sit in the limited space, while small mice scurry maniacally across his bare feet. For close to a month, Yusuf has held his body together rather well, tensing and loosening his joints and muscles in stifled isometric contractions up to three times a day, the only movement the small space will allow him, in order to keep the blood flowing but also to maintain some sort of mental as well as physical discipline over his psyche.

"They will not take my mind," Yusuf repeats to himself over and over again. "They will not take my mind."

Located in the General Security compound in Baghdad, the Sijn Al-Tarbut prison is currently home to almost four hundred people. The majority of prisoners have formally been charged and arrested and their paperwork properly processed through administrative channels. Still, a small number of the others have been taken off the streets or pulled from their homes in secret, often without reason or explanation. They are mostly men, but there has also been a steady increase in the number of women detained since the outbreak of war and as the number of casualties of husbands and sons has broken one hundred thousand.

There are all different types of prisoners in Sijn Al-Tarbut– murderers and thieves, corrupt business owners accused of inflating the prices of their wares, and illegal smugglers operating outside governmental jurisdiction. The majority are enemies of the state and its methods. It is not uncommon for the elderly men who have lived through the revolution and British rule to want to make one lasting change as their final will and testament before they die. There are also revolutionary students filled with the vigor and impulsiveness of fanatics yet innocent to the intricacies of a working society. There are those people who have experienced the full brunt of force of the ruling fist and have had their fathers and uncles taken under the blue shadow of the Arabian moon, and those rare examples of men and women whose happiness upon being reunited with a missing loved one is tempered because that same loved one is unable to properly sit down as a result of having glass bottles broken inside them. Yusuf is considered part of the group known as revolutionaries or "underground movement members."

The reputation of the casket prison is well deserved. The long, narrow boxes used to detain prisoners are kept in pull-out drawers stacked neatly into the walls like in a mortuary. Sijn Al-Tarbut was built to maintain only two hundred people. The increased sweeps and widespread crackdown by the regime against insurgents as a result of the war has resulted in all the prison systems operating well past full capacity. Subsequent construction of several harsher institutions has temporarily been suspended due to the lack of funds and the insurmountable debt incurred and growing since 1981. The walls of the operating prison systems bulge out like an inflated balloon from the pressure.

Yusuf is prisoner number 407, the digits written on a white patch pressed against his shirt breast pocket, and he is spared the funereal-like accommodations of the casket prison due to its overcrowded conditions. He is detained instead in the basement of the prison, four levels below the ground. When he first arrived, Yusuf could tell many of the prisoners were still alive only by their moans and grunts in the darkness. He could barely see their sparse movements, their narrow shadows falling across his cage in exaggerated proportions. In several boxes lay rotting corpses, decaying bodies slowly melting away each day into the rancid and stained concrete pavement.

Prison guards periodically patrol the mazelike paths in the fourth basement level. They draw down the columns in the morning and place individual bowls of water and a small loaf of bread at the foot of each cage. In the evenings they repeat the same process, only in addition to the same portion of bread the prisoners receive a small splattering of fragmented gravy as well. It is the long, anxious hours in between the meals when the mere presence of the guards strikes fear into the tenants of the cages. It is with a feeling bordering on relief when the guards come and remove a dead body. On those occasions when they come for reasons other than to serve meals or remove the deceased, you can almost feel the silent vibration in the room, the inaudible buzzing of movement too quick to be seen, of the prisoners trembling. Men are tortured in full view of the others; the agony of a man being burnt by live electrical wires a form of detached torture in itself to those who witness the brutality.

The first night in his cell Yusuf understandably did not sleep.

The moans and screams coming from the other cages did not dishearten him, but rather they increased his determination to remain unbroken. I will not become an animal, he told himself. He had always felt himself stronger than his fellow country-men; his fortitude and resolve were strong enough to break the bones of men and even the shackles of the past. He knew by cutting off the ear of the Republican Guard bodyguard he was going beyond the measures of good judgment, but he wanted to scare those who held power; to have them see that he could be just as cold and ruthless, to turn the tables. The bodyguard claimed he'd overheard a conversation between two members of the ICP, and Yusuf took the man's ear as an example. It did scare them; it scared them so much that the Mukhabarat took Yusuf the night after the meeting was raided in the basement of the Papous Bake Shop.

He began his isometric exercises, tightening his hamstrings for five seconds and then releasing the thin muscle for five more seconds. He counted to himself, mouthing the cadence in har-mony with the silent tapping of his finger and only stopped when the overhead lights in the room suddenly flashed on and he was able to see the full description of his conditions for the first time.

Closed metal cages were stacked against the surrounding walls and piled on top of each other in rows of four in what looked like an underground human kennel. He was able to see the causes of the smell of burnt skin and bodily waste that had sought to overwhelm him when he was first brought in. He was disgusted at the sight of human excrement falling through the open square partitions from underneath the cages and onto the ones below them. Streams of urine displaced themselves to form puddles on the ground, a putrid caste system in which, Yusuf would later find out when the guards mocked the unfortunate faith of a priest, the offenders are stacked according to impor-tance, the bottom occupants residing in the rank phosphorescent puddles and refuse of others. Yusuf memorized what he could about the area from his cage, the third one amidst a series of boxes falling dramatically underneath the length of an overhead fluorescent light and set up in the middle of the room.

Now the lights have turned on again and Yusuf notices three guards enter from the closest door. The firmness of their shoes against the cement drowns out the cries of the other prisoners. Yusuf had already received his morning meal, and by the way the shadow of daylight was still moving across the far corner of the floor, it was too early for dinner. He is immune to the anxiety and the fear the guards' entrance causes, and in his heart he is filled with fibers of strength coming from the knowledge that all he has fought for in the past ten years was the abolition of everything that was now taking place around him. He had heard stories from men who came to the shop or from students telling him about their missing fathers or brothers, but now Yusuf al-Mahoudi was witnessing it firsthand. He feels the enormity of pride in his bones knowing that he was, after all, a better man—a moral man—and his beliefs were not only worth fighting for but would also make for a better life for his countrymen. While people might have considered him a crazy old radical, he was pleased to note that despite what others may have thought, he had been right all along.

He can hear their footsteps getting closer. The guards are standing only feet away with their backs to him. To Yusuf they all look the same, short-cropped black hair and black eyes, bushy, unmanageable eyebrows, and the requisite thick black mustaches. They all look to be the same height, and Yusuf can judge the order of their rankings by the width of their satisfied paunches. It is a costume that has grown to sicken him. He has not been able to get any of them to look him in the eye. He has tried but the guards have silently refused. They unlock the gate on the front of the cell across from him.

"Be strong, Anjaf," Yusuf yells out, and one of the guards kicks at his cage.

"Keep quiet, infidel."

"Help me please, praise O great Saddam," Anjaf cries. "Please, I beg you—I praise Iraq and I praise Allah. I praise whatever you want me to praise."

Yusuf sees the impression of the man's ribs against his pallid skin, and in the brightness of the cement room the guard that had kicked at Yusuf's cage places a revolver next to the man's ear and when steady fires the trigger, a small explosion burning the man's flesh and temporarily hollowing all sounds under a thick and heavy drone as the bullet ricochets off the adjoining wall. Only when Yusuf's hearing comes back does he acknowledge the heavy sighing coming from the cages stacked against the far wall and he realizes the stray bullet may have found a target. Anjaf has slumped to the ground screaming and clutching the right side of his head, his blood emptying out over auburn hands.

One of the guards runs over to the far wall where the bullet has landed, and from his cage Yusuf can see the luminous eyes of a woman cowering away into the back corner of her cell. An open wound crosses her shin, like the arched markings left behind after a kiss, and her lips are pursed to a color that now seems to be coming out from the hole in her leg. She continues to try pushing herself farther back into the cage with the instincts of a cornered animal. It is impossible for her to stifle her pain to avoid detection. Yusuf knows this because he knows most of his fellow countrymen and countrywomen are too weak to surpass the thought of pain in their own minds. That fiber of discipline he has mastered so well they let swell with a heat so strong it could melt glass. The woman prisoner stares up at the guard in front of her, and if he were closer, Yusuf would be able to recognize the stare as one filled with an exhausted resignation. He feels no emotion and watches the guard fire five shots into the recess of the cage, and the despair held by such luminous eyes vanishes.

Each night brought similar incidents. A thief was lashed with an electrical wire until he could no longer move. The guards left him where he fell on the floor, and Yusuf heard what sounded like a child vomiting from across the room. One night the muffled resolution of a woman prisoner being raped by two of the guards barely woke him from a compressed sleep; they have come back for her every day since. Yusuf blocks these happenings out of his consciousness; he has to or he will crumble like a house of cards. He numbs his mind by concentrating on memories and what he plans to do if he ever sees the light of day as a free man again.

He has also become fascinated with his fingers. More importantly, his fingernails. When there is enough light from the sun outside the hallway, usually for close to two hours a day, he will stare with his back hunched like a bow at the cracked markings of his fingernails, at the white moons rising in unhealthy patterns underneath. The nail on his third finger has grown extremely brittle and has already begun to splinter down the middle. Yusuf tries to forget about the man whose nails were pulled straight off the flesh with a thin pair of pliers, the sound it created like that of striking a match. There are many things he needs to forget now. Yusuf would stare at his own cracked nails and was amazed that such a trivial part of human anatomy could be used for such purposes, fingernails as a subject of torture.

"They will not take my mind," he repeats to himself, and turns his hands over, "they will not take my mind."

When not eating or concentrating on his exercises, Yusuf spends the hours daydreaming. When the sun lowers across the hallway and the shadows of full darkness descend upon the room once again, Yusuf remembers back to the time in his life when Shalira had been just a child and he a young father and a shop owner selling French bracelets and watches and African diamonds on Arasat al-Hindiyyah. Looking back, it seemed like such a simple life, but he had been naïve in ever thinking so. He enjoyed as much as he enjoyed anything in his country the half-hour break during his lunchtime when he sat with the younger students and played the jewels over in his fingers to let the light pass through them, creating a spectrum of colors. He amused himself and would smile at their concentrating faces as they watched him bend light, each one thinking Yusuf possessed the knowledge of witches. Each day they returned fearful with wonderment to watch the tall shop owner, thin as a lamppost, break the sun into its individual pieces.

Their trivial nature lent to the beauty of such matters, and then Yusuf would remember back to the days when his own good nature began to erode, before he anxiously sensed the grains of his personal hourglass falling into oblivion, before he became the type of man to carry out violent acts against another man—even murder—and before he became the type of man who was fast becoming a stranger in his own country, a man unmoved by the barbaric and inhumane, the type of man who carried around a severed ear.

"Under the eyes of Allah," he whispers to himself, "we are our own worst enemy."

And then he starts to count to five as he begins his exercises once again.

18

MAY 15, 1984

IBRAHIM GALEB AL-MANSUR AWOKE earlier than usual and his heart raced with an unmistakable excitement. The continued silence of his wife, the disappearance of Yusuf, the capture and murder of Tapiz—all these concerns he temporarily left behind in the world his sleeping consciousness had created. Today he would try his best not to worry about such things. He was excited and didn't want the blackness of those evil clouds to block out any of the happiness he intended to bestow upon Hassan Jaffa. Ibrahim had already scheduled a meeting with Jazeri for the following afternoon. He wanted to clear his head before he confronted the deputy minister of information about the brutal images in the photos. The department's secretary informed him that Jazeri was away until tomorrow morning. For a brief moment Ibrahim entertained the idea of sleeping outside his office and waiting for him. But he would try very hard today, he had poured a lot of himself into this project, and he felt it would be a good test of discipline to act for a short time as though nothing were wrong.

He found upon waking the feelings already stirring in his belly and limbs, and they proved what Shalira often told him: "You are selfless, my Ibrahim, always wanting to give something to others. You are more concerned with giving than receiving."

Ibrahim had responded to her at the time that it was simply his wish to be divine and, in a way, all his work held that same characteristic, driven in part by his inner desire to give life to others and to be some sort of creator.

"I would choose for you to live forever," he would joke back to her, his words carrying a sentimental tone rather than the hollow abruptness he had recently begun to recognize in himself.

The intimacy they once shared seemed to leave their relationship as soon as they married. A silent bitterness replaced Shalira's once exuberant and worldly nature, and Ibrahim tried to understand the impact Yusuf's disappearance had on her. She no longer visited Ibrahim at work to share lunch with him, and she did not even want to meet Tapiz after he was first assigned to Ibrahim.

"Ibrahim, I do not have enough care to even be somewhat courteous. Please keep your work out of our house," she instructed him.

Not used to her firmness, Ibrahim did spend more time out of the house, offering her the distance he thought she needed.

"This is not Paris, Shalira," he tried. "And I am not some European bohemian."

Then he resented his tone and honored her wish without question. He doted on her when home, though she was less responsive than he had hoped, and on those rare occasions when the world seemed to revolve once again around only them, her smile would reenergize him.

"My Ibrahim—never change your nature for me or for anyone. I just resent them for making you so unhappy. They made my father, who at one time was a very happy man," she said, then briefly paused, "well, he is nothing now if not broken."

"But I am happy," he replied halfheartedly, and regretted his inability to be more persuasive.

Ibrahim knew that although she rejected the nature of his employment, she was extremely proud of his personal work. This morning he carries the painting of his mother, Fazeera, carefully under his arm, not wanting to let any of his weight come into contact with the face of her portrait. Although it is dry, he has always held true to the superstition that once a painting is completed, he should not touch it again until it is viewed by someone other than himself, and no one had seen this work yet, not even Shalira.

It had taken him three straight nights and he'd even worked a half day on Friday despite it being a holy day of rest. He felt so invigorated when he began that he forgot time and place and was completely immersed in his activities, only stopping once when Shalira had come down with a strong fever and he put his brushes aside and sat over her laid-out figure for hours while he pressed cold towels against her forehead.

Two thin bungee cords are wrapped around the frame and are attached to the small metal ringlets on the underside of the canvas, securing the tarp covering in its place. He hoped with the greatest of intentions that the painting would somehow help Hassan Jaffa keep a part of his wife with him and also stir up certain memories that may have hardened over time. It was the closest Ibrahim could come to giving them both Fazeera back. He can only hope Hassan Jaffa will find the colors he used in good taste and not too decadent compared to the black-and-white images he would remember of the photo Ibrahim had used as his model.

In his six weeks back at work, Hassan Jaffa had found little rest in his position as the curator of the Baghdad Museum. A slight, permanent limp along with a reddened, bulbous protrusion resembling a coin under the skin on his right shin were the only remaining aftereffects of the accident, though an ample layer of skin had also begun to form around his waist from too much idleness. As a result, Hassan Jaffa was working later hours to catch up on missed paperwork and to correct and adjust the work performed in earnest by his colleagues during his absence. He would never admit to anyone that he was also working the longer hours due to the political ruminations in the capital that had recently increased with the bombing of a nearby military facility and were now threatening to once again divide the proud city.

Lately, Ibrahim did not see much of Hassan Jaffa. Shalira thought it was a good idea to check up on him, and one evening during Hassan Jaffa's first week back to work she and Ibrahim came to surprise him for dinner and found him already asleep, a half-finished bowl of chicken noodle and herb soup resting on the wooden table in the dining room and his small transmitter radio emitting an orchestral piece from Hamid Al-Saadi in low decibels from where it sat upon the sink ledge. Sleep and work, it had been his father's life for as long as Ibrahim could remember. But the sounds coming from the radio pleasantly struck Ibrahim because it seemed to him that during his life his father always seemed to miss out on the music.

"Idleness is the devil's playground," Hassan Jaffa was prone to rationalize to Ibrahim, and his son the artist understood all that his father had sacrificed in his own principles and even his self-respect in order to make the best possible life for his son and for his wife before she'd passed away.

Around the university and in the neighborhoods surrounding Baghdad, people were disappearing into shadows. All signs of dissension were quickly and abruptly extinguished like the flames of an open fire snuffed out by buckets of chilled water. The age restrictions set by the conscription laws had been lowered to allow for a larger number of boys to be drafted into the ongoing war. The older men who brazenly spoke out against the government and its policies were privately being carted off to prison camps where a fate too horrific to be imagined awaited them. The ill winds of distrust crept over Baghdad like an endemic sickness. The foundation of the regime was crumbling. For the past several years all funds were directed toward the war effort, and with the dire conditions of the economy the only thing the Baath had left to stand on was fear, a harsh ruling principle that it was not going to let go of too easily.

Hassan Jaffa safely kept his thoughts to himself and spent his time in the underground storage facilities of the museum or seated at his desk judiciously going over his ledgers and records. He became overzealous with regard to a British display the two countries were working on together, his excess of enthusiasm prompting his British contemporary to remark, "You would think your museum has nothing else to exhibit."

To Hassan Jaffa it wasn't the exhibit itself but rather how it helped him to pass the time. He knew he had to keep his mind in his work to prevent it from wandering. His country was falling apart, and even if it somehow managed to survive, Iraq had turned into a place he no longer wished to be. It was not the same country where he had once imagined he would spend his old age. He was relieved when his leg had healed to the point he could once again get around by himself and was only too happy to return to work. All the time he had spent at home had offered Yusuf the opportunity to come and see him repeatedly, even after Hassan Jaffa had finally relented and dismissed his proud manners and openly pleaded with Yusuf to leave him and his son alone. But Yusuf did not listen, he never did, and the old shopkeeper continued to call on him nevertheless and eventually succeeded in making Hassan Jaffa nervous with his constant talk of revolution.

"The only thing to come from revolution is death," Hassan Jaffa spoke sternly after biting his tongue long enough.

"Does Islam not teach that death is change?" Yusuf replied, and Hassan Jaffa suddenly grew scared, not because of Yusuf's preachings and outspoken nature, but because Hassan Jaffa knew deep down inside he was right.

Local visitors to the Baghdad Museum consisted of members of the upper and middle classes, people educated on the detailed characteristics and cultural value of world and, more specifically, Middle Eastern art history. But it was also not uncommon for members of the military and governmental authorities to be in the building's grand halls as well. Soldiers were stationed at appropriate distances to safeguard the transport and subsequent display of important and valuable historical artifacts. Members of the regime often came to learn about a changing history they hoped to build upon and eventually use to instill a widespread sense of nationalism. Due to the large-scale official presence, the Baghdad Museum was more secure than most banks and financial institutions in the capital. Hassan Jaffa knew Yusuf would never come to such a place, not after his jewel shop had been taken from him. He was viewed as a crazy old man divested of wealth and status, and to Hassan Jaffa you could always smell him coming from a mile away. He felt safest in the museum; it was already controlled by the government and it was *his* world.

It has been over a month since Hassan Jaffa has last seen Yusuf. Rumors of his imprisonment were widespread but could not be confirmed. If Yusuf was in fact still free, he would be a fool to risk his presence in the Baghdad Museum, an occurrence almost as out of place as camel tracks on a snow-covered roof. And if Yusuf was in fact in the casket prison as speculated, well, the man knew the consequences attached to his actions. Hassan Jaffa understood as much. A long time ago he and Yusuf had both been cut from the same cloth, but somewhere along their paths a small tear turned into a complete separation, and the life that Hassan Jaffa had sacrificed most of his inner dispositions to maintain stood in silent opposition to Yusuf, a shop owner who long ago had his livelihood taken away from him by soldiers from the elite Republican Guard. The men had entered his busy store one afternoon and proceeded without reason to break all the glass partitions enclosing the jewels, smashing the mirrors lining the walls, and in the process granting Yusuf an infinite amount of bad luck. After a brief struggle they seized control of the shop and stripped his ownership away under the will of the military, forever marking the day and the changes it caused within his spirit like chapters of a sacred text in his stark memory.

Ibrahim walks across a pair of similar green lawns and through the side pathway around the portico and past the delivery docks to the back of the museum to the employee security entrance. Aid Et-Wari, the on-call security officer, sits at moderate attention reading a Western entertainment magazine and drinking a can of soda. He recognizes Ibrahim almost immediately from across the short distance.

"Good morning, Ibrahim."

Even at such an old age the man still had the eyes of a hawk.

"You know we haven't seen much of you around here lately. You've been up to no good, no doubt?"

Since Ibrahim's commission his visits were less frequent. With his political status on the rise he rarely went out anywhere, not even to the Baghdad Museum to visit Hassan Jaffa. His temperament had shifted; he had felt it suddenly like a mountain moving deep inside him from the force of a volcano, its warmth continually coating the back of his throat. This, Ibrahim calmly accepted, is what it must mean to be jaded. He used to enjoy working in the museum, the experiences among the artifacts helped spark his own creativity, and Ibrahim had always been friendly with everyone he encountered while an employee. They were always happy to see him too. In those days the museum had felt like a second home; and being the curator's son didn't hurt either.

"Good morning to you." The familiarity of seeing Aid Et-Wari at his post made Ibrahim smile.

"Your father tells me your new position is going well."

"As well as can be expected with the war. I cannot complain. And how are things with you?"

"My sons headed off south almost a month ago, and the last word we received was that they were securing a border field outside Duaiji. Children can never see the pain they cause their parents by leaving. A family is like our own private little kingdom. What can I do but pray for them?"

"I will pray for them too, Aid Et-Wari."

"Thank you, and Allah be with you, Ibrahim."

The security guard noticed the wrapped object underneath Ibrahim's arm.

"What are you trying to steal from us today?"

When Ibrahim had worked at the museum for Hassan Jaffa, Aid Et-Wari and the other security guards would often tease him about the prospect of taking works of art and passing them off as his own in order to sell them for profit in the open markets.

"You would have better luck stealing the *Mona Lisa*. It is known that the president finds her very attractive. Maybe there is some money to be had in it," Aid Et-Wari jokes.

No future existed for a painter in Baghdad, knowledge as common as the sun's rising each day, and Ibrahim's appointment came as a surprise to almost everyone and a blessing to himself. It enabled Ibrahim to continue to do what he loved while receiving government paychecks. Granted, it wasn't the type of work he'd envisioned himself performing while a young boy, but work of any type was rare in the country and he felt lucky indeed to be granted such an opportunity. So what that he painted the faces of the regime as a form of propaganda, as Yusuf had so bluntly put it. Did not Islam forbid the depiction of humans in art? In painting his country's leaders, Ibrahim felt like a rebel. No one else knew how much he was paid, and the joke had stayed with him since the first day Ibrahim had gone to the museum with Hassan Jaffa and they'd asked how it was that the greatest artist the world had ever known had been bought by the Baath.

Ibrahim carefully clutches the painting of Fazeera at his side. He wants to get to Hassan Jaffa as soon as possible but does not want to appear rude.

"If I was trying to steal something today, Aid Et-Wari, I would be smart enough to wait until you were off duty and had gone home. If I remember correctly, the night guard sleeps like a mule," Ibrahim replies. The old man still had an ounce of pride and his cheeks flushed with the remark. "This is for my father. A gift for his office."

"What a wonderful gesture. I wish only for the gift of my sons' safe return."

The museum was between exhibits so there were no visitors. Most of the security guards could be found playing cards or dominoes in the air-conditioned chamber in the basement. Aid Et-Wari held the longest tenure by twenty years, and he never gambled in his life, even for the vanity of boasting.

"Now you must disregard the sentiments of an upset old man," the security officer says, suddenly tired. Ibrahim can feel the warmth begin to rise in his throat.

"An old man with the keenest eyesight this side of the twin rivers," Ibrahim adds.

The two men laugh and Ibrahim passes Aid Et-Wari and continues down the corridor until he is in front of the last door, the one leading into Hassan Jaffa's office. He can hear his father's voice in conversation behind the half-opened door and walks straight in, unable to contain his anxiousness any further.

"Please, do not do anything stupid. The consequences may have been given to you unfairly, but you have done nothing to be ashamed of. Please understand this."

Hassan Jaffa is pleading with someone on the telephone. When he sees Ibrahim, whatever color remaining in his plump face drains away, and Ibrahim immediately knows something is wrong. Hassan Jaffa quickly hangs up the phone. Then he stands up and grabs his coat from off the back of his chair.

"Ibrahim, my son. Is everything alright?" Hassan Jaffa asks.

"Yes, Father," he replies, and extends the painting out in front of him. "For you, Father, please take this gift."

Hassan Jaffa is almost out of the room already before he stops as though there had been a rip in time and stares at the wrapped package and then back up at his son. His shoulders slacken and Ibrahim sees the years in his father's face, the lines etched by time and the abrasive winds of the desert. In that aged face Ibrahim recognizes a more urgent priority than what has brought him to the museum, and he places the unopened picture on the floor and leans it against Hassan Jaffa's desk.

"My son, my son," Hassan Jaffa begins, "I wish so much for you. So much more than all this rubbish that exists around us. And now, more than anything, I wish for your strength. Please sit down. Unfortunately I have no choice but to make this quick."

Ibrahim sits at the head of his father's desk, and Hassan Jaffa, wisely understanding the staunch limits of time, does not waste a moment searching for his words. He reaches out and lightly touches the irregular curve of Ibrahim's nose.

"It is your wife, Shalira. That is no virus or sickness causing her such frequent fevers. She is pregnant, Ibrahim. She just called looking for you and couldn't contain her secret any longer. She has just gotten back confirmation from her doctor and so it has been that she is with child. She has been with child for over three months."

"Hassan Jaffa, please, what is this nonsense you are saying?" Ibrahim begins to plead. Their wedding day was only two months ago and they had consummated their relationship for the first time the night after the ceremony. All the excitement and goodwill that had earlier held Ibrahim like the comforting threads of a warm blanket stripped away and was replaced, instead, by the growing anger and rage he had tried hard to leave behind within his lost sleep.

"She is a scared and tormented soul, and like all of us she prayed and prayed and hoped with all her faith and her strength that this would somehow go away. She used all her energy to pretend this wasn't happening. Well, today it is officially confirmed and in doing so she could hide it no longer."

Hassan Jaffa walks over and places his hand on his son's shoulder.

"It was that night when the guards broke your nose. She kept silent, hoping to force it into the back of her mind where it would disappear with all of the other diseases we store away and want to forget. Iraqis are known for their steely dispositions. She is home now and we must go quickly," Hassan Jaffa continues. "She does not sound well, Ibrahim."

Hassan Jaffa follows Ibrahim past Aid Et-Wari, who is now snoozing delightfully in his chair. The magazine sits folded across his lap, and although his eyesight may still have been strong, his vigilance has softened with age and they rush straight past him, leaving him undisturbed in the basement of the museum. They hurry down Qadisiya Street toward the flat Ibrahim and Shalira share in Al-Mansur, past the busy storefronts and spectacle of the outdoor vendors. As they run, people begin to take notice of them: a frail, white-capped professional man and a slender, youthful one running frightfully down the street with a purpose that causes a small group to not only watch them but to begin to follow as well.

Fifteen minutes later, covered in a thin film of sweat and dust, they run into Ibrahim's neighbor Jaffar Kamza, sitting uncharacteristically sober outside the front gate leading into the courtyard of their apartment. The town butcher smells of lamb's blood and arak although he has not yet started drinking this morning. Instead, Jaffar Kamza holds a respectful solemnity within his bloodshot eyes, appearing almost meditative while sitting sentry at the entrance, and as he rises from his wicker chair, he accidentally blocks the entrance to their complex with his beefy shoulders.

"I am sorry, Ibrahim," Jaffar Kamza manages to cough out, and Ibrahim feels the muscles in his chest and shoulders tighten up. He pushes the butcher, who doesn't resist the force, with all his strength out of the way and runs past him into the courtyard.

"May Allah be with you, Ibrahim," Jaffar Kamza yells out from behind him. "I am so sorry. I only wanted to make sure you were the first to see her."

A large shadow falls across Ibrahim as soon as he enters the courtyard, its breadth moving unnaturally with the slight breeze coming in from off the Tigris. The pigeons that usually ate and congregated at the broken birdbath are gone, and instead two crows idle maliciously upon the bevel of cement. Ibrahim is halted, and although he tries to move himself forward, he is overcome by a paralyzing fear that prevents him from going any farther. His feet become part of the ground underneath him, and it is at this moment, when we learn more about ourselves than we ever care to know, that he is forced to understand what it means to be helpless. He stares up at the third floor where a gilded nameplate GALEB sticks over their doorbell, personalizing their apartment among the many other mundane flats, and within the shallow grounds of the courtyard sees his wife suspended from the third-floor balcony, the bed-sheet they shared wrapped tightly like a cord around her almond-colored neck.

19

OCTOBER 9, 1984

AT FIRST GLANCE THE nights in Baghdad are not too dissimilar to nights spent in other metropolitan cities. Streetlamps and neon signs spring to life and illuminate the settling dusk. Car headlamps map out the roads ahead and hurriedly begin to dominate the downtown area as workers scurry to restaurants or shops or back to their homes out in the surrounding suburbs where the hiss, screeches, and machinations of the city are quaintly replaced by the solitude of what one can no longer hear and the tranquility of the rural desert winds blowing dismissively through the poplar and date trees.

In Baghdad, young adults walk along the Cornice, the paved pathway of restaurants, cafés, and shops running alongside the Tigris River, talking of dreams and ambitions and quite often of soccer with a fervor that reminds me, being from New York, of the Yankees fans back home. Their ardor and heated allegiance rivals the passion of the provincial English football fan. In Iraq, the sport of football, what Americans call soccer, is the one major non-Islamic predilection. Besides religion and the state, Iraq's citizens pour their souls into their local and national teams and wait patiently for the hands of Allah to deliver them into the arena of international recognition.

Half-covered outdoor patios are filled with men playing dominoes and drinking coffee while small televisions broadcast replays of recent games. Historically, it is not customary for men and women to intermingle in public, but since the war many old customs are bending. Couples can be seen lingering along the water's edge under the bright white canopy of stars and whispering sweet nothings to each other against the backdrop of the passing river.

Merchants are still out in large numbers selling sweet meats, oranges and bananas, silk veils, toy soldiers and porcelain dolls. The prices of their wares continue to adjust according to the changing position of the sun. The halting blue domes of the mosques have become invisible, melting into the blue pool of the receding sky. The rounded tops that were originally built by architects in a vain attempt to reach the heavens have instead succeeded in becoming a part of them. From a snapshot's view it is easy to see the same city exemplified in the renowned story of *A Thousand and One Nights,* and it is changing very slowly.

I stop off at the Say ad Manood Hospital to visit Qadro before meeting Daniella for dinner. It feels like it has been days since he accompanied me to the war front. And it feels like weeks since both of us traveled south past the city of Basra and onto the stretches of greenery outside the Haur al Hawizeh marshes, an area where the number of troops from both sides currently pushes close to half a million. But my memory is mistaken; it was only yesterday. This morning Iranian warplanes struck a Kuwaiti tanker sailing one hundred miles off the coastline in the waters of the Persian Gulf. The shooting was intended to enforce the newly adopted Iranian policy that until Iranian ships were able to safely pass throughout the area, all ships using the waterway would be in danger.

I can already hear Qadro's wavering voice from the elevator halfway down the hall, and I am pleased to find that the prospect of living the rest of his life with only one foot has not tempered his tongue. As usual, he is speaking freely.

"Just wait until we get the official orders to unify all of our teams. Once we join together, all of our strengths can come together. Right now our league—the pool is too diluted. If the enemy would only agree to a friendly game of football then"—he pauses for effect—"then maybe this madness would stop."

I expect to find someone else in the room and I am surprised to see he is alone, lying on a white bedsheet and talking to himself.

"That's the first sign of going crazy, you know," I call out as I enter, the stench of ammonia or bleach beginning to lightly scratch the passages of my nose and throat.

"Mikhail," he cries, and attempts to sit up, momentarily forgetting that a portion of his lower leg is gone and accidentally rolling over onto his side. But I do not sense any frustration in his efforts, at least not yet.

"As you already know, a man must be crazy in order to survive in a crazy place," he says sarcastically while rearranging himself.

He is the only patient in the room. A young soldier suffering from a mysterious rash that had spread out across his face and neck was sent home earlier this morning and will, presumably, be back at the war front very soon. There was also a new mother, the wife of a high-ranking field general, who had given birth to a son two days prior and was released the night before I came to visit. I read their details from off the attendance chart that is posted publicly during times of such high casualties.

Hospital space is limited and rooms are sometimes double-filled, with patients even forced to line the walls in the outside hallways. Qadro will not have the room to himself for long.

I walk over to his bed, trying not to stare at the space where the clean bandages end. I have seen worse, but with Qadro I also feel a sense of responsibility. It was me he had been escorting to the front when his lower leg and foot were blown off. I notice a slight haze covering his eyes in a thin coat of gray restlessness, and there is a transparent brown bottle of pills on the nightstand next to his bed.

"No pain at all," Qadro says without taking his eyes off the television. The soccer game he is watching is scoreless.

The hospital conditions are moderately sanitary and typical of what I am accustomed to in the East. I look at the monitors next to his bed, and although I am unsure of the numbers or details of the readings, none are beeping and all of the signals are green. Qadro clutches the remote control to a compact television set hanging high up in the corner of the room. It is showing a match between Karkh, a middle-class district in Baghdad, and Nasiriyah, a city in the southern war sector, and contains less action and skill than an adolescent rock fight. The players follow the white ball across the parched field the way children do in a schoolyard game, absent of any strategic or tactical arrangements, chasing after the ball like the clouds of dust stirred about by a growing sandstorm. It is blatantly apparent that both teams lack the athletic skills to properly play the game. The best players have either gone off to Europe or are presently in training at one of the modern facilities newly constructed by the regime for the national team. The players that have remained behind seem to lack the desire to actually score any goals; all they seem to be doing is just running away from each other. Most of the games I have seen or read about in the papers usually end in a 0–0 tie or, if the gods happen to be shining down on them that day, in a 1–0 final.

Qadro, born in Baghdad, is rooting strongly for his Karkh team. They are one of the capital's three local teams, and its players are dressed professionally in red silken uniforms crossed at the shoulders with vertical white stripes.

"I know they end in a tie, but I am still rooting for a different outcome," he offers dejectedly.

The date on the television is March 17, 1984, St. Patrick's Day back in the United States. The game is a replay from almost seven months ago.

"These matches," Qadro continues, "we watch them over and over again–new ones, old ones, it doesn't matter–and it always ends the same way; deadlocked with no victor. But so goes the way of the game; just because there is no winner doesn't necessarily mean that the trial has been a waste. We are used to things ending in a tie."

"How do you feel, Qadro?" I ask him and sit down in the chair next to his bed. I glance up at the television screen. "Besides some offense, do you need anything?"

"Mikhail," he answers, "I do not feel as bad as I should. Thank you for asking. The part of my body that should hurt is gone; "phantom limbs," the doctors call it. The sensation in my brain recognizes something that is no longer there. The mind is as strong as a bull and it doesn't let go of things too easily. Medication is the elixir we should all desire for."

Out of the corner of my eye I notice the level of pills remaining in the bottle on the nightstand. It is half-empty.

"But I could use a cigarette," Qadro says.

Twenty minutes later, he is seated in a wheelchair situated on the small cement deck outside the cafeteria door and heartily puffing away on a Marlboro. A sudden charge of artillery fire bounds out in the streets below and is quickly followed by the sentinel sound of sirens racing off in the direction of the activity.

Qadro does not shudder. He remains immune to such noises common in the country since the time of Ottoman rule.

"You Americans may have baseball," he says. "Iraqis, for all our history, have always had war."

When the cigarette is half-gone, he begins to draw less and enjoy the comfort.

"I sometimes wonder, Mikhail, is it too much to ask to die with a bit of dignity?" he asks me with an emphasis on the second syllable in my name. His pronunciation is similar to the Russian pronunciation, a fact I find quite curious since the red borders are less than eight hundred miles from downtown Baghdad, a distance notably less than that between Chicago and Miami.

"This afternoon they brought in the remains of a local barber. The hospital, I guess, needed to sign his death certificate in order for him to be considered an official casualty of war. To tell you the truth, I am not sure why he was brought here. He was past the point of recognition and was already long dead. Regardless of the reasons, he had been taking care of his intestinal duties, if you understand what I am trying to say. The poor bastard was sitting on the toilet in his home when a small plane flew overhead. I can only imagine that it happened with a bright flash and then he was catapulted straight out through the roof of his house and across the street with the toilet seat still stuck to his ass. A simple barber. At first his family didn't know what to do so they formed a circle around his remains to obstruct the view until the police arrived. Their first inclination was to protect him from embarrassment. They wanted to protect him, and themselves, from the shame of his spectacle. What a way to go."

And with that he laughs heartily, gasping at times to catch his breath, until he sees I am not laughing along with him. He can tell by the look on my face that I am a bit disturbed by his reaction, and he turns to me.

"None of this is funny, Mikhail," he confesses, and shakes his head. Then he leans back and presses the cigarette out against the metal railing attached to the side of the wheelchair.

The surgeon and doctor attending to Qadro have told him that he should expect a full recovery. The bleeding has stopped and the surrounding tissue is miraculously still alive.

"I believe it is the power of the nicotine, yes," he theorizes to himself.

He is prescribed painkillers for the throbbing and burning he will feel from the nerve endings transmitting sensations to the brain from a foot that is no longer there. There is a high probability he will become addicted to the medication and his mind will continue to long for the missing limb. He has not experienced any shock, which amazes the hospital staff, and he is only being kept under observation to ensure that the area doesn't stroke and the remaining flesh doesn't become infected with gangrene. The doctors still can't believe not only how Qadro survived the explosion but how the tissue was completely severed at the "dead line," as they call it. All the living matter above the dead line, the invisible marker where the ankle-high portion of his leg was severed, remained unharmed. He is to be discharged by the end of the week.

I wheel him back to his room. A young orderly is making his bed and another is cleaning the floor. Outside Qadro's door an older man is lying upright in a hospital bed reading a newspaper. He appears to have no external injuries and takes a moment to look us over rather disdainfully before burying himself back within the tribulations of the daily news. I push Qadro into his room and help him get back into his bed. We have been gone almost thirty minutes, but in the snowy reception on the television set the soccer match remains even at zero.

"Mikhail, when I leave here, I would like to take you to a match. It is much more exciting in person."

I can't see how this is possible. At least on television you have the luxury of changing channels or turning the set off, or even going outside for a cigarette. But a large portion of Baghdad and most sections of the country have been ruled off-limits to foreign journalists, and I expect the game to be as well. I agree to go with him.

"You will meet my friend," he continues, "the painter. I did not forget."

It is amazing that considering the events of the past twenty-four hours he would remember our simple conversation during the ambulette ride back to Baghdad as we drove past the large, rising murals of Saddam Hussein.

"He does very good work considering the subject matter and he should be very proud of himself. Yet, as an artist, he sometimes loses the link to the passion that drives him."

Qadro goes on to explain the brashness of his friend, the new-world artist. He tells me he fears his friend has been tainted, that his soul has been poisoned. This painter of murals and governmental headquarters had once had more talent in his two hands than the entire country combined. I make a mental note of the past tense he uses in his description.

"When I am out of the hospital," Qadro continues, "I will take you to a soccer match and you will meet my friend Ibrahim, the state-sponsored artist. You will see the creator behind such things."

The pain medication is beginning to wear off. I can tell because Qadro is breathing heavily through his clenched teeth and he is also trying hard to stop himself from rubbing the edge of the bandages. His hands dart down to the area only to quickly pull back up to his sides, mechanically repeating the gesture though he appears unaware of doing so. The pale gray haze in his eyes is now gone and he begins to mutter to himself between short, heavy sighs.

"I am sorry, Mikhail," he apologizes, for what reason I am not sure, "it sometimes gets unbearable."

"Please, Qadro, there is nothing to apologize for."

He reaches across the table and fumbles with the bottle of pills, accidentally sending it tumbling to the floor. A dozen orange tablets scatter about the tiles.

"This," he screams, "this is fucking mule shit.

"These godforsaken–," he curses, and then pops the two pills that I hand him into his mouth and is momentarily silent while he struggles to swallow them without the aid of water.

After a few seconds his jaw loosens and he slicks his hair back with both of his hands and begins to massage his temples. In another part of the world he could have been a doctor or a college professor. He is immediately likable. Maybe it is in the way he looks at you when you are speaking, as though he is truly and completely interested in the things you have to say. Maybe it is the way he refuses to let himself get beaten down or the strength with which he continues to keep his spirits high. His presence somehow influences you and your desire to do the right thing. I understand such influence; I recognized it years earlier in a priest I had known while I was a young boy. The pills take their hold after several minutes and then Qadro smiles.

"They make me nauseous, though," he says. "My wife, Hayat, is bringing me lamb kebabs and *khubaz*. I am nervous to eat it but I will try anyway. To show her I appreciate her thought and her work. But I was very sick this morning . . ." He trails off, drained of his energy.

The match between Karkh and Nasiriyah finally ends, once again, approximately 205 days, nine hours, and thirty-six minutes after it was initially played. And it ends in a tie. I am sure that when Qadro is sent home, if he has a television set, he will watch the same game again, and although he knows how it will end, he will still root for a different outcome. Lying in the hospital bed, he doesn't look well and has started to sweat profusely. The bedsheets are pulled up tight underneath his chin.

"Thank you for coming, Mikhail," he says.

"You're welcome. Is there anything I can do for you?"

"Next week when I am discharged and hopefully feeling better, you will come with me to a real soccer match. And you will meet my friend."

"I look forward to it," I respond almost truthfully.

We say goodbye and I walk out into the blue-tiled hallways. As soon as I turn away from his room, I can hear Qadro begin to talk to himself again.

"Hopefully, the outcome will be a better one," he wishes aloud. "Yes, next week I hope for a better outcome."

The older man waiting outside Qadro's room puts down his newspaper to mark my departure and then the two young orderlies come running over and begin to wheel him inside.

"My friend, my friend," I hear the fading voice of Qadro start talking to his new roommate as I turn the corner and step into the waiting elevator, "you are late."

20

OCTOBER 9, 1984

DANIELLA IS SITTING ALL alone at one of the outdoor tables in Saadi's Café. The dark hair of her Iraqi heritage lends itself to her blending into the crowd, but the ice blue of her eyes is almost hypnotic, and as usual she is the most beautiful woman in the room and can't help standing apart. I leisurely stare at the nape of her neck, not wanting to startle her as I walk up toward her table from behind, and I am distracted by a feeling that has grown only stronger since last night. I get close enough to touch her but she senses my presence before I can even reach out my hand.

"You are late," Daniella states without turning to face me. "Michael, I was getting anxious."

And then she smiles and I kiss her and sit down across from her. She is all I can see in the café. Her silk hair shines like a new chador and is pulled back to reveal her face, accented by the smoothness of her delicate cheekbones rising under each of those bottomless blue eyes to frame a nose that is at once both feminine and studious. She pouts her lips teasingly as if I have kept her waiting all night, a gesture that makes me check my

watch again only to confirm I am actually considerably early–
by thirty minutes to be exact. She adjusts the turquoise shawl
draped across her shoulders, its color intensifying the shade
of her eyes, and underneath I can see the straps of her dress
pressed against the thin hint of freckles on her bare shoulders.
Recognizing the prudish society of this country, she gently pulls
the material back up and around herself, a small clip clasping
its edges together about her slender neck.

"Michael, it is so good to see you," she says, and her long,
athletic fingers squeeze my hand across the table. "I felt like a
schoolgirl all day."

I squeeze back and I sense a difference about her, a self-
assuredness replacing her often-stoic nature. It is in the way
her hand lingers over mine. She doesn't rush to move it away
like she has so often done in the past once she has initiated contact. Instead, she lets her fingers rest securely atop mine. Before
last night it had been almost three months since we'd seen each
other last. I flew to London during the interval we both had
scheduled between assignments and we spent a week together.
I remember that as each day passed, she closed off a little bit
more of herself, until by the last day I couldn't help but feel as
if she had placed an insurmountable mountain between us.
When Daniella dropped me off at Heathrow Airport, she almost
extended her hand upon saying goodbye as though we were
merely business associates. She is not used to opening herself
up–I know that because she has told me as much. Instead, she
lets her feelings run through her thoughts where they will
eventually settle, only after meticulous consideration, within
her recorded words. They race through her mind and accumulate until she is able to release them into stories written about
the lives of others, her reporting a reservoir into which she has
hidden her own emotions. By expressing such heartfelt, and often raw, emotion in her reporting, she has helped to distance

herself from her father's reputation. Johnathon Burkett may have been the war, but his daughter was its people.

"If I knew you'd be early, I would have come sooner," I tell her, trying not to lose the irony of two journalists presently covering a war and yet being able to be early for anything.

Several soldiers dressed in casual khaki attire, not their field uniforms but rather the clothes issued for leisure, occupy a table across from us and appear to be having a good time. One of the soldiers is attempting to juggle several rolls of bread while the others sit back and with increasing amusement watch him fumble about.

The soldiers holler out loud in applause and kick their heels up in excitement as the juggler accidentally drops a roll into a water glass and then laugh even louder at each other's laughter. As I watch them, the simple adage about the world's best medicine comes to mind. I hear Daniella laugh along too, and I wonder if I have ever heard a more pleasant sound. I smile and then look away as the juggling soldier shakes the crumbs from his lap and a waiter rushes over to deposit another basket onto their table.

"Michael," Daniella begins, "Baghdad is our place. As a little girl I always dreamt of falling in love in Paris or Rome. Even Bombay with its harsh smells and underlying sensuality; but nope, this is it—our place."

This is the first time she has mentioned it, love, or falling into something like it.

She is smiling a bit demurely and I remember her foolishly leaving my hotel room last night against the regulation of curfew and the threat of arrest. I had tried to stop her but she is as stubborn as her father, a man known to walk straight into the line of fire despite the stern warnings of others. She is not a leader or a follower; she moves freely and alone, hindered only by her own sense of frustration while quietly absolving herself of any obligations so as not to hinder the process. Johnathon Burkett traveled by horseback into a foreign country after the closing of the two great wars despite efforts from his superiors who told him his safety could not be guaranteed. He strode into a world of nomads and bedouins, a world unfamiliar with things of the West, and against the better judgment of others, only to be awarded the Pulitzer Prize as a result of his audacity and refusal to be directed. This world grows more dangerous every day—I witness the growth—and I have feared the presence of that same trait in his daughter. Staring into the eye of a storm, she will curiously step toward it.

I sit across from her and want to wrap my arms around her and protect her, protect her from the stares and the desires of others, from the dark recesses of anger and frustration that seem to be the cause of so many of the world's problems, to protect her from her own sense of freedom and from herself. This is the reason why she visits me in dark hotel rooms in the middle of the night, why she escapes from my sleeping arms like a tender dream. She only gives what she feels won't hold her back, and just like the man who flew to cover the assassination of a quasi-monarch on the date of this country's revolution and, as a result, missed his daughter's second birthday, her competitive nature is not one against others but rather only against herself and what she perceives are her own limits and fears. Daniella Burkett, with an earnestness in her eyes that she will never be able to fully hide, puts enough pressure on herself so as not to be concerned with the prospects or competition of others; she has always been her own worst enemy. Yet, in many ways, it has served her well, driving and pushing her further and more quickly than she could ever have imagined.

Several photographs are laid out in front of her and I recognize some of them immediately. She releases my hand and places one of the pictures in it.

"Do you remember Washington?" she asks me.

The photo is a bit worn around the edges from travel. In it we have our arms around each other, and on our faces are the excited smiles of two people who have left the cares of the real world temporarily behind. We are standing proudly in front of the Lincoln Memorial during a four-day weekend spent together in the capital. Toward the end of our vacation I remember I had rented a small boat to take us out sailing across the Chesapeake Bay. Surrounded by the orange and red tints of the changing leaves, the seasons slowly undressed before us. I placed my fingertips in the water, its temperature warmer than the brisk Virginia air, and let them drift along with the pace of the boat. Our shoes were off and we were stretched out next to each other as the captain and his deckhand secured the tarp of the sails and we slid lazily across the water. It was the anniversary of her mother's, Shahrazad's, death. The lung cancer that metastasized in her bones silently drew its way up her throat until there was no room left for air to be inhaled. She suffered, but for a short period of time. As a result, Daniella never found out her mother was sick until it was too late. And Shahrazad never knew that her daughter didn't know she was dying.

The wind pushed hard against those sails, the pressure buckling the material until the deckhand could tighten the pulleys and steer us rigidly about our course. The motion of the men at work and of the boat was soothing, and Daniella grabbed my hand as the world slid past in frames of changing colors around us.

"I am here for you when you need me," I told her, a bay breeze tossing her hair across her face.

"Yes, I know," she said while pulling strands away from her eyes. "Thank you."

Hours later when the boat was in its slip and secured in its moorings, we sat at the maple bar of Stan O's, a local tavern, enjoying a final beer before we took the ride back across the

Potomac and back to D.C. Daniella was comfortable and we were laughing and joking with an older couple enjoying a weekend getaway themselves, up from Virginia Beach, and Stan, the aged bartender, fisherman, and fan of the Baltimore Orioles referred to in the establishment's name. The tourist season for the area had ended with the close of summer, people now choosing the majesty of the changing foliage up north in the New England states. A small group congregated at the bar, and judging by the conversation they were mostly locals. Everyone seemed at ease as the area settled back to normal after a crowded and profitable summer; especially Daniella, who seemed relaxed as she leaned across the bar and put her hand on my wrist.

"I want to be there for you too, Michael," she whispered.

I place the picture down on the table in front of me. There are a dozen others. The two of us skiing in the mountains of France, our skin flush from the cold air. There we are poolside with fresh, healthy-looking tans outside a hotel in Grenada. There is even one of us and the couple from Virginia Beach, with our arms around each other, smiling underneath the flashing neon lights of Stan O's. I don't remember it being taken.

She may have kept herself at a safe distance but she has always remained in my scope. Although she may not have opened herself up to all the possibilities or given what she fears she is not strong enough to give, we have been following each other, side by side, either in person when we could or in each other's thoughts.

"I am sorry," she suddenly says, "and I am finally able to admit it. I am sorry for being so stubborn and so cold. You deserve more and I am grateful for your perseverance."

"Dee," I respond, "without even knowing it, you gave me no choice."

She continues, "I was overwhelmed last night when I knew I was coming to see you. And then I left because of the strength of my feelings. But this morning something released itself inside of me and then I was angry at myself for leaving. I have been angry at myself for so long it is overwhelming."

Sitting across from her in Saadi's Café, I sense she wants to open more of herself, to loosen the demands of her own making and the drive and ambition she has put first in her life for so long.

"You see, Michael," Daniella says, "regardless of what I may or may not have screwed up, there is a history between us, a good history. And I like it, I like it a lot."

She pauses to gauge my reaction, or to temper her words, always playing them out beforehand in her head. Then upon realizing that she is doing so, Daniella only smiles as though to prove she is trying.

"I know you have wanted more," she continues, "and I am sorry that I couldn't give you what you needed. But please understand that I gave you—and only you—all that I was able to."

Then she sits back and stiffens her shoulders, trying to regain some of the composure she feels she may have lost with her openness. She doesn't understand that her words only help to illuminate her. I can see she is nervous. We have known each other for over three years and we have spent more time together in foreign places than in the comfort of our own homes, courting each other in the worlds of dying kings and falling dictatorships, on the coastlines of a rising theocracy and in the hallowed respite near the papal throne. We have grown toward each other—for that is what she is trying to say now—in countries where the passions of their people are second to the demands of their leaders, in places where the stories always were of the tremendous struggles of everyday life and most often in a land where words were used like swords and wartime soldiers juggled bread like carefree children.

"I was afraid, Michael," she whispers after a moment. "Eventually, I grew to look forward to the time I would see you again. I would plan ahead and drive forward without distraction until we would get together. And then something happened the last time I saw you—as each hour, each minute passed—I began to resent you. I began to resent us, everything—my job, my preoccupations—because I did not look forward to the time I would see you but rather I began to resent the time that we would be apart."

There is a conclusion in what she is describing. I know it is coming to the surface because it is something I have been waiting for.

"There doesn't have to be time apart," I tell her.

"I hope so," she answers me. "Not anymore."

A tumbled commotion comes from the table in the corner behind me where earlier the soldier tossed dinner rolls. I turn around and watch as the soldier leans too far back in his chair and one of its wooden legs splinters. The laughter from the other soldiers grows more rambunctious, and as the juggler tries to juggle his own balance, he cocks his head slightly to the side and instinctively drives up his boots to gain some support. But he only gains momentum and accidentally kicks over his own table. He hovers unsteadily for a split second and then the leg completely cracks and he falls backward into the table of an official-looking elderly couple eating their dinner behind him. Unanimous applause rings out from the other soldiers who now stand up and surround him.

Outside the café, a stern voice calls forth in Arabic from the loudspeakers hanging propitiously from the minarets close to the river.

"Baghdad is our place, Michael," Daniella repeats herself and then laughs aloud with the rest of the café, along with everyone except the elderly couple, who appear quite shaken at being made a spectacle of and are now having words with the owner.

Daniella is not taking mental notes, at peace with the trivial nature of her current thoughts, and is momentarily amused. For a brief second, I can recognize the little girl in her, understanding we have come a long way in one night. I watch the soldier lying on the floor covered in the dinners and drinks of the two tables he upturned around him. A waiter has run over to offer the soldier a helping hand, and he is instead pulled down amicably into the mess. The other men all stand around their fallen comrade and grab the dinner rolls from off the floor and start to throw them back at the two men lying on the floor, who can only do their best to cover themselves with the stained tablecloth.

Outside, the final daily call to prayer plays over the city, and people stop whatever they are doing to practice their faith. Lights shine off the Tigris from the riverboats coming in to dock for the night, and the last merchants slowly close the gates down over their shops.

I breathe in the surroundings—the brine odor of the pier extending out past the café patio, the milky sweetness of the puddinglike desert *ma'mounia* wafting out from the kitchen, the slight burning of frankincense lit by the devout worshippers praying behind their shops—taking it all into my lungs and understanding the fact that the ancient city of Baghdad has survived for over twelve hundred years, from its origins as the capital of the Abbasid caliphate when it prospered and was known throughout the world as the City of Peace, through the severe devastation of its buildings and fabulous gardens brought on by the force of such foreign invaders as the Mongols and the Turks, and the chaotic internal strife that has permeated throughout it all like a cancer. It belongs to no one but simply to history.

21

DANIELLA BURKETT JOSTLES ABOUT in the backseat of a converted military truck as the small group rides uneasily through the flowing grass hills preceding the jagged black rocks of the Zagros Mountains and into Kurdish country. Two government minders sit at full attention in the front seat of the truck, one driving while the other quietly points out directions. The pair is escorting Daniella and two other members of the international press—a Parisian woman and a Syrian woman—up north in an attempt to quell widespread rumors of Iraqi chemical attacks against its own citizens, the Kurds.

The vehicle angles over the small dirt road they have driven on for more than an hour, the same dirt road they have been on since passing through the town of Kirkuk and the last remnants of civilization. On one side, the rising mass of cement and dark rock hovers threateningly over their truck like a night watchman; on the other side the low flatlands wash away in the distance like extended rolls of green velvet.

The Parisian and Syrian women grow more restless the farther north the group travels. Once the memories of the signs for Kirkuk fade, the two women try to hide their nervousness by conversing with each other, only to quickly realize the impediment of their different languages. Upon first meeting the women, Daniella had given a cursory glance at their press badges, as she assumed they did to hers as well, attached like ski-lift tickets to their jacket breast pockets and stamped with the flags of their respective countries. A recent legislative announcement by the National Assembly has granted permission to foreign-born women to travel in the northeastern country region. Foreign men are presently not allowed past the village of Samarra in central Iraq. In a part of the world where women have commonly accepted the submissive role, it is a historical proclamation in itself, though it will barely last a month.

With the revolution in neighboring Iran, the Iraqi government is hard-pressed to try and prevent the turmoil from spreading to its own people. Their own men, they fear, would quickly disappear into these dark foothills, diminishing the already falling number of soldiers currently conscripted into the army. The Republican Army does not want its soldiers siding with the pesh mergas, or worse, crossing the borders into Iran. They also fear foreign men sent as spies or the coercive tactics of the Iranians recruiting support and sympathy for their own causes. The Baath presumes women won't possess the inclination to flee. They also presumed the gesture to be a hollow one. The National Assembly did not expect any foreign women to use this proclamation as a means to travel in the area.

Daniella holds a sense of relief after our conversation last night as though a burden has been lifted from off her shoulders. A feeling like happiness awoke with her this morning, and for the first time she can remember, she felt content.

"Even this pungent, stale air seems to smell better," she said.

"Maybe you're just coming down with a cold," I replied, and she playfully turned away from the window and rolled back into bed. It felt good to watch the sunrise together.

We both left Baghdad early, she going north and me heading south to the war front yet again. Before departing, I explained to her about Qadro and the senseless explosion that took his foot.

"It is as if no one is even watching the ground around them," I said angrily. "It's like they are only looking straight ahead, concerned with their own being, and then boom—you are screwed."

She sensed the outrage in my voice when I described the young soldiers urinating on the picture of the ayatollah before the small mine exploded. Then she implored me to use more caution when choosing my friends.

"Especially during a time of war," she said, the sarcasm in her voice a cover for her growing concern.

But I have always been alone in this world—she understands that part of my past. As a result, I make acquaintances easily and rather quickly as though reestablishing a familiar yet shallow bond with the first handshake. And just as my weakness for always giving people—even strangers—the benefit of the doubt has sometimes frustrated me, it now frustrates her that I put myself in harm's way.

"I wish you didn't have to go do this, Dee," I told her as she checked her gear one final time and I tightened the straps on her backpack. "You know it isn't pretty dangerous."

And Daniella smiled. It was a new nickname I had recently begun to call her—"pretty dangerous," although she never thought of herself along those lines.

"It is extremely dangerous. Whatever resources exist here by the capital to actually protect us, as silly as it seems that they may want to protect us, there is nothing of the sort up in those hills. It is lawless. And there is nowhere to run."

And Daniella knew I was right. Whatever their group might

encounter in that region of the country, the government of Baghdad would be too far away to provide any immediate protection. The National Assembly may have granted women passage, but they did not guarantee their safety.

At the time only Daniella knew her reasons for going–she wanted to prove to herself that she didn't need these dangers anymore; that she could leave them behind without any regrets. She thought to herself, "What kind of wife . . . ," and then took it one step further–"What type of mother would subject her family to such worry?" Then she thought of Shahrazad as she recently seemed to do more often. If she were still alive, she'd be happy to know that Daniella wouldn't be doing this much longer. If correct–and deep down inside herself she knew that she was–this would be her last assignment of the type. She still needed some kind of internal reassurance that when she was actually put into the moment she wouldn't realize she was kidding herself. She was ready to settle down–she knew she was–and this trek up north was her last test to herself, a send-off, and also one to which she had already committed herself.

Contemplating this, a wave of serenity fell over her in contrast to the rest of the people in the truck. Daniella was excited yet at ease. She pondered what she would do with her time instead; maybe she would teach or try to write a book, definitely travel less. And maybe she could begin to enjoy her life.

A slight pause takes hold of the truck's carburetor and then the engine bucks forward with a hesitant kick. A darkened exhaust cloud escapes from behind them as the truck struggles to meet the earth rising slowly up ahead. The tan, weathered faces of hooded men have sprouted up along the mountainside, pushing out past the branches and shrubbery. There are many of them, lined sporadically along the mountain's rising edges. Daniella can make out the Kalashnikov rifles the men carry over their shoulders as more pesh mergas appear out of nowhere, like ghosts falling from the sky.

Almost a year ago, the Kurdish guerrillas and members of the Kurdish Democratic Party helped Iran seize the border post of Hajj Omran after Baghdad had strategically relocated its troops to the southern front during periods of intense fighting. Baghdad soon responded by reentering the security zones taken by the Barzanis of the KDP and swiftly rounded up between five thousand and eight thousand Kurdish males and drove them south, never to be seen again.

Further uphill the truck steadies itself and more men have assembled right in front of their path. Atheer, the driver, slows the truck to avoid hitting the small group blockading the road ahead and is forced to stop when the men refuse to move. Thickly wrapped turbans with colored tassels called *mishki*s adorn their heads, and gleaming belts of ammunition crisscross their chests. The guerrillas appear to be replicas of one another, each dressed in uniform brown pantaloons, white flowing shirt, and headgear. Daniella notices the thick green cummerbunds wrapped around each of their waists and the iron dagger slipped in neatly underneath the wrapping, a cultural sign of manhood. Although the Russian rifles smuggled in from across the border pose a far more formidable example.

Three men approach the truck, one toward each front seat window and another comes up to the hood of the truck. Their rifles are kept drawn and the guerrilla directly in front of the group aims at the windshield. Atheer puts the truck into park and slowly raises both his hands so the approaching men can see them. Then he motions with his left hand to mimic the motion of rolling down his window. The guerrilla closest to Atheer continues forward while the other two men stay farther behind, their rifles readjusted in preparation of being used. Daniella wonders why they are standing directly in front of the car. They are far enough away for Atheer to give the engine ample gas to cause some serious damage and too close for them to even get out of the way.

Atheer smartly rolls down his window and shows their official transport documents from the National Assembly to the man at his side. The guerrilla dubiously shakes his head and starts yelling out at the other guerrillas who have begun to surround the front perimeter of the truck. A few of the men break out into laughter.

The pesh merga glances furtively at the documents and then shakes his head again. Understanding that the decree is not of the normal kind, Daniella wonders if any word of the new legislature made it past the major cities and into these foothills; and if word did in fact spread, if the law would be followed. For a moment she recalls her visit to her uncle's horse farm and remembers the green cummerbunds as the distinctive "colors" of certain Kurdish tribes.

"You haven't even read them yet," Atheer submissively pleads, and with these words it becomes clear—the man is unable to read them.

For the second time today, the barrier of language has become evident. The guerrilla slings his rifle over his shoulder and out of his way and begins to rip up the papers authorizing their transport into smaller pieces. He turns the paper over several times in his hands and, after he is satisfied, quickly slaps his hands together in a gesture of mock explosion and lets the pieces fall over the ground. Then he brings his rifle out once again. Daniella notices the petite hands of the Syrian woman shaking in her lap. Even the government-appointed minder in the front passenger seat is cowering under the window, slumped down in his seat yet keeping his hands up high and within the sight of the pesh mergas. He is only a boy, much too young to hold such a job.

Close to thirty pesh merga soldiers surround the area, and the three directly in front of the truck have their guns drawn and aimed aggressively at the journalists' small party. The mountains overhead are blocked by the cover of trees, and Daniella can only estimate how many more guerrillas they can't see up above them in those hills.

"This is as far as we go, ladies," Atheer says, turning around. The morning had been cool, but rings of perspiration have quickly darkened his gray shirt. "I am sorry."

Atheer slowly places his hands back on the wheel, careful of any sudden movements, and deliberately maneuvers the truck, careful to avoid any contact with the guerrillas who are still standing very close by, until the three men previously facing the windshield are rotated out of sight, and then Atheer steadily gases the truck off in the direction from which it had just come. When a warning rifle shot is heard in the distance, the Syrian woman gags, and then as if to catch herself, she breaks out into nervous laughter.

"They take threats to their way of life very seriously," Daniella says not as a statement to the others but more as a reminder to herself.

"And we do not," the Parisian woman argues back, surprising Daniella with her knowledge of the English language. The passenger-side minder has finally put his hands down and is grasping at the sides of his chair.

"Yes, I guess we all do," Daniella replies, "but the mountains make them so isolated."

The truck continues on in reserved silence. Approximately six miles down the road they pull up next to a narrow dirt pathway the width of a laid-out streetlamp and bordered on both sides by high-rising hedges. Daniella implores the driver to turn.

"They will warn us first if we overstep our bounds," Daniella pleads with Atheer, and then to strengthen her position and conviction she continues in what little Sorani, a southern-Kurdish dialect, she remembers. "Tell them we come to see the tradition of their culture. We come as students, to see the horses."

They are the only words she can remember. Two generations ago, Kidhir Effendi drove his horses to the edge of the same foothills of this region, riding east along the Iranian border with his brother Neffi, Daniella's grandfather, to trade with the southern Kurdish tribes. The quality of the rich soil was optimal for cultivation, and the wheat and meat products were far better than those produced around Baghdad and in the southern territories. Kidhir traveled the distance for the best grain and beef he could find for his Arabian stallions. Although trade amongst Arab and Kurd wasn't too unfamiliar, Kidhir had traveled from outside Baghdad, a considerable trip for only two men to make on horseback. His father and uncles before him had also traded with the southern tribes, exchanging their lesser horses and often money for the quality of the produce in the region.

When she was a little girl, Daniella's uncle would tease her when she came to visit, doing so in Sorani and Kurmanji to the displeasure of his own mother, Daniella's grandmother, who had come from a family of wealthy landowners. Daniella's family had never held itself to the strict customs of society and instead forged relationships with foreigners and strangers alike, failing racism in all its most primitive forms just as they did when Daniella's father ambled onto their property, all blond hair and blue eyes, even when the sounds coming forth from his motorcycle scared the horses so much that it took Kidhir until sunset to gather and calm the stallions.

The other women are too stunned by Daniella's request to reply, and Atheer, taken aback by this woman's knowledge of the Kurdish dialect, quietly submits and begins to steer the truck east. Quickly, the road narrows further with thickets of ferns rising from off the sides of the path and reaching overhead to form a tunneled passageway through which the truck can barely pass without ripping off branches and leaves with its side mirrors. Then the path ascends sharply into a darkened patch overhung by fern and oak trees, and they lose the shadow of their own vehicle that had followed them at a safe distance to the west and a few car lengths behind. The engine hesitates once again and then kicks forcefully forward, knocking the words of the two other women who were just about to voice their objections aside in silence.

Shortly up ahead they come upon a small clearing before it fully opens into a circular area surrounded on the outside by various-sized bamboo huts. Smoke smolders from off the ground like a rising mist, and for a brief second Daniella recognizes the faint smell of pecans. The smoke extends out in a series of hazy lines past the bamboo huts and off the far path, continuing in decline well into the distance.

"There are no watch guards or sentries," Atheer says quietly. Then he whispers it again, "Why are there no guards?"

The small village of Shiek Wiha Aan lies west of the larger town of Al-Sulaymaniyah in the southern mountains. None of the occupants of the truck would be familiar with the name, at least not yet. The agitation that had almost completely left Atheer since driving away from the guerrillas on the road to Irbil starts to rise again in the throat of the frumpy man. Daniella notices his hands are shaking, and rings of sweat renew themselves across his shirt. Half expecting an ambush at any moment, the group keeps as quiet as possible so as not to disturb any of the inhabitants, who are currently nowhere to be found.

The truck slows as they approach the first bamboo hut and almost comes to a halt as Daniella leans across the other two women in the backseat and peers into its opening. Inside the room several rifles are leaned against the doorway. Wicker baskets hang from hooks nailed into the ceiling and parchments of animal skins decorate the main wall. Off to the side a low bamboo table is laid out, and upon it a man is sleeping. Atheer takes his foot off the gas and lets the truck roll along naturally. As the vehicle passes, they closely watch the sleeping man to see if he moves, but he remains undisturbed by their movements and then passes out of sight. Ten similar bamboo huts enclose the village, and farther inside the main area clotheslines are drawn tightly between several of them. Laundry looking excessively aged hangs brittle in the air, as if washing it were simply an act of vanity. Shirts and robes drape from the lines in tatters but are not merely torn as though incomplete, like pieces had purposely been removed to produce more weathered pieces of incomplete garments.

A three-foot ridge of stone surrounds a well not too far off from a fire pit marking the epicenter of the main area, their proximity to each other for safety reasons, as in most of the villages. As Daniella notices the setting, something catches the corner of her eye. Underneath the small roof of the well a sandaled foot hangs suspended and upside down, secured by the ropes from the water pulley system. Daniella pushes the two women aside and leans over to get a better view. The truck hits a slight impediment, dragging a blunt object underfoot until the vehicle gently lifts itself up in the front and over, and then there is the loud popping of expelled air from underneath the front tire.

"Oh my God," Atheer cries.

Up past the base of the village is a well-maintained path bowing down to a flowing stream before which dozens of bodies have fallen short of its waters. Men, women, and children lie motionless and twisted on the ground as though they are sleeping, a thought that quickly makes Daniella think of the man in the first bamboo hut. Unlike the sleeping man, who appeared comfortable in his slumber, these bodies are strewn about in unnatural positions.

Atheer stops the truck and the two government minders and three women rush out. Atheer picks up a flattened object from off the ground behind the front wheel and does not go any further. The three women rush toward the water, and Daniella is suddenly overcome by a fear that maybe they will fail to reach the stream as well. She stops and leans over the first body she reaches, a young teenage girl lying atop a younger girl. The smaller girl's head is buried beneath the older one's weight and suggests one had tried to suffocate the other.

In fact it appears as though everyone had suffocated. No blood or visible signs of injury or harm are evident on anyone except in the eyes of those which remained open. In those blankened stares, the whites around the irises are gone, burnt a ghastly red.

"Not one person has made it to the water," Daniella yells, "not one."

The other government minder runs back to the vehicle and compares the empty silver canister he has found to the crushed one Atheer picked up from underneath the truck. While he matches their dimensions, a tiny drop of yellow liquid escapes from one and lands on top of his hand, instantly causing the skin to burn and bubble. The minder quickly drops the canister and runs past the fallen bodies and bamboo huts, oblivious to the carnage around him, straight into the stream, where he first drops his hand and then submerges himself completely underneath the water.

Gathering whatever composure she can, Daniella calls the others together and suggests they search the bodies to make sure no one is still alive.

"There is still smoke from the fire," Daniella says. "This happened not too long ago."

Then she cautiously removes the layer of her first shirt and wraps it around her mouth and nose. The others do the same.

They search each body, listening for a stifled breath or hoping to see an expansion in a chest cavity, and after two hours have all but finished. No one has survived. The Syrian woman is still sick. The moment she got too close to the bodies she instantly froze, unable to walk or bend at the knees. Daniella and Sophie, the Parisian woman, helped her to an empty bamboo hut where the woman sat back stone-faced on a lamb's-wool cot and whimpered quietly to herself while the others continued with their inspections.

As she walks back over to the truck, Daniella again notices the wrapped leg she saw when they first pulled into the village of Shiek Wiha Aan. What they encountered after that had completely occupied her mind, and she had almost forgotten about it until she turned to the well after examining the last villager and saw the sandaled foot still hanging upside down and secured by the well rope. Walking slowly toward it, she wishes that with each footstep she takes the well would magically recede itself farther away from her, somehow miraculously staying beyond her reach. Without any conscious effort her footsteps grow smaller. The hardened nutty aroma she recognized when they first exited the vehicle has grown stronger. She remembers reading during her research that certain chemicals retain the odor of nuts and even vegetables after they have been released as gases into the air. The most common smells are those of almonds and even pecans. Then as she draws closer, Daniella recognizes the thick calf muscle and dark hair along its length representing a man's leg.

With Atheer's help she starts to pull the man up, but when they first move the body, a long second passes before a faint splash echoes out from deep inside the well. Daniella and Atheer grab the man's waist and pull the body out as quickly as their strength will allow them, and only when the body is on the ground next to them and the opening of the well is clear does Daniella look into its depth, and in the radiating darkness she can make out the newborn baby floating still in the water below.

22

OCTOBER 10, 1984

THIS TIME IT WOULD be different. I knew as much before we even left Baghdad when a Ministry of Information official named Jazeri Khayrallah introduced me to the minder that was taking me to the southern war front and crudely joked, "Please be careful. We do not have many left."

As friendly and talkative and personable as Qadro is, Nabonidas is reserved and quiet, giving off a calculating air that lends itself to the reason why minders were appointed in the first place. He carries about a general distrust regarding everything around him. He simply nodded when he first entered Jazeri's office, not even offering a cursory glance in the direction of my extended hand. Nabonidas's nature rubbed off on me almost immediately as I withdrew from any further conversation with these government officials, feeling suddenly suspicious of them myself, and we soon embarked down the same road Qadro and I had journeyed on only days earlier, past the outposts of wounded soldiers and dying men and boys, past the smoldering gray wickets of abandoned homes and towns, without the incessant honking Qadro believed fueled the car, but rather accompanied by an awkward silence.

Thousands of Iraqi troops sit entrenched in the marshland borders, heavily fortified with supply caches and excess munitions crates hidden from the sky under an abundance of palm fronds and reeds. Flying overhead or in close proximity is a considerable amount of air support strategically providing cover for the platoons, which have been dug in the ground for close to five days. Not too far away, off the southern coast, Iraqi planes earlier fired Exocet missiles at the Iranian oil terminals on Kharg Island. In anticipation of the small, mazelike layout of the island and the recent installation of surface-to-air missiles and low antiaircraft guns protecting Kharg, the pilots were required to take a higher flight and attack zone than usual. Consequently the rockets failed to hit their intended targets, striking, and thus sinking instead, several Panamanian- and Saudi-owned vessels carrying Iranian oil away from the island.

Threats of retribution against ships in the Gulf transporting Iraqi oil were nonexistent. There were no ships in the Gulf transporting Iraqi oil since Iraq had no oil refineries in the area. In addition, Iraqi soldiers had retaken much of the land in proximity to the city of Basra that Iranian forces had secured earlier in the war–reclaiming almost 90 square miles of the more than 130 previously taken under control by Iranian soldiers. Since the war had now shifted in emphasis, the threat of a land invasion caused an increase in fervor among the Iraqi populace, and the Shias who once might have aligned themselves with the Shia majority in Iran were now fighting for their own soil. Threats of desertion decreased and were replaced by a strong familial desire to protect the homeland. Publicly, the ayatollah overconfidently proclaimed a counteroffensive to be launched within the next two weeks in an attempt to retake the area once again. The Iranians, unable to hurt the Iraqis in the Gulf waters, were determined to exact revenge on land, and the Iraqis waited anxiously in their trenches for the first sign of opposing forces moving farther into their own country and away from the cover of the Iranian mountains.

It has been close to a week. Thousands of Iraqi men and boys remain stretched about in the damp earth. Each day that passes does its part to lessen the impending threat in their minds, and the soldiers openly laugh and joke with each other, more confident to be protecting their own land than invading a foreign one, but, more importantly, ever hopeful that an attack might not even occur at all.

As soon as we arrive, I quickly wonder if this is going to be another one of the government's hide-and-seek adventures and tell myself this might not be so bad—a wasted trip is usually also a safe one. But no sooner do I close the car door than a contingent of Iraqi jet fighters soars overhead in the direction of the Gulf to continue their assault on Kharg Island and the coastal cities of Gaveneh and Bushehr. A loud roar bellows forth from out of the thick furrow in the earth and the men begin to cheer with the presumed offensive.

"Saddam, Saddam, Saddam, O great leader," all of them profess with a national pride that has grown tremendously with the recent and successful defense of their homeland.

Earlier in the war Iran tried unsuccessfully to capture Iraq's only port city, Basra, with the hopes of cutting the country off from every waterway and landlocking the republic. But up until this point each attempt has been put down. Unable to capture the city, the Iranians have instead taken to shelling it. U.S. intelligence received from satellites flying over the area claims close to fifty thousand Iranian troops have recently crossed over the border from Khorramshahr and are now heading west toward Basra. Many of the soldiers that were already inside Iraq were waiting outside the town of Abu Khasib. Surveillance photos showed the Iranians hastily building wooden plank bridges and crossings for their tanks and other vehicles in order to gain access over the stretches of the eastern marshlands. The Iranian offensive is expected at any moment, but as the minutes turn to hours and the hours to days, preoccupations often shift, and it took the ominous sounds of war to bring their purpose back to the soldiers. Iraqi attack helicopters patrol overhead, flying the length of the strategic Basra-Baghdad road, when several suddenly open fire toward the southern stretch below the Jasmin Canal.

I quickly dive into the trench and press my back against the front wall. Helicopter gunships whip overhead, stirring the air through the remaining palm and date trees dotting the scarred battlefield. The Iraqis own the air. Their French and Russian helicopters and planes are more advanced and reliable than the outdated American planes deployed by the Iranians. It is ironic considering the United States' outward public support of Saddam Hussein and open disdain of the ayatollah.

With my back against the front wall, I quickly glance down the length of the posting. The two-mile-long trench resembles the pink and elevated marking left behind by a cat scratch and is curved at its distant edges to form a flattened U-shape. At its tips, SAMs explode in staggered response and rockets are launched over the marshy terrain, falling in the distance into clouds of debris and orange and gray smoke. I peer over the ridge but I am unable to make anything out. My sight has become quite limited by the thick screens of smoke, dust, and rubble circling through the open spaces between us and the invading Iranian troops. Three French Super Étendard planes fly up from the Gulf region below us and abruptly rise into the sky at almost ninety-degree angles, leaving behind pockets of vacuous sound resonating throughout the green helmet handed to me by Nabonidas when we'd first arrived. He stares at me derisively, silently sending me the message that the only reason he is on this front is because of me; although after admitting to Qadro how I felt partially responsible for his accident, he'd harshly responded that if there weren't a requirement for government minders to accompany the international press then they would all be at the front lines instead and in immediate and constant danger as combatants. *It doesn't matter one way or the other,* Nabonidas's eyes now say, reflecting the hollowed-out acceptance of both good and bad and one's belief in his inability to do anything about it.

"They're here, they're here," a soldier to my left screams.

The earth trembles with a stampede and men pull up and pump their rifles over the gravel ridge, sending sparks flying in all directions. Others begin to jump the wall and storm out toward the east and against the attacking army. Farther down the line I notice a man's shirt has caught on fire. I watch as he jumps back and forth against each wall, trying unsuccessfully to extinguish the cloth on his back. Another soldier immediately drives his shoulders into the man's ribs and tackles the burning soldier into a wettened reservoir bordering the entrenchment.

One by one the Iraqi soldiers seem to be falling around me, and I am too frightened to leave my position in order to peer over the ridges at the advancing Persian forces. I look to my left and see a soldier screaming next to Nabonidas who has pulled a rifle from off one of the fallen troops and has started firing out into the smoke. Some of the men cry out in unison before they jump over the ridge and into the fray. But no sooner are they gone than I get up the courage to peer up over the three-foot-high wall, and I see them all heading back.

"This is strange," one cries.

"There is no one there," another yells.

The firing of artillery has abruptly stopped, and nothing is coming at us from across the field. I can't see anything past ten yards because of the smoke. A few moments pass as the dust whirls begin to settle and the black clouds slowly part and rise. An eerie calm descends over the area. The cause of the commotion, word is passed, were two Iranian fighter planes that had flown overhead and opened fire against the outer posts of the embankment. A lone Iraqi helicopter left behind on its patrol unexpectedly turned around and began to deftly chase the two planes, inflicting serious engine damage on one before being shot down by the other.

Men curse loudly and the boys moan to themselves; a few curse the ayatollah. The man whose shirt had caught fire is lying outside the trench, propped up against a car tire and sipping slowly from a water canteen he also periodically runs over the length of his back. The area east of us is now clear, but there is a change in the air; the same kind of change noticed when a stranger first enters a room but you do not yet see him.

And then I do see them. Hundreds of Iranian children, boys and girls—some of them even holding hands—walking in rows toward us. The smoke clouds part before them, and as the children move closer, I can see the ropes attached to their legs, binding them to each other to prevent their desertion.

"Halt fire, hold fire," a soldier down the line yells.

We watch in amazement as the rows of Iranian children slowly make their way across the burnt and dried land, each wave coming in succession and separated by approximately twenty-five yards. Their clothes are dirty and worn; their faces expressionless. I try to make out as many of their individual features as I can—the fullness of their cheeks, their drawn-out eyes—not fully understanding my own reasons for doing so. Then the first explosion comes. Off to the north, several children are drawn up off the ground into blackened clouds, simply dissolving into the air like fragments of shattered opal glass. The remaining children stumble forward to the ground, unable to flee due to the ropes, and the silence that has gripped them since they first shuffled up the distant hill has cracked with the explosion and they begin to cry out in fear. A quarter of the first line is quickly gone. Those farthest from the explosion still feel its immediate effect by being tied to the others, and the line becomes weighted down by the fallen. Some of the older and sturdier children try desperately to pull the ropes forward, but they lack the physical strength needed to pull along the others.

The next wave behind them passes and another explosion quickly knocks out the middle of the row. The two remaining edges continue on until separate detonations sound off and then the row is completely gone. I grab my small camera and, feeling slightly nauseated, begin to click away, resolved in the knowledge that people must see this horror in order to believe it and, thus, hopefully to prevent it from ever happening again. Wave after wave come, making their way over every square foot of land, purposely detonating the land mines laid in the ground in defense by the Iraqi military. I stand and watch in awe the most horrible thing I will ever see as hundreds of Iranian children are sacrificed in order to clear the way for advancing tanks. *A country sacrificing its own children.* I wonder how I would proceed if I were somehow able to stop this travesty, but I can only watch the adolescent flanks crashing into the stone and sand and wetlands beyond us.

The last row struggles forward and I can see that most of the children have their eyes closed, their tired faces shutting out the world around them. It is a feeling I have to fight myself–the urge to close my own eyes. The sound of their small feet shuffling hesitantly across the ground has grown almost deafening, and the ropes linking them together are now straining against their legs as some of the children are not moving fast enough and have fallen behind. The last row passes by the first group, where several children are clinging desperately to each other, and then on through the second, the dangers preceding them having already been found and erased, and eventually they make it the farthest, almost to the halfway point between the tanks that have now suddenly appeared behind them and my position within our entrenchment.

I can almost see the faint breath blowing in innocent puffs of a little girl struggling to pull her side mates forward when suddenly she is gone and another explosion takes the far wing. Before I can cover my head, a dozen Iranian tanks rumble toward us, confident in the knowledge that no more land mines remain in the ground. Their machine-gun fire cuts down any remaining children, eliminating all the disturbed faces that the land mines left behind, before taking a group of soldiers to my left who have been standing watch outside the protection of the trench in amazement at the human wave.

Glass cracks underneath my feet and I am struck by the thought that maybe photographs aren't meant to lend testament to this inhumane tactic, incapable of capturing the full scope within their motionless stills. My camera lies in the rusted damp earth, its lens shattered and the outer protective casing broken open to expose the tape of film. I did not realize it had fallen to the ground.

There is no time for pensive reflection. I peer over my right shoulder and across the ridge. The Iranian tanks are closer, barreling forward now about three hundred yards away. I quickly duck my head back under the trench wall when the trajectory of fire makes its way toward my end. With my back to the advancing tanks, I look up and down the length of the trench. The rest of the men are in similar positions, their backs pressed against the front wall and out of aim of any machine-gun fire. Some are scurrying to lift the dead soldiers off the ground with their boots, trying to free a place where they can burrow themselves deeper and away from the line of bullets.

The soldier standing next to me looks no more than twelve

years old, his skin still swollen with youth and without any hint of facial hair. It is taking all of his strength to keep himself upright while holding on tightly to an AK-47. He is frantically trying to move a body away from the floor and up the side with his feet so he can take its position underneath for himself. I recognize the light blue shirt the young boy is pressing his boots against, leaving small brown impressions on the dead man's back. Nabonidas is facedown in the dirt, his fate sealed, I am forced to believe, the moment he was assigned to accompany me to Basra.

The line of fire coming from the tanks is close, and now shards of rock and metal dart forcefully overhead as the tanks shoot up the ground directly across the line at our backs. Pellets and debris fly up into the air and land against the back wall of the depression, the tossed sediment beginning to fill up the open spaces.

Overhead the three Iraqi Super Étendard planes have rerouted and soar past us. Before the sound of a descending missile can be identified, one of the tanks stops short and smoke begins to pour out of its sides. The latch quickly opens, there is a faint scream, and then the orange and red of rising flames. Another decrescendo and then a second tank rocks back on its tracks and is halted in a mist of smoke and fire. Five land mines have also detonated under the weight of the advancing tanks, the previous waves of children falling short of their location, and the Super Étendard planes continue to drop missiles from the sky until all ten tanks have been destroyed and no advancement on either side or exchange of land has taken place.

The remaining soldiers rise slowly out of the trench, and when they are confident the attack has been halted and no further fire will be directed upon them, they break out in a victorious cheer.

I am not a participant in this mindless war. I do not have a stake in its outcome nor do I agree with the reasons either side chose to fight. I am here only as a reporter. I do not feel the victory nor the defeat, though I cannot help but be affected by the death and suffering. I realize that these boys and men aren't necessarily cheering a victory or the successful defense of their homeland but rather their own survival. They roar loudly and I understand that they are praising their own mortality and the fact that they are still alive. With that idea in mind I feel like yelling as well.

But as I step up out of the trench into the broken sulfuric air, the sight of Nabonidas's light blue shirt covered with small bootprints and partially submerged under red mud stops me.

23

IBRAHIM DOES NOT FLINCH when a second bird flies mindlessly through the window and straight into the adobe wall behind him, bouncing backward in a fit of shock before falling to the ground in a mass of disheveled feathers and with a broken wing. The heat of the early afternoon is unbearable, and Ibrahim submerses a towel in a large bowl of cold water and then drapes it across his bare shoulders to keep cool. It can drive people crazy—even birds—this heat, he thinks to himself.

Somewhere beyond the vicinity of his apartment complex, explosions have gone on for ten straight nights. It is the longest continuous succession since the war first began. Ibrahim often felt as if he were the only one to notice the change the war had on the animals. In the coops, some of the chickens were producing more eggs than usual, while some had stopped laying eggs altogether. Several of the cows had begun to leak a silky, white substance, which, due to the food shortages, was not discarded. The emission was first boiled and drained and then boiled again before it was considered safe for use. Last night the

Toonis' dog had run itself around in small circles for close to an hour before finally turning and jumping straight off the rooftop. The neighbors' children found the broken animal where it had landed on the ground, when they left for school. The same night several of the chickens had also escaped, and after the commotion of the dead canine subsided, the following morning they were found in the large basin located in the outside loo after they'd apparently drowned themselves. Since then all the wooden doors of the coops had remained locked and the animals trapped inside.

Ibrahim is not as aware of these other living things as he used to be. In fact, he used to be aware of nonliving things as well, as if they had their own breath. He would stare for hours at a vacant cutter, almost invisible through the tall grass on a knoll outside the gates of Ishtar, or at the descending arrangements of the colored gardens at Babylonia and the splintered beams circling overhead. At an early age it seemed to Ibrahim that some higher being had pressed its dry and hardened lips against these items and blown a sense of an actual living identity into them. To Ibrahim those days felt like a thousand years ago. Although he was still more aware than others, it angered him, his diminished ability to see things as he once did. He was changing. There were many things he didn't notice anymore. He felt that slippage like the gears of a shifting engine, and his disconnection with the physical world seemed to be expanding. Recently his consternation only seemed to be mitigated by the inner drive of his creativity finding a new outlet.

It is his fourth speech in as many weeks. Ibrahim deliberates over each word like a cartographer studying the intersections of a large city, the possibility of a wrong word like a wrong turn that could somehow lead the listener astray. As shy and reserved as Ibrahim knew he was, the public speeches–if they could really be called public considering the size of the groups in the basement of the Papous Bake Shop—not only got easier each time but he even began to enjoy them. He started to relish the entire process, from researching and writing the speeches to reciting them along with slight bits of improvisation in front of the growing groups of disenchanted men. By the second week Ibrahim began to draw strength from his position, and he was so exhilarated by the end of the night that he had to walk around the city for hours just to calm himself down and let the electricity dissipate. He was emboldened by the curious faces listening attentively to every word, every syllable, until the sentences came together and finally settled themselves and the overall message of the words began to make sense. The eyes of the men widened with their understanding, and then they would all began to nod their heads in acknowledgment.

Ibrahim felt more alive on those Wednesday nights than he did during the days before his appointment as a historical generator and sanctioned artist of the Ministry of Culture, when he and Shalira would hide from her father and seek the comfort of the darkness under the evening sky. They would point out the brightest stars they were able to find and name them for one another. The first time they exchanged stars, he had shocked Shalira when the following day he'd lent permanence to what they'd seen together by placing the heavens he had christened in her name on canvas.

He would never have believed it himself, but these speeches stirred him in the same way. Although this creative energy was different. It came from anger, there was no doubt about it, and although he knew rage was a strong motivator, his personal paintings had always come from an inspiration he understood to be driven by love.

Instead of the answers he sought for himself, he saw a sense of relief in the eyes of those boys and men who came out every Wednesday night to listen to him speak; relief in not only finding certain answers to their own questions but also at the mere recognition of the same issues and problems that had for them always remained unspoken. To Ibrahim, the sensation of these faces staring back at him was almost religious, although he would never admit that to anyone. Especially since he found no use for religion immediately after tossing the first shovelful of dirt onto Shalira's grave. His father, Hassan Jaffa, sadly clung to his spiritual beliefs like a desperate beggar clutching his last coin. If Ibrahim needed religion to be saved, he was sure Hassan Jaffa was doing so much praying that he would be covered by his father's overabundance.

Ibrahim would never feel such desperation. He refused to. He found hope, instead, in his anger, and for him that suddenly was enough. It drove him farther down a path Yusuf had fervently discussed with him months earlier when Ibrahim had, at the time, cringed at its mere mention. Now that same path was laid out in front of him, and with an immense clarity Ibrahim had moved forward.

My wish is not to be a leader. I do not want to tell people what they should or should not do. I cannot tell them what is in their hearts or in their spirit. I do not want to lead, he wrote on his notepad, *my only desire is for change.*

It had been three months. Ibrahim, now like his father, is a widower. But unlike his father, Ibrahim has no son or daughter to care for, and he is amazed at the anger and aggressiveness that has sprung forth inside him like a dam suddenly burst open. He vowed to himself that he was going to put an end to this blind acceptance of the way they were supposed to live and the fear that permeated every crevice and every crack of their existence like a cancer. He had never felt it himself, immune to such feelings, but he could recognize it in the eyes of many of his countrymen. He had been thrust past that stage.

And unlike Hassan Jaffa, Ibrahim would never hold his

tongue. He had never paid any attention to social or political matters before, yet his previous silence wasn't an acceptance but rather aloofness. With Shalira laid to rest, Ibrahim felt no better purpose for himself nor was he burdened with the safety and concerns of a family to consider. The copy of the autopsy report he'd received as a favor from Jazeri described Shalira carrying an almost fully formed fetus, its fingers, feet, and ears still slightly curled and transparent. The fact that his wife was carrying a child while simultaneously deciding to withhold this knowledge from him—her husband—made Ibrahim furious at himself and also at Shalira; then he became furious with the idea that he could feel anything but love and longing for his dead wife. The anger gave birth to bouts of frustration. The fact that Shalira's womb had held another man's son was the catalyst that ignited Ibrahim's feelings into action. It had scared him to the point of tears when he'd read that the shock of Shalira's body dropping had caused the unborn child to shift violently inside her stomach, disrupting its air passages and causing it to suffocate, and he had felt no remorse for the infant. In a strange, unsettling way, he found some sense of satisfaction in the child's death.

The night of the first speech he had stopped at Hassan Jaffa's house after backing down a maze of side streets and escaping through the just closed bazaar of Kadhimain Square to make sure he wasn't being followed.

On that first Wednesday night, Ibrahim found his father up and reading an old newspaper, his mouth mindlessly moving while his index finger slowly followed the sentences from paragraph to paragraph. Ibrahim felt an immediate impulse to turn around and leave his father at peace and relaxing by himself. He is better in the past, Ibrahim thought to himself, with his sentimental memories. He may still be able to maintain some happiness.

Hassan Jaffa barely slept anymore. The dark patches under his eyes were an unhealthy blue, and they had recently begun to threaten the sagging flesh of his cheeks. After work Hassan Jaffa often went to the Imam Hussein Shrine, where after removing his shoes he would kneel down despite the difficulty in his lower leg and pray until the sun slowly descended underneath a bruised sky. It was not until later in the evening that Hassan Jaffa would come stumbling home, eat a late dinner, and eventually fall into and out of a light sleep in front of the television set.

But Hassan Jaffa felt the change in the air, and after having lived with his son for twenty years, he could easily smell him enter the room. He turned and smiled at Ibrahim.

"Hello, Father," Ibrahim said.

Hassan Jaffa remembered back to the day when he'd watched his son painting in the courtyard. He recalled with dismay the unavoidable absurdity of the images in the sky—twin helicopters fleeing past the gilded dome of the Kadhimain Mosque. He had been most impressed with not only Ibrahim's obliviousness toward everything else going on around him but with his accurate depiction of the scene overhead down to the most specific of details. Hassan Jaffa remembered the military logo on the helicopters and was impressed by the strength of his son's vision. Hassan Jaffa knows they were much too far away for him to be able to make out the green lettering or the encircled emblems stamped on the doors. It was only from Ibrahim's painting that he was able to see the detailed insignia. And from that day he prayed for his son to also have the strength of his emotions. Hassan Jaffa was born again into the power of prayer because for the first time in his fifty-one years, his prayers had been answered; an internal strength of conviction and spirit was all his son now seemed to possess.

"Ibrahim," Hassan Jaffa cried out, and limped over to his son to lightly kiss him on his cheek.

"How are you holding yourself together?" he asked, and then smiled again as though this mere gesture could assure the lifting of his son's spirits.

"I am doing the best I am able to do," Ibrahim replied. He reached out to touch the dark circles underneath his father's eyes. "I wish the same could be said for you."

"Me?" Hassan Jaffa asked. "Don't be foolish. I have survived this long."

Like a mouse nevertheless, but I have survived, Hassan Jaffa thought to himself.

He still carried a moderate amount of influence due to his education and position. He also made a fair salary. In fact, with the economy failing and the war still raging on for close to five years, he was lucky not only to have a job but one that was stable and afforded him a nice lifestyle. Many of his friends were working several jobs to make ends meet; and those were the ones who were able to even find the extra work. He had always been able to provide for his wife and son. There had never been a time when they struggled financially or wanted for anything except out of excess. He had quietly succumbed to the temptations and appeasement of comfort. More recently, Ibrahim had gained his employment through the government contacts Hassan Jaffa dealt with from the museum and the relationships he had established over the years. Yes, there were sacrifices in living quietly, but there were also rewards too. Why couldn't anyone else see them?

But Hassan Jaffa knew the convictions that raced through his blood weren't as strong as those in the blood of his son. Then he remembered al-Sharistani and quickly changed his mind. Maybe not his convictions, bless us no, swallowing his convictions was like ingesting swords; maybe it was the acknowledgement that his spirit had been broken like that of a well-trained dog. Hassan Jaffa recalled all the years he had instructed Ibrahim not to be naïve. Now he understood that he was just trying to protect his son and, in the process, it was he who had been naïve. All those years Hassan Jaffa wanted to protect Ibrahim but also to prepare him for the day when he, Ibrahim, would also have to decide, as Hassan Jaffa had decided a long time ago, if he was able to live under the conditions set forth by those in positions of authority or whether he would try to do something about them instead.

That day had come for Hassan Jaffa almost thirty-five years ago when as a young man of seventeen he had curiously watched as the shops were being closed down early on Arasat al-Hindiyyah Street, the parched shades drawn down tight to the bottom of the windows one final time. Later, as dusk fell, he watched the cars packed high with suitcases strapped across their roofs slowly kick up faint dust clouds before they drove dejectedly away from the capital. He witnessed the departures until late in the evening when the last remaining caravan pulled silently away, taking with it the last of the Jewish blood forced to leave the country by official decree and to surrender their Iraqi nationality and citizenship. It was one of those vacant shops Hassan Jaffa had watched empty out that would soon become Yusuf's for a reduced price.

Some twenty years later Hassan Jaffa would again watch in silence when more than fifteen thousand Iranians living on Iraqi soil for generations were also expelled and sent into exile.

It made him nauseous to think about how he chose to bury these acts deep within himself; how, at the time, he'd felt the urge to rise up and strike the fist, as Yusuf called it, only to quickly swallow the feeling back down. But it wasn't that simple. He had been in love. And so with a soft heart he had become a husband first and soon thereafter a father. And it was as a father that he was as proud as he had ever been in his life when he heard his son tell the vice president he did not want to be a soldier. No, his son, with an eye for detail like his mother and the love of history shared by his father, had wanted to be different. "A painter," the child confessed, and Hassan Jaffa felt the pride in his chest rise up until he was forced to expel it in tiny, gasping breaths.

It was a month after the Iranian exile when he found Ibrahim transfixed by the back kitchen window. The sun was at its peak and Ibrahim stood trying to hide himself in the darkened shadow falling across the pane from the east.

"My son," Hassan Jaffa called out, "what is it you see?"

But Ibrahim did not hear him; the same concentrated intensity that would later impress Hassan Jaffa first caused him to worry. Unable to move the child with his words, he made his way over to see what had Ibrahim's attention, and what he saw stopped him dead in his own tracks, robbing him of any strength or fighting spirit he might have still held up until that point.

His friend the schoolmaster was kneeling on the field behind the houses, the thick tufts of his gray beard were aflame and Hassan Jaffa could barely make out the man's defiant expression before smoke completely engulfed al-Sharistani's face.

Hassan Jaffa forcefully retraced his steps backward and out of the room, the only control he could muster, leaving his son of eleven years to wonder what meaning lay behind such a horrific act.

It took Hassan Jaffa a long time to accept the fact that he was a weak man, resigning himself to the duty of caring only for his family. Love is a weakness. And so was the responsibility he associated with love. Anything more was putting your head in the lion's mouth, he reasoned to himself.

"We have lost everyone, Father," Ibrahim suddenly said.

Hassan Jaffa remembered back to the promise the two had made.

"We have not lost each other," he tried. "Our promise can not be broken."

But his words did not have the intended effect.

"Maybe Yusuf had it right," Hassan Jaffa now tried after setting down two tulip-shaped glasses of tea in front of them. "Maybe I should have listened to him all along."

"Are we all not right?" Ibrahim replied rather harshly. "Don't we all—each and every one of us—want change?"

Hassan Jaffa had never heard Ibrahim speak with such authority, let alone show any concern or emotions about such matters. His son's fire intrigued him and it also showed that Shalira's death had not robbed him of everything.

"Every man goes home each night if he is lucky enough to have found work and a home, and before he and his wife lie down to sleep, their hearts lighten with the hope that maybe, just maybe, things will be better, freer, tomorrow. That somehow that black shadow of fear will be gone. You have felt it too, Father. But who, I ask you, who do they think will remove it?"

Hassan Jaffa watched his son contentedly. It took all of his strength to lift himself up and out of the chair, his tired limbs cracking with the subtlest of movements. He hadn't had a good night's sleep in the three months since Shalira's suicide. At first, his daily excursions to the mosques were more for her soul, praying that the Almighty might forgive her her transgressions and set forth for her an eternal and peaceful rest. Eventually, Hassan Jaffa returned to also pray for the soul of his son and his departed wife and for the strength to bear all that had happened to them and all that was still to come. But more importantly, for the first time in his life he also prayed for a voice.

"Besides," Ibrahim continued, "Yusuf was a fool on many

matters. Who is going to believe a forlorn and disheveled old man? Not the young of today, not when you have movie stars riding around in fancy cars and businessmen lounging in private clubs and dressed in tailored suits. It has always been the young that provide the foundation for any movements of change. Why would you follow someone whom you don't aspire to be yourself? We want to see ourselves in our leaders. With Yusuf, he missed the boat. Who wants to see themselves as a scraggly, bitter, and hollow man who appears empty of all other emotion except self-importance and asceticism? He appears no better than the ayatollah."

Then to ease the tension of the exchange, Ibrahim added, "An unkempt disposition is not an aspiration. Yusuf's followers could smell that on him, among other things, from a mile away."

Ibrahim smiled at Hassan Jaffa. "Father, one must be *alive* to lead."

Hassan Jaffa thought of Yusuf in the casket prison, the horrific rumors and stories intensifying the visions he held in his imagination. He wished, for a moment, that he could have done more for the old fool, but quickly remembered the threat of danger that always followed him around.

"I have only wanted peace and love for you and our family," Hassan Jaffa confessed, the expulsion of words vibrant like the emission of energy. "I thought anything more was asking for too much. Be that as it may, I also wrongly assumed that through love and peace all else would fall into place."

"I understand, Hassan Jaffa," Ibrahim replied, calling his father by his proper name. "You have always been a man that is to be respected. That is nothing to be ashamed of. It is more than most men can ever ask for."

"I used to think that was enough."

Hassan Jaffa again lifted his teacup to his mouth just as he had done only seconds earlier when he'd first emptied its contents.

He slowly rose up and made his way over to the stove and switched the burner back on. He felt his head thicken and his eyelids suddenly grow heavy. The slackness returned to his arms and legs, and when he came back with a fresh kettle of tea, he placed it on a porcelain warmer and stretched himself out across the low table in front of him. Tonight he would finally be able to sleep; his body was telling him as much. It was a welcome feeling.

"Maybe it is time for change," Hassan Jaffa said with a surprising calmness.

<hr />

My only desire is for change. Ibrahim continues to write the words out in his head before putting them down on paper, the same way he would construct the images in his mind before touching the canvas or cement walls with the tip of a colored brush, preventing the mistakes of hesitation through careful thought and deliberation. He hasn't attempted any personal or creative painting recently, not since completing the picture of his mother, Fazeera, which, as far as he knows, is still sitting unwrapped against Hassan Jaffa's desk at the museum.

His work has now become labor. Ibrahim methodically shows up at the predesignated locations for his assignments, but without the excitement he used to feel prior to starting something new. He simply performs that for which he earns a paycheck. Less than six months before, he fought the urge to paint a crimson bullet hole in the forehead of the president's mural on the escalator platform across from the Baath Monument. He entertained the idea of superimposing Tapiz's face on one of Saddam's images. He does not care about the dangers involved and is not concerned with who may be aware that he has become some sort of spokesman for this underground group, the ICP. The Iraqi Centrist Party. It made him laugh, the confusion the

name caused with another opposition group–the Iraqi Communist Party. He is only concerned about progress, in lighting the
first fuse to begin the chain of events. He does not want anything
to get in his way, so he remains cautious and careful, not for the
purpose of self-preservation but rather for the preservation of
principle. He can only trust himself. What good would he be in
jail or killed before he had the chance to put the process in motion? He just wants a platform, not selfishly, but–as he is writing
the words–all Ibrahim really wants is change. He cares not for
recognition or disruption–even revolution. Change, he believes,
can begin with the simplest of actions.

I am not a leader, he writes again, and is thinking of a vast
open field where he and Shalira can run through the grass,
staining their clothes in blushes of emerald while teasing each
other playfully, content to be in each other's company. The two
of them would watch as their children prance through the yard,
the youthfulness of their expressions innocent and full of all the
life still ahead of them. Then Ibrahim can't help thinking about
one of the children who sits off to the side by himself, his back
deliberately turned toward the others. The child is quiet and
does not join when the younger children come and needle him
to play, his blond hair and fairer complexion a contrast to the
almond skin and dark hair of the merry ones who continue to
laugh and tumble through the grass around him.

Ibrahim has stopped writing for a moment. A line of sweat
across his brow sends a drop to the desk below it, smearing the
ink and the first paragraph of his message. He rubs the spot
with his finger, still thinking of this strange unhappy child, and
does not notice when a third bird flies mindlessly through the
window and hits the wall behind him.

24

AUGUST 3, 1984

WITH THE HELP OF Savos Adonan and Kamel al-Saadi, the old retired general from the Iraqi army, Ibrahim cuts through the barbed-wire fence surrounding the perimeter of the presidential airstrip. The three men cross the empty barracks and under the pale blue light of the moon crawl slowly across the two miles of bare land leading up to the gates outside the tarmac. Two sentries are posted at the main entrance, where all arriving airplanes first touch the ground upon landing. Current security is lax due to the manpower needed on the southern and northeastern fronts. Also, with the president out of the country, the airstrip is not needed for immediate use and stands, except for the presence of the two sentries, vacant.

Savos snips through the bottom of the mesh gate and the men roll underneath one at a time, waiting for the shadow of the man in front of them to disappear from off the landing before following behind. The beacons of light from the two sentry towers are turned off as a precaution against attacking Iranian warplanes, and the night is still and silent. Ibrahim can hear his heart drumming loudly within his ears and wonders for a moment if the other men can hear it also. He is amazed at what they were able to accomplish within such a short span of time.

⌄

Jazeri, the deputy minister of information, had let it slip out one morning while going over Ibrahim's new civil assignment, the painting of the ceiling in one of the presidential palaces to be a replica of Michelangelo's work in the Sistine Chapel. The only difference was that Saddam Hussein's image, Jazeri explained, would replace that of St. Peter.

"The president is going to inspect this project as soon as he comes back from Paris next week," Jazeri informed Ibrahim, not realizing the importance of this pocket of information that gave the group close to five days to complete the sabotage.

As Jazeri's words first registered in Ibrahim's head, he concentrated hard on maintaining his expression, careful not to give any signs away. Since Shalira's death, Jazeri had been more open and conciliatory toward Ibrahim, as though his inclusion in certain secrets of the state would help maintain, if not completely sway, his allegiances.

Five days the president will be out of the country, Ibrahim played over in his mind, that bastard will be out of the country for five days.

The men, he knew, would be excited to finally put their plan into action.

⌄

He meets Savos behind a landing light post, and the two men start to unroll the wiring for the explosives along the edges of the runway, running parallel with Kamel al-Saadi as the old general does the same fifty yards across the road from them. It takes twenty minutes before both sides of the strip are lined and fully packed and all the wiring connecting the shots has been covered with dirt and sand. The explosives are spaced evenly apart at ten-foot intervals according to Savos's strict calculations meant to destroy the entire strip and also take down the sentry towers as well. According to the group's estimations, by the time the police arrived at the destroyed site, all that should remain will be a still rising dust cloud between two small mounds of brick and clay. Any presidential arrivals would have to be accommodated farther away from the capital, an annoyance sure to draw the ire of the regime.

Ibrahim hesitates before digging the hole for the first mine. At first the theory seemed on the verge of overkill, but upon reflection he realized he could never be too careful. The idea was a simple one—just when the authorities thought the explosions were complete, a second wave of land mines would be detonated, inflicting further damage and, more importantly, increasing the fear associated with such attacks. He resumes his shoveling, pushing the handle of the spit deep into the ground with both his hands. So this is what it must come to, he thinks to himself, and bites down on his lower lip until he draws the faintest taste of blood. Then he continues to dig hole after hole, fifteen in all, without once stopping.

Covered in sweat and out of breath, he meets the two older men after they have completed the opposite side of the tarmac. All three sit to rest for a moment at the far end of the strip, their backs against the emergency landing post, the top of the sentry towers out of view, and each smoke a cigarette in silence, feeling overly confident in not only their ability but in the silent energy of the moment.

"This is sure to rattle some heads," Savos whispers. Ibrahim almost hushes his friend but decides to let the comment pass back into the silence of the night.

He had spent the previous two weeks thinking over and evaluating an acceptable location—a spot that would symbolize the goals the ICP was trying to achieve, a definitive end Ibrahim wasn't quite yet so sure of himself, without also affecting or disrupting the everyday life of the working people. The idea had hit him one evening while driving away from one of the palaces located in the Karkh district. He noted the length of the private presidential airstrip as it spread out beyond the outskirts of Baghdad. His intimate knowledge of the area had also provided him with an opportunity for detailed planning and a bit of advance scouting. He had painted the sky-blue pillars heading into the base of the runway months earlier and also the emblazoned gold depictions of the Lion of Babylon across each support. It had never occurred to him that he would be destroying some of his own work in the process as well.

When he'd proposed the site to Savos and several other members of the ICP, they were astonished by his brazenness, and an immediate consensus rose from the group. Shortly thereafter, while going over their demolition techniques, they had all agreed without question to plant a parallel series of explosives within the ground along the length of the runway and ancillary explosives wrapped like serpentine wires around each pillar. That is everyone, except for Korobash, the arms dealer, who, Ibrahim realized, was getting too rich on smaller, safer incursions that posed no threat to his identity or any of his affiliations.

"You will all be dead within a week," Korobash blankly stated. After the planning was completed and Korobash realized Ibrahim was going to follow through on the attack, the arms dealer had conveniently disappeared.

The silence continues for the next few minutes while the three men privately enjoy the taste of their cigarettes. Then they toss their finished butts to the ground and make their way back to the cutout partition in the fence. They crawl back across the two-mile stretch of open land in the opposite direction of the runway. All three quickly embrace and then part ways when they reach the outskirts of the capital. Ibrahim walks down to the river and sits at its edges for a while, listening to the flow of the water, until he hears heavy footsteps coming from up the path. He stands up and starts to make his way through the dark side streets and alleyways between the buildings and shops until he is safely back in his apartment without, he hopes, being seen or followed.

Two nights later, he takes a long, cool shower to help calm his nerves before lying down on his bed. The blinds are all lifted and the windows in the apartment are opened. The pleasant humming sound of the crickets from the small orange patch below fills the rare solitude of the evening. Ibrahim listens and stretches out his legs and locks his hands comfortably behind his head. He stares at the ceiling and notices the small cracks in the paint branching out from the corners of the room. He hears the first explosion at one ten in the morning. It takes barely sixty seconds until the entire apartment is awake and moving about, nervously wondering what is going on outside. Ibrahim ignores the first set of knocks on his door and then thinks it better not to arouse any suspicion by his absence, and after a few minutes he answers to the smell of lamb's blood from off the pajamas of his neighbor Jaffar Kamza, the butcher.

"The Iranians have just bombed the university," Jaffar Kamza yells frantically at him before proceeding down the hall to the next apartment.

Ibrahim closes the door behind him without responding and goes back to his bed, where he lies down and sleeps peacefully through the night for the first time since becoming the head of the ICP, the same position held by Yusuf, his father-in-law, only months earlier.

25

IT IS A MONTH later and Korobash has resurfaced.

Ibrahim can't help but notice the hefty bulge hanging over the expensive-looking leather belt on his waist. The arms dealer looks pleasantly stuffed to capacity, and the small charges of flatulence he periodically emits make it hard for Ibrahim to take him seriously. It is not that Ibrahim finds the man comical–the portly Syrian *is* in the business of selling mass weaponry on the black market–but rather he finds it hard to take the man, at least when in his physical presence, seriously. Yet one look at the stale yellow invoice quickly adjusts Ibrahim's outlook:

> 10 missile launchers
> 15 AK-47s
> 5 cases of ammunition
> 4 boxes of hard-nosed grenades
> Approx. 50 Russian rifles

"All with enough bullets to shoot continuously for three months," or so Korobash had put it. "This war of yours is definitely not a children's game. No matter who they may have fighting it."

The crudeness of the Syrian arms dealer had disheartened Ibrahim ever since the first time he'd dealt with him, and the formal tradition in which Ibrahim was raised offered him no prior experience in dealing with the man's fondness for the indecent.

Hayat, the attractive wife of the street sweeper Omadan, also showed up prior to the meeting to tell the group that her husband would not be in attendance for at least the next three weeks. His municipal bosses had included the Shaykh Hamid area along his current route, adding an additional two hours to an already overfilled workday. Omadan refused to balk at the increased responsibilities and in return was rewarded with a small increase in pay. His allegiances were important and he didn't want the group to grow nervous over his extended absences. Such consideration was important, and the danger Omadan put his wife in by exposing her and sending her with his message was evident by the chaste strain across the poor woman's face.

"Why don't you come join us instead?" Korobash had asked her, beads of sweat beginning to glisten off the gold jewelry he wore around his neck and wrists.

When Hayat made the mistake of looking at Korobash, he rudely pointed to his lap to confirm the spot he had intended for her.

Ibrahim fought the urge to immediately slap the hefty Syrian. But he was currently their only link to the weapons market, and Ibrahim understood that in order to achieve anything of substance, armed force was a necessary requirement. It was also the Syrian's first meeting back with the ICP. Ibrahim had grown more suspicious of his intentions since his sudden departure, and he wanted to passively observe him and his interaction with the group's members.

"Korobash," Ibrahim started, and only when the arms dealer continued to ignore him did he rush over to his chair and grab him by his beefy shoulders from behind.

"Korobash," he yelled. The arms dealer outweighed Ibrahim by close to a hundred pounds, and perhaps in another part of the world Ibrahim may have feared the man. "We do not like exposing our women to such foul air. Please refrain next time and indulge us with your Western manners."

The reference to his Western education caused Korobash to proudly straighten up, and he soon became preoccupied with his own comfort, jostling violently in his seat until he was satisfied.

Before he started the meeting, Ibrahim turned and scanned the rest of the room. He immediately felt his confidence begin to rise again when he saw the able bodies of the young men seated before him. The earnestness etched across their faces implied that mere words would be all that was necessary to get these men to act. It would be up to Ibrahim to find those correct words. In fact, now a month after the destruction of the airstrip, a more formal action was the next logical step.

The government suspected Iranian sympathizers from the north were behind the recent attacks, and the umbrella of suspicion fell, at least publicly, short of the capital and the ICP.

"My brothers," Ibrahim began, "we welcome you here this evening to renew our purpose and the strength of our convictions; which, up until now, have served us well. Our leadership"–with the mention of the word he looked over at Savos–"is preparing for our next action statement. And rest assured, we hold all of your concerns as our own. We have been successful in the destruction of the presidential airstrip, and you can take some satisfaction that our next project will be a bold one."

The fifty men in the room quickly stood up and broke out in applause. Ibrahim was proud of his friend and their actions together. The retired general Kamel al-Saadi had also been worthy of the current adulation. But the old man had suffered a heart attack as soon as the first explosion went off. It was the second wave of detonations, which had also taken three military police cars, that stopped his heart completely.

Less embarrassed than fulfilled with the success of their recent project, he called Savos out onto the platform to join him. Ibrahim found comfort in the education minister's presence. The mild-mannered appearance and demeanor of the professor always put his students and those around him at ease. It was a trait that had lent to his success. The fact that he was also secretly skilled in the wiring and detonation of explosives was hard to imagine. He and Ibrahim often spoke freely to each other when they were alone, each confiding a small portion of his fears and hopes to the other, only to happily find out that they shared many of the same.

"With each successful mission, our continued silence becomes more and more important. Let our actions be our words. Do not let our minor accomplishment force your tongues to boast, for if you do, then this will also be our last accomplishment." Ibrahim spoke with authority once the men had returned to their seats. "Because soon, they will all come to know who we are."

Mohammed Baznil, owner of the Kabajesh Grill, moved up to the podium next and proceeded to read a formal declaration concerning the financial holdings of the group. At the mere mention of money, Korobash, Ibrahim noted, straightened up in his chair. The restaurateur acquainted himself with the wealthy clientele his establishment served, and these men commonly paid more than double the price of their check as a donation to the ICP, not the Iraqi Communist Party, but the Iraqi *Centrist* Party, as Ibrahim continually stressed, a group synonymous with new beginnings. Their influence extended to local farmers as well as wealthy businessmen and even government officials, like the tentacles of an octopus, and each successive week meant more men were filling these meetings. The group's reach was extending so far Ibrahim had confided to Savos that he was unable to see its distant edges anymore.

Savos had objected to mentioning any financial information, but Ibrahim wanted the men to know the financial, as well as the physical, cost of promoting and performing such activities. Change was by no means cheap. When Mohammed Baznil finished reading the anonymous listing of donations, the names of the donors Ibrahim kept to himself, he sat down and the debate quickly began concerning the next target to strike.

Korobash and Savos Adonan, the assistant deputy minister of education, each wanted a bank, though for different reasons. The assistant deputy wanted to achieve the maximum results and greatest possible impact with the limited number of resources the group currently possessed. Korobash, on the other hand, always had money floating through his mind. Ibrahim thought back to his meeting with Jazeri at the Ministry of Information when both men stared out from the second-level office toward the ruins of the Bank of Sadou, its lobby and rotunda sadly leveled out like a gutted whale carcass, against the backdrop of a quiet Saturday morning.

"A bank is like a kick in the nuts," Korobash belched.

"He's a fool," Ibrahim told Savos out of earshot of the Syrian. "How does he expect then to get paid?"

"I agree," said Omadan, the street sweeper, "hit them where it hurts."

Of course, Ibrahim thought to himself, the ones who are either too stupid or those without any money want a bank. He was able to hold a clear conscience as long as no civilians were hurt by their actions, not realizing at the time, or perhaps more shortsighted to the power of his actions, that people were being punished, somewhere, for what the Iraqi Centrist Party was doing. Ibrahim confronted his demons every night under the solitude of his own roof and under the millions of stars shining like diamonds across the sky as he watched and prayed through his open windows. It felt selfish that his morals were preventing him from acting further, and so with a stolid fortitude he erased his conscience from the arena of his ideology and replaced it with a tunneled sense of purpose. It wasn't too hard to do considering men and children were dying every day by the hundreds and thousands for an imposed and sanctioned national pride. The purpose, Ibrahim kept telling himself, was the freedom from fear, and although the acts the group committed were also causing fear themselves, it was a means to an end, just as wars are fought to bring peace. Ibrahim left the ironies of the world outside the door of his own conscience, for although he wanted the life his father, Hassan Jaffa, had silently subscribed to in his own mind, Ibrahim was also filled with the hot-burning fires of revenge and an intense growing desire to satisfy those urges.

"No financial institutions," Ibrahim abruptly cut off the men in debate. "Our people are going hungry as it is. The economy is already crippled and it would send the wrong message. In addition, our means will only begin to dry up even further."

"The Say ad Manood Hospital will be next," he proclaimed to a chorus of rising sentiment. "It houses no children, only wounded and dying soldiers, and the leaders of the regime. We will be doing them all a favor. No one will be heading back to the fronts."

"They will begin to fear us soon enough," Ibrahim commanded, not recognizing the mass he quickly swallowed back down as dread, but instead feeling only the rising satisfaction of hurting those who had destroyed his spirit.

While the men in front of him shifted nervously in their seats and a few verbally disagreed, Ibrahim knew that they had their sights set upon the totality of such a project and not the concept of setting a precedent.

"We do not have to destroy the entire hospital—in fact, to do so would be murderous. Just a controlled portion to show them that we can be just as ruthless. To show them we could have taken the entire building"—then he paused several seconds for effect—"if we wanted to."

After the meeting ended, Korobash lingered in the front of the room and waited to confront Ibrahim when everyone but Savos had left. The length of time the group occupied the basement did much to lessen the sweet aroma of fresh breads and pastries that frequently lingered in from the upstairs bakery. As was most often the case, the overcologned smell that surrounded Korobash like bees hovering outside a honeycombed hive soon hit Ibrahim's nose.

"I see you have come back to us, Korobash," Ibrahim noted while gathering up the handfuls of leftover pamphlets that Omadan, the street sweeper, and Muthanna, a student of agriculture, were handing out at the university and its surrounding shops. "It is very thoughtful of you to come out of hiding."

"Your ambitions are getting bigger my friend. What are you trying to do?" the Syrian questioned.

During the course of the meeting, Korobash had acted uncharacteristically well mannered, if not entirely behaved. Except for the heavy sighs that accompanied his head perking alertly to one side at the mere mention of money, his presence would almost have gone unnoticed.

"Korobash," Ibrahim instructed, "we will not need you or your suppliers for this operation. You do not need to worry anymore.

I know you think your risks heavily outweigh the ones we undertake, but remember—you do not wish to go home because you do not possess one. While on our own land, we would be left behind to be skinned more terribly than the lowliest of sheep. We are becoming bigger, you can see that for yourself, and our needs will soon outgrow what even a fat camel's ass such as yourself could provide."

Then Ibrahim laughed tenderly, and Korobash smiled confusedly at the young man.

"You may be growing too big for your own britches as well. You are becoming a very dangerous man," Korobash told Ibrahim.

"A dangerous man in a dangerous country," Ibrahim responded pointedly. "How appropriate."

"A danger to himself most of all. I must insist that you refrain from addressing me in such a condescending tone. I am a powerful man myself, lest you forget, and in more countries than you may care to admit." Ibrahim didn't think it was possible, but the threatening tone of the Syrian added to his distaste of the man.

"At first, I thought you too much the pensive type for such activities. And now I fear that I may have misjudged you. Your ideals are like steel and I have seen what happens to men who are unable to bend. Why don't you blow up an elementary school or a mosque if your real desire is to end up in eternal damnation?"

Ibrahim stopped what he was doing at the table and turned to face Korobash. Their eyes met at the same level.

"Korobash, just keep track of your own growing pockets and expanding waistline. The hospital houses several men very close to the regime. If we take them, the chain will weaken. We are not yet strong enough to overstep our means, as if I need to take the time to explain myself or my reasoning to you."

Upstairs, the scuffling of the baker across the floor caused the men to glance up toward the ceiling. Savos stood off to the side silently, listening with an appearance of ease at the two men jockeying back and forth for position.

"Besides, as I said, it is no longer your concern. Thank you for all of your efforts—your services are not needed anymore."

"Who then?" Korobash yelled out with earnestness that made Ibrahim want to strike him. "Do not be so foolish. Who could possibly provide such services as I do now?"

Ibrahim felt a buoyancy in his steps replacing the burden he'd carried across his chest since the destruction of the presidential airstrip. It felt good not only to see growth but to be an integral part of it. He stared out across the room and at the rows of empty chairs. Pretty soon they would outgrow this room as well. He turned and walked up next to Korobash and leaned over to whisper in his ear.

"You have heard of the Iranians?" Ibrahim replied flatly.

26

OCTOBER 1, 1984

AND SO KOROBASH WAS dismissed quite easily by Ibrahim. Yet Ibrahim knew he shouldn't be too concerned. There were other more pressing matters that required his immediate attention. An increasing number of men had recently begun showing up unannounced at the ICP meetinghouses. Night after night the group was running out of chairs and tables despite the careful detail Ibrahim used in setting the attendance lists. Every participant had always been accounted for, each man known and evaluated prior to his admission. But now, far too many strange faces were crossing over too many different social-class boundaries. Neither Ibrahim nor Savos nor Mohammed Baznil knew how these men found out about the meetings.

The extravagant portrait Ibrahim had been commissioned to paint was still going forward as planned, and with the rise in insurgency he was forced to proceed with more diligence despite the attacks. The fat bastard wouldn't do or say anything that would implicate himself, but Ibrahim nevertheless regretted the white lie he had so easily told Korobash.

Yet it wasn't necessarily a lie but rather a subtle extension of the truth; that Ibrahim had secured a contact with another source of arms was true. That this source, Reza Hojjati, was an Iranian was also true. But he was not affiliated with the inner circle of the Persian government suspected by the Baathists of funneling weapons and money to the northern Kurds and Shias in Iraq. Rather, Reza Hojjati enjoyed the modest reputation of a powerful international businessman who rejected the religious authority and ideals of asceticism that the ayatollah carried around with him like a worn set of prayer beads. The same set of principles the old fanatic had brought with him out of exile from Iraq and France upon his return to Tehran. Reza Hojjati was a capitalist in a country taken over by theocrats, and as a wealthy man of means, he understood that religion was bad for business.

Reza Hojjati did not concern himself with the purpose or intended uses of the materials he was contracted to supply. He did not care to know names, places, or dates—even the affiliations of such groups—he operated truly underground, like an invisible spirit that passed out loaded guns from its transparent hands. He spoke in codes, the names of weapons changed to ancient Greek gods: Athena for the commonly used Russian rifles, Achilles, the weak-footed standing missile launcher, and on certain orders he even referenced biblical characters. He did not attend any of the ICP meetings, a welcome contrast to Korobash's malodorous presence, and when a face-to-face meeting was required, he did so under the cover of darkened rooms or within the shadow of unlit corners. Whereas Korobash had become some sort of parasite, sucking the group dry with his buffoonery, Reza Hojjati remained unattached.

Ibrahim, unhindered by the vulnerability of love, made the dangerous acquaintance without thinking twice about its consequences. One night after Korobash had insulted the Indian agricultural student, Muthanna, to the point of fisticuffs, Ibrahim saw the look of disgust in the eyes of several of the men, a look so strong that Ibrahim could recognize the overwhelming sense of disruption behind it. Savos then mentioned to him that he might have procured another route through which the ICP could continue to purchase weapons and explosives. Although it was too late to abandon their plans for the airstrip, Ibrahim still wanted nothing more to do with Korobash and his pestilential presence. And after the Syrian conveniently disappeared, well, he couldn't be counted on much longer. Ibrahim praised Savos's diligence and loyalty; the teacher always kept his ears open and continually looked for ways to improve the group. Such attention was what led to his eventual meeting with a history professor from the university who, in return for his own anonymity and a clandestine payment of five hundred American dollars, instructed Ibrahim to go to the school's library the following evening after the lights had gone out and the building had closed. Ibrahim did not concern himself with the complications of such relationships and the thin threads that connected contacts—the entire state was ruled by threads no thicker than a spider's web. It had passed his ears many times that with the war continuing on, there was a constant mass movement of weapons and supplies, with as many as twenty different countries involved.

Reza Hojjati was not the man's real name. Ibrahim found out as much after walking through the closed and unlit university library to meet the stranger, a bit disarmed by the building's vacant silence. He found the man only by following the small circles of smoke rising up from between several rows of books and suspended in the pale blue light shining through the windows from the outdoor lampposts.

"I will assume the name of Reza Hojjati," the man said coolly through a slight opening between the books.

At the moment, Ibrahim did not understand the current significance of the man's alias. Only later, when he saw the name of the displaced Shah of Iran pass across the bottom of the television screen in his father's living room, was he struck by the idea that others might hold feelings as intense as his own.

A week later and under the same conditions as the first meeting, Ibrahim pressed a paper listing five of the twelve apostles in alphabetical order and the name of the prophet Moses inscribed in India ink between chapters 4 and 5 of *The Prince* by Machiavelli, to symbolize the transition in years each country had endured during the war.

The difference does not arise from the greater or lesser ability of the conqueror, but from dissimilarities in the conquered lands.

Ibrahim paused and read the sentence twice, lingering in the library so as not to arouse any suspicion with such a quick arrival and abrupt departure. Although the author had intended to imply the conquest of many areas, Ibrahim interpreted the words relative to the fabric of his own country and the different groups that made up its populace.

In any other part of the world this would be at least three different countries, he noted. They have combined us, groups as different as the sun and the moon, into one unidentifiable mass of gray, and it is to our credit we have survived together for as long as we have been able to bear. The dissimilarities of his country, Iraq, were so pronounced that it suddenly struck Ibrahim the absurdity with which it was composed.

Three days later another note replaced the cryptic order slip he had previously left behind.

Moses and his apostolic friends have settled in safely behind the police station on Al-Haryat Street. They cautiously await your prompt arrival. –RH

A police station? Is this man crazy as well? Ibrahim thought, exasperated.

At first, Ibrahim did not understand the logic behind the location; but by unloading next to the police station, Reza ensured that anyone who had happened across these messages or had been watching their movements would be scared off from any further interception by the proximity of the authorities. Although the closeness was a risk in itself, the letters themselves might lead to Reza Hojjati and his mysterious presence in the university library, whereas the pickup of the actual supply would only result in Ibrahim's capture and his link to the ICP. With the police station nearby, the delivery would either fall into Ibrahim's hands or those of the authorities. Ibrahim smiled. Bless, Savos, this man appears to have the strainings of a conscience.

The pickup went easier than Ibrahim had expected and, from what he could tell, without notice. In fact, everything seemed to be going smoother than he ever thought possible after his dealings with Korobash. All their recent meetings went by without detection, unlike the first meeting he'd attended when the caustic stare of Yusuf had made him somehow feel less than a whole man. Their cache orders were received quickly and without any questions. It was as if they were operating without the possibility of detection, and as a result they began to loosen their thoroughness and their tongues.

After the destruction of the presidential airstrip, Omadan, the street sweeper, had boasted to one of his customers, a wealthy banker with financial ties to the leaders of the regime. At the time, the man simply pressed his finger to his lips without uttering a word, a simple gesture of silence enough to scare Omadan into later confessing the encounter to Ibrahim and Savos. The two friends agreed it was best to follow the banker's advice and remain silent about the encounter, though they watched the man's house for the next two weeks without witnessing any irregular activity. Several days later, a small group of students knocked on the door of Savos's university office. The assistant deputy minister of education did not recognize the four young men from any of his classes, and he feigned surprise when they told him they had heard about the secret meetings of an underground group opposing the current authority. The four men asked him if they could attend one such meeting.

"I do not know of such dangerous things," Savos promptly answered. "And I suggest, for your safety, that you all refrain from knowing."

The following session, the same four young men sat among the registered students in the lecture hall for one of Savos's history classes. Savos entered minutes before the class started, and upon seeing them huddled together, their faces as yet unmarked by corruption, he simply nodded in their direction where they sat in the back of the hall. He was not surprised when they followed him to his car after class.

"It is unwise to ignore the advice of a teacher."

"It is unwise to ignore the tyranny of our leaders," they responded.

Until recently the ICP had searched out its members rather than having people come directly to the group. It proved a far safer measure to open the door to those they had already carefully reviewed rather than those people who initiated contact for their own reasons and without any prior acquaintance. By recruiting its members, the ICP could choose only the strongest and most influential people, people who would spread their message and recruit others of similar means, like an ongoing pyramid scheme. Most of the members also had their own secrets to hide, which helped foster a mutual understanding and allegiance. The group picked individuals only after careful study and informal interviews. Once they were satisfied, they offered information in bits and pieces to see if the person not only became interested as much as empowered.

And the group had grown. They soon outgrew the Papous Bake Shop and moved their headquarters into an abandoned warehouse near the Central Railroad Station. As a result of the increased responsibility that came with its growth, an anxiousness began to stir in Ibrahim, almost replacing the ardor of purpose that had gripped him since Shalira's death. He found himself unable to concentrate. Even Savos had commented to Ibrahim that he no longer looked you in the eye when talking to you. Ibrahim dismissed the comment as he did the wealthy banker's silent secret, his thoughts quickly racing elsewhere.

And it was his thoughts that soon turned toward Tapiz when one afternoon he came home from work and found a note left mysteriously behind on his dresser top.

I recommend a book for you. It waits at the first meeting place. –RH

The following morning Ibrahim strolled around the border of the library, reading the various postings on the telephone poles and boards, until the building opened and he was one of the first to enter. He found the book by itself wrapped in coarse brown paper upon the seat of the same chair Reza Hojjati had used that first night.

Your deceased assistant was correct. They ARE watching you. –A friend

Ibrahim noted that Reza Hojjati did not initial the message as he routinely did with his other correspondences. The Iranian was beginning to distance himself even further. If in fact this note was actually from Reza Hojjati. Ibrahim looked cautiously around the large room, the buttressed hallway, and along the outstretched mahogany balconies. Although he couldn't see anything, he felt the glare of a hundred eyes staring back at him.

Encounters that had happened in the past, things Ibrahim was unable to focus on at the time because of his restlessness, now found their way back into his mind, sometimes months after they had occurred. Ibrahim would often lie awake at night, unable to sleep, and without knowing where the link came from or what set the thoughts off, the arbitrary statements and conversations he had had with others came back to him. He was speeding through the hours of his days like an obstinate bull with its head kept down, and the dialogue and the ideas and concerns of others were finally trying to catch up. But it wasn't that close, it was more like a movie tape whose audio had been started ten minutes after the first scene began, the action moving forward while the words struggled behind it. It seemed like not so long ago when he had napped without care under the shade of a palm tree during his afternoon lunch, daydreaming about what his life would have held had he gone to Europe.

He would then remember Tapiz, his portly assistant, with his cherubic smile and facetious demeanor, who shocked him with his knowledge of Yusuf as Ibrahim felt his head lighten and a peaceful sleep creep into his muscles.

"They are watching you," Tapiz had said, and Ibrahim had forgotten about the statement not so much for its abstraction but rather because of the events that came running forward and pushed it out of his mind.

The picture of Tapiz, his eyelids cut away like those of a paper mask, still haunted Ibrahim. He had burned it immediately afterward, yet the image stuck with him. At nights he would wake up in his own dampness, slightly afraid to trust the transition between wakefulness and the subconscious of sleep, and almost half-expecting to see Tapiz's bloodied body hovering above him in the air, small, focused beams of light shining through the circles of his eyes.

It was only after Ibrahim confided to Savos that the professor softened and started to explain to him how Tapiz had been one out of many of his students at the university showing a quiet yet strong disdain for the government.

"That poor fellow had not an ounce of harm in his body. What could they possibly have expected from him? What did they really think him capable of?" Ibrahim asked. "They kill the weak because they are weak themselves."

The educator broke into his calming smile, gentle enough at times to almost contradict his inner fire.

"You became so driven, Ibrahim, there was never a time to confess to you. He was not as much chosen to help you on your commission as to help us learn about you," Savos said. "We needed to understand your intentions, your direction. You have become very important, Ibrahim."

"So, I have been scoped out just like everyone else." Ibrahim felt betrayed.

Savos understood the look that passed across his friend's face. "They studied me too," he offered.

In addition to the first lie he had told Korobash, Ibrahim understood that he was also lying to many of the men in and around Baghdad. Lying by secretly watching them leaving their homes and studying how they conducted themselves during business hours. Watching them as they left their offices at the end of the day not to go home but to less substantial apartments where they fornicated with their mistresses or visited sick relatives, or even to the outdoor cafés where they played dominoes, more like children than grown men, and shared stories about the irresponsibility of their youthful days. Then offering his hand by a chance meeting, as though it were merely a coincidence, and securing them a dangerous future with the polite gesture of an affirming handshake. Savos had watched him. Tapiz had watched him. He was watching too, another link in the chain.

"They are watching you," Tapiz had said, no longer an abstract sentence but a complete statement.

They were watching him just as he was watching others. *They* meaning simply everyone. To Ibrahim a lie was not telling the truth. He didn't proclaim falsities or untruths, but rather he did not make his real intentions known. To his way of thinking, he did not tell the truth but he also did not lie. With Korobash, he did lie, and the ease with which he was able to do so gave him another power. Now he could not only mislead but he was able to force direction. Although Savos proclaimed that he had indeed watched Ibrahim prior to his arrival at the ICP to know his intentions, his directions, by lying Ibrahim was giving or forcing the direction of others and their own intentions, no matter how pure and clear they may have been, and no matter how soon they were to get cloudy and lost and misjudged.

The restlessness Ibrahim felt only grew stronger. They were getting close. Ibrahim sensed the proverbial wolves at the door. Five new men mysteriously showed up at the vacant granary outside the Karkh district, uninvited and unrecognized; a different group from the one at the university and much older. Small groups of changing men waited by the entrance to the marketplace, and with eyes blinded by success and sense of purpose, they had accepted them all as new members of the group without question. Ibrahim knew that although Savos, Tapiz, and even he himself were investigating people, potential members and possible enemies, it was highly likely that they were being scoped out as well, not just by other groups or underground figures but by the authorities. The secrets and confidences Ibrahim held close weren't so unknown. Their meeting places were established in advance, as were the persons they sought out for membership and inclusion once their identities became known. With their power grew their reputation. It was one of the reasons Ibrahim had dismissed Korobash, albeit a less than personal one.

Korobash disgusted Ibrahim so much that he sought out help from an Iranian, which carried a death sentence in itself regardless of the relationship's purpose or intent. He ruffled some feathers, as he had done in the past. But Ibrahim felt he had no reason to fear the Syrian. He prudently watched every step he took and also those of every individual he dealt with. Now there were many eyes to watch; too many. Ibrahim knew that Korobash would never put himself in any danger by contacting the authorities about the ICP. His affiliations, though disavowed, would have proved to be his own death sentence.

But Ibrahim underestimated the extent of the man's pride. Savos, using the circumstances as a further means to warn him to be careful, had informed him of the arms dealer's fate in person.

"Korobash was so enraged by his abrupt dismissal that he set up a meeting with the minister of defense, Ali Al-Maas," Savos said. "He must have been shocked to learn that after giving up our identities and the various meeting places of the ICP, Ali Al-Maas did not act surprised at all, as though the man possessed this knowledge all along."

Ibrahim listened intently, his friend once again succeeding in surprising him with his knowledge. He felt his own rising discouragement, with himself and with each facet of betrayal going on around him as it slowly revealed itself.

Savos continued, "They had met in a crowded outdoor park at Korobash's insistence. The Syrian kept a driver cautiously waiting for him by the opened gate and instructed him to keep the car idling. He was not as stupid as we may have thought. Things just got too tight. He felt it. He did not want to linger around afterwards, and upon divulging his secret information he intended to leave before it became even more dangerous.

"But the minister of defense was several steps ahead of him. As soon as Korobash turned down the main pathway and made his way past the large cracked fountain and out of Ali Al-Maas's line of vision, his driver suddenly pulled the car out into traffic and sped away from the area before Korobash got back. The Defense Ministry had already, in fact, been watching our movements and the ICP.

" 'There are men who believe more in their country than their egos. Several moles exist in the organization,' Ali Al-Maas stated matter-of-factly to Korobash.

"And Ali Al-Maas had also been following Korobash for some time as well. The arms dealer from Syria was well-known and fairly recognizable. They knew he was here for a reason. Yet he had no idea that when he ratted out his ICP contacts and proclaimed to Ali Al-Maas with a satisfying pride in his large belly, 'They are securing weapons from the Iranians,' that this piece of information alone would enrage the minister of defense so much that in doing so Korobash had also ironically sealed his own fate.

"Hours after being forcibly escorted back to the minister's office and put in a cell, Korobash was stripped of his clothes and then scorched for hours with the bare ends of a live wire against his exposed skin. The knowledge he freely offered up indicted the messenger as well as its subjects. Once they were content with the information they had obtained, one of the soldiers placed a large burlap sack over Korobash's head and led him out to a cool and open space."

"My God," Ibrahim muttered, "they now walk among us."

"It took the soldiers close to two hours to cut the fat man's body into portable pieces," Savos continued. "After the minister gathered his breath—he couldn't stand the smell; the burnt aroma of flesh did not bother him anymore, but the mixture of oil and fecal matter that the flesh emitted when the skin was cut open had caused the man to vomit in front of his subordinates–the remains were gathered up and collected in the same burlap bag and then driven several miles out into the desert. The soldiers scattered the pieces around like rotten garbage left to dry out under the sun where eventually the body of the Syrian would be devoured by vultures."

It was under that same Arabian sun, as the first vulture arrived, that Savos and Ibrahim sought their own relief under the palm of a date tree in the outdoor patio behind Savos's house.

"Each of us cannot be too careful anymore, Ibrahim," Savos warned him, more as a response to Ibrahim's feeling of betrayal at his being watched and studied by these same men he had recently grown to trust.

"It is obvious," Ibrahim responded. "There is no one left to trust."

The shade of the palms felt good and Ibrahim wiped his forehead with his napkin. This time the manner of the assistant deputy minister of education had not succeeded in calming his nerves, instead disarming him with the knowledge of Korobash's fate.

"I was there when the meeting with Korobash took place," Savos confided. "I found out the rest from a soldier who had watched Al-Maas get sick. The soldier seemed more amused with Ali's weak stomach than with the sins of his own actions. We live amongst barbarians."

Seated across from Ibrahim, Savos carefully sliced apart the last remaining piece of smoked fish into two equal pieces, tossing one half into his mouth and pushing the other half on the plate over toward Ibrahim.

"If our fate has been decided," Ibrahim said, "then so be it."

And with those words of acceptance the leader of the ICP

picked up the last half of the smoked fish from off the plate and put it into his mouth. He slowly chewed the delicacy, contemplating the growing lack of moderation in his fellow countrymen and the fervency with which everyone seemed to carry their beliefs, savoring its strong and preserved taste along his tongue now more than ever.

27

IT TOOK THE NURSES several hours to calm Daniella down. She had been given a mild sedative in the hopes of settling her nerves and was in a pensive haze when I found her alone and resting in her room at the Say ad Manood Hospital, the same hospital where I had visited Qadro days earlier. The two other women from the trip were in the adjoining rooms, and their proximity helped to accommodate the private-nurse service the three shared, a rare exception during the five years of conflict.

Along the sides of the hallways injured men lay scattered about, unattended and writhing in pain atop rusted aluminum cots. Most of the new arrivals were being turned away at the downstairs admittance station, and there was occasional fighting among the relatives and hospital orderlies. The administration could not build new hospitals fast enough to meet the rising demand. All the emergency parking lots and underground garage facilities were empty. Every resource was out or being utilized. At the onset of dawn ambulances methodically made their way through the countryside picking up and transporting the casualties of the war, their drivers staying conscious of the position of the sun as the day progressed. Tired and coated with dust, they returned to the hospital in the early evenings when the darkness also brought the threat of thieves and bandits lurking on the open roads.

Manpower is in short supply but the three journalists are being offered nearly every amenity. Daniella's room is furnished with crisp white sheets and an abundance of laundry–towels, clothes, robes, and pillowcases. A private catering service from a nearby hotel, the Palestine, is charged with bringing the three women their meals. Piles of European magazines are stacked neatly on the bed stand, adjacent to a small television set incapable of reception.

I understand that the accommodations are an attempt by the government to somehow influence the memory of what these three journalists stumbled upon yesterday morning in the village of Shiek Wiha Aan. I have not met the other two women, but with Daniella I know the attempt is in vain. Besides, these gestures of goodwill are also short-term–all three women have been ordered by President Hussein to exit the country as soon as possible. Their foreign press passes for Iraq have been revoked by the Iraqi government. The orders claim that their removal is primarily for their personal safety, as though the attack on the village was, by the default of their happening upon it, somehow a personal attack against each of them. All three women are charged with violating the country's strict press code previously laid out for them in detail when they had first arrived in Baghdad. They visited an unauthorized area, and in doing so, the punishment was banishment. Atheer and the other minder accompanying Daniella's group were also abruptly taken by officials as soon as their truck entered the capital. They were being detained for questioning in a local holding cell. Regardless, tomorrow Baghdad will begin its slow and silent retreat into memory as each woman will be forced out of the country and flown off to her respective home.

Daniella's hysterics have almost gone and she is finally able to speak in full sentences without breaking down. I had held her in silence for close to an hour until I thought she had fallen asleep. I slowly released my arms so that she might lie back more comfortably against the pillows only to realize that she was still awake when she pulled me tighter to her. Her strength is gone; it is the adrenaline that comes with emotion that keeps her from fully closing her eyes and the medication she has taken for the shock that has caused the rest of her body to go limp.

"I have to leave this place," she says with a sob, and I know she means Iraq and not just this hospital room.

It is intentional, her words—we *are* journalists—and it is the abstracts she now begins to cling to. No more definites, no more facts, no more statistics. No more getting lost in large piles of data. It is her emotion, picked lightly like a scab on a kneecap.

Earlier I had arrived back at Baghdad subconsciously praying to myself over and over that Daniella was safe. A handwritten note on hospital stationery was left folded on the corner of my bed at the al-Rashid, and before I could close the door to my room I was back out in the streets of Baghdad once again and hailing a taxi. The message informed me Daniella was unharmed but that her group had encountered *a very unfortunate display of our enemies' willingness to push the limits of decency.* It gave her room number and the salutation in Arabic *May Allah Be With You.* A postscript listed the details of her official escort out of the country scheduled for first thing tomorrow morning. And it was unsigned.

She is being kept in the hospital under observation as an act of international diplomacy for which I am thankful but also understand too well its inherent hollowness. Two cold and uneaten trays of food lie on the floor next to her bed: one French toast with sausage links and the other a salmon-fillet dinner. Both are covered by thick glass lids. I glimpsed underneath, having myself not eaten in over twelve hours. A dozen empty juice containers overflow from the small plastic garbage can next to her bed. Daniella may be suffering from shock, but there is more concern about the effects of dehydration on her body. I pour out a small portion of the remaining orange juice and bring the cup to her lips. She drinks it without hesitation, and then, escaping for a mere moment, the image quickly comes back and I place my arms around her as she begins to weep silently into my chest.

A newborn child with an expression of curiosity—not unlike a puppy investigating a new smell—but with a look of *curiosity*—so strange and beautiful and as yet unblemished—frozen forever on its face. She begins to explain it all to me.

A low-flying crop duster had passed over the small village well after midnight and dropped several metal canisters the size of Brazilian coffee cans from out of its interior. After the last canister fell, the plane quickly turned away and sped off in the opposite direction. Upon impact with the ground, colored bands of smoke began to hiss out through small cracks in the sides of the cans. The contents quickly dissipated into unseen vapors captured within the shadows of the night. Within hours the entire village would suffocate. The pilot of the duster, an Iraqi farmer from Mosul suspected of spying, was identified the following morning by his dental records. Army officials found the wreckage of the plane and his charred body thirty miles away after he apparently crashed into the rising foothills of the north, unable to see them in the darkness. That dental records existed was strange enough, but later I will recall that not one person interviewed in the man's supposed village claimed knowledge of him. The capital maintained dental records, but the local government held no account of the man's existence.

A well-intentioned Kurdish villager tried to save the baby's life as others fled to the sanctuary of the water. The man shuffled out of his hut with the child pressed underneath his shirt, hopelessly gasping for moderate breaths, and made his way to the well, where he attempted to hide the baby underneath the cover of his own body in hopes of preventing the caustic fumes from descending upon and choking the child as well—a final act of martyrdom.

But there was no way to escape the gas unless equipped with special masks or sealed suits. An entire village was wiped out. There had been similar stories from the towns of al-Wikan and Shamilayiha, where chemical weapons were also rumored to have been used. But no such activity was ever proven. There were no witnesses and the areas in question, if indeed scorched by chemicals, must have been tidily and hastily cleaned up. No traces had ever existed, until now.

"It is too much," Daniella says. She continues to sob and I notice her passport and flight papers on the far side of the bed wrapped tightly together with several rubber bands.

An escort politely waits outside her hospital room. The young man is scheduled to drive her to Baghdad International Airport tomorrow morning where she will be searched, questioned, and then flown directly to London, thus officially ending her assignment covering the Iran-Iraq War for the London *Times*. Special and private government planes were ordinarily flown to Syria or Tripoli to remove foreigners under an unwritten rule of Iraqi protocol, and usually without hesitation. But several private airstrips had recently been blown up by opposition groups, and all air traffic was being redirected through the international airport, now overflowing uncontrollably with the added activity.

I understand she must leave here. In a way I am glad she will soon be out of danger and away from the omnipresent sound of gunfire and mortar shells. I am glad for the result—that she will be safe from the war—but the causes seem too inhumane to bear. In my heart I can't help but wonder how long it will be until we see each other again. We seem to have crossed a bridge in our relationship. My hope is Daniella will not turn her back again now that she is going home. It is selfish of me, especially at such a time, but it is a feeling I am unable to help.

In other countries, when members of the foreign press witness activities or events they weren't intended to see, they are usually unofficially whisked out of the area as soon as possible as though their deportation would somehow hinder their memory or that their banishment would serve as some sort of punishment. It is not uncommon for journalists in Africa, for example, to watch the brutal mass killings in Rwanda or Liberia only to be blind-folded themselves sometime during the night while they struggle with sleep, the covering only removed hours later as they sit stunned and weary in a carrier somewhere amidst the rising blue caps around them.

Outside the closed door, the escort has fallen asleep on the floor. He is a young boy—yet apparently old enough to drive—and I make the decision to question him when he wakes up. His breathing is heavy and labored and for a moment I think Daniella is about to smile. I wish I could console her and I try my best, explaining to her that those villagers would all have disap-peared without a trace—without justice—if it weren't for her. That so many tragedies in this world go unnoticed is a brutal fact, but by her group's happening across those grassy hills, this tragedy could now become public knowledge and those responsible pun-ished. But she is past the morality of such reasoning, looking be-yond the facts and instead to its inherent meaning.

Daniella is a respected journalist, just like her father, but her work is respected for its personal touch. No matter how distant she has kept herself emotionally, she has always been able to re-veal the emotions of her subjects, despite intentionally sacrificing her own rather easily. But now the heat of the battle has gotten too close to her own heart. I bite my tongue at the idea she has only opened herself because of me and my persistence.

"I don't want the memory," Daniella says, a hint of steely composure straining her face. "It corrupts my good ones."

And then I sense the rest of her resolve soften, as though all the years of her stubborn will and determination have been stripped away, like layers of hardened paint, each revealing a different color. As though it has all been a mistake of judgment. She is exhausted. I am tired as well, but her weariness seems ancient. There is heavy shading around the patches under her eyes, and a slight vertical tear divides her lower lip. All the years of composure and ambition, the inability of and aversion to emotional attachment, unraveling within her like the string of a kite.

Later, she tries to smile to show me she will be alright, to somehow reassure me. Yet the pain she feels for the others–the same pain she has done her best throughout her career to keep from interfering and purposely put aside–has been set free, floating within the light of that early-morning sun along with the remnants of colored smoke.

"Michael?" she suddenly asks, and then with an earnestness that momentarily disarms me, "come back to London with us?"

And she grabs both my hands within hers and pulls us closer together. For a moment I can see the ocean within her eyes and then her words register, and it is the moment of clarity I have searched and waited for since that conference room in the ancient city of Cairo.

There is a fable older Iraqis tell their children when they reach the age of wisdom regarding the human body. Although it is becoming harder to believe with the passing of years and the hardening of society, it is held dear by a few people who still believe there exists in their long history a time of peace and harmony, before the imperialistic tendencies of marauders and invaders. It is a tale told in the cafés while outside the last remnants of daylight slowly dissolve. It is spoken of at dinner parties when the mood turns sentimental after too much drink. It is told to others who don't recognize the story until they themselves feel the inexplicable pull of their own heart.

The story begins, like most things here, with hordes of conquerors riding through these desert lands carrying with them unimaginable weapons and brimming with ferocity, putting down the natives and their local resistance quite easily. In a land invaded so often that this is its primal characteristic, future invaders began to fear the inhabitants would not only catch on to the technology of war and the growing modern world but would also exceed their own advances. Just as birds developed wings, so too they feared that these people would adapt. The foreigners recorded the intelligence and capacity of the people dressed by the sun, worried that one day the natives would grow their own wings and be able to soar higher than even the strongest of winds. Fearing their progress, a new band of imperialists from the West came with a strategy much more communal and civilized than their past rivals, and they brought with them overseas a new weapon. They brought it to the shores of new lands and into the heart of a desert whose stories are as numerous as its particles of sand. The new invaders brought it silently, the most dangerous weapon of all. They brought the idea of love and they brought it within a new world order of politeness and courtesy and order. They became friendly with the villagers, and after several nights of food and drink they told them of their new philosophy, and as the men and women of the village turned and gazed upon each other with longing eyes, the invaders knew they had won once again. Men and women turned toward each other for the first time in a newfound life, as though the different gods they worshipped had been found, and as they did, their treasures and livelihoods were stolen from underneath the darkness of their shared beds. When they awoke, without any anxiety and with a serene sense of calm, they became too passive to understand that they had been overrun, and they succumbed to the beatings of their hearts rather than fists beating for war against their breasts. The rivers were said to form the shape of a smile during this time. A period of peace followed, but soon the embers of this new flame eventually began to fade, and so too did the history it helped shape. Conquest once again took hold of the land and it has not let go since—earmarking the culture between two immovable bookends. "We have been taken over because of love," some still whisper with pride, because only love will survive. Because the idea is what they want to believe. But that was a long, long time ago.

"Us?" I ask, and she demurely tilts her head downward and looks at her stomach, lightly rubbing our joined hands across her midsection.

"Yes, us," she responds, and for the first time in my life I felt closer to a place I had never known.

28

ALL OF THE ROOMS on Qadro's floor are filled past their capacity, many exceeding triple the normal occupancy rate. The ranking-military personnel ward is a clear contrast to the special-patients floor where I left Daniella minutes ago after she finally closed her eyes and fell asleep. Her breathing had relaxed, and when I pressed my palms lightly against her stomach, she sighed within her sleep. I bent down and kissed her gently on the forehead, then turned off the overhead lights and left the room so she could finally get some rest. I silently closed the door behind me and made my way past the crowded hallways and the long lines at the service stations down to the second floor to see Qadro.

As I approach his room, nudging past men on crutches and patients laid out on stretchers, I can see his door is also closed. Three men dressed in hospital gowns are waiting directly outside in the hallway smoking cigarettes, and as I pass, they eye me suspiciously. I stop next to them and knock on the closed door. Since my spirits have been lifted by Daniella and her surprising announcement, I offer them a polite smile.

"Mikhail," Qadro exclaims as soon as I enter, "so glad you came back, my friend."

He is sitting up and appears in his usual good spirits. His wounded leg is covered by a heavy camel-hair blanket pulled up past his waist. A small metal table stands next to the bed with a chair directly across from it, upon which a young and handsome olive-skinned man is sitting. The legs of the table wobble unevenly with any sudden movements, and when Qadro leans over upon my arrival, the opposite sides alternately thump back and forth against the tile floor.

The stranger rises up and inspects me with an eager curiosity while trying his best not to appear impolite. He is thin and muscular like a marathon runner, with long, delicate hands and charcoal hair falling down to his shoulders. As our eyes meet, I notice his facial features are quite refined. A solid, square jawline rolls tightly backward toward his neck. There is a straight ridge of white teeth common in the wealthy, and an innocent brow that is both smooth and distinct, not yet hit with the consternation of age. The youthfulness of his expression adds to his accessibility until he turns his head slightly toward Qadro and I notice a high arc crossing the bridge of his nose and bisecting his face unequally, a pale pink demarcation line buried within the skin between his eyes.

Qadro is unable to stand up, offering his hand and then a small glass of spirits instead. I bring the cup up underneath my nose. The fluid is colorless and without odor. When the vodka hits my tongue, I welcome the warmth it carries down my throat and then spreads evenly through my chest. On the table between the two men lies a handful of yellow folders, documents and photographs arranged in piles. A thick-volumed book sporting the cover of the Koran is open, and I can see the hollowed-out partition in the middle, a secret storage place in the holiest of books. The folders and pictures don't look as though they will fit into the compartment as the young man hurries to fold the papers and then presses the small pile of photos against the floor of the book. When the table is empty, he closes the counterfeit text and secures the small attached locket to prevent it from accidentally opening.

"Mikhail, this is the friend I told you about," Qadro introduces us with pride in his eyes, staring at the other man as he places the book within his jacket. When he is satisfied that the text is secure, he walks across the floor to formally greet me.

"The great artist of Baghdad, Ibrahim Galeb al-Mansur," Qadro says, beaming, and begins to laugh as though our meeting in a crowded hospital room in Baghdad during wartime can only be construed as a stroke of good fortune.

We shake hands firmly, and when done, he momentarily places his hand over his heart in a cultural gesture of sincerity. He is taller than my six feet and I understand what Qadro meant on the ride from the front when he talked about the man's stature. Like most governmental employees, he carries himself confidently and with an air of authority, but there is no reservation in his movements. Whereas most civilians move about their daily lives with the knowledge that the eyes of the president are always upon them, this man appears not so much as unaware of that possibility but rather that he does not seem to care. He is without the usual veneer accompanying those working for the regime, and it is hard to put my finger on the exact reason why. Most people working for the government, whether they believe it or not, go about their business with a public display of loyalty toward their leaders. This man appears to transcend such ingrained behavior, a trait common only among the clerics, and with his deliberateness appears to hold no secret agendas.

In the beginning of the war, Baghdad poured hundreds of thousands of dollars into a widespread arts program. The hope was to ignite a sense of nationalism absent since the country was first declared a British mandate by the Cairo Conference in 1921. In 1983, the Baathist regime erected the Martyr's Monument on the eastern bank of the Tigris River. Two separate blue-tiled halves of a pointed dome encircle a twisted piece of metal representing the Iraqi flag. The government built the structure as a testament to the ideas of faith, represented by the two separate halves, and nation, represented by the crumbled flag. But many Iraqis have been devastated by the loss of so many lives and attribute the monument's meaning to those killed during the ongoing war with Iran. The implications of faith and nation are too abstract for many citizens to find any deeper meaning. It is faith that has helped to keep this country broken, dividing it into its separate factions and resulting in most Iraqis feeling no sense of nation at all. The Martyr's Monument is a direct example of the government's propensity for re-creation, an attempt to establish a contrived network of beliefs and history to foster a sense of unity and consolidate the fragile country.

Qadro has told me that this young man standing in front of me paints the pictures and murals commissioned by the Baath to further that contrived sense of history. I wonder if he is at all affected by the incongruity evident in his post, that an artist can be directed solely by the ideas of others without hints of his own personal inspiration and that that work can ultimately be devoid of any real truth. I do not want to judge these people because their circumstances and varying traditions are very different from my own, and I feel like I can only plead ignorance with regards to their solemnity. But from what Qadro had spoken of him and from my introduction, this man, Ibrahim, appears like a man grounded in his own beliefs. After viewing some of his work myself, the idea that he is commissioned by the Baathist government is hard to believe and almost blasphemous.

"This is the man decorating our beloved country," Qadro says.

"I have heard much about you," I respond.

"Hopefully not too much." And he smiles over at Qadro. "Soon we will run out of secrets to share."

"What made you accept this government position?" I ask him, and after thinking it over for a few seconds he answers.

"When I paint, I am alive. Besides, a painter in a place such as Baghdad is not in such high demand. I can only accept what is offered."

"Our president, dressed like a downtown Miami pimp," Qadro chimes in, laughing. "Yes! Next thing you know, across the Jumhuriyah Bridge you will see that bastard smiling and cavorting around in a polka-dotted bikini."

We all laugh at Qadro's comment, and for the moment neither man seems concerned with the disparagement of their president.

The room is filled with smoke. Both men continue to inhale their cigarettes effortlessly. I do not notice either of them ever lighting a new one, but there is a growing half-filled plate of ash sitting on the windowsill. I take another mouthful of the vodka and find it hard to concentrate. I spent only one half day with Qadro before the accident, and yet after visiting him several times here in the hospital, a delicate bond seems to have formed between us. I move to lift my glass again but Qadro stops me and gently taps the bottle against its side. I reach over so he can fill me up, and after he does the same to his own glass, I drink heartily, a personal and silent toast. I am to become a father, I remind myself. I find the thought exhilarating yet still hard to fully believe. I am anxious to get back to Daniella's room. A light knock comes from outside the door, and a small, well-dressed man cautiously enters the room carrying overstuffed bags of fruit dangling from off his shoulders.

"Who are you?" Qadro orders, but he is immediately cut off by Ibrahim, who slices his hand religiously through the air.

"I am sorry," the small man tries nervously. "I was told you were here."

And he looks up at Ibrahim as one looks upon the altar, penitential and reverent. Ibrahim takes the bags of fruit and leans them down against his chair.

"Thank you," he responds, "that is a very kind gesture. But my friend here is ill. Later, perhaps, would be a better time."

And in his tone the small man recognizes the implication of unspoken words and gives a small bow toward the artist. He looks nervously about the room and says, "Yes, I understand."

"Before you go," Ibrahim says, "this is a military hospital. Maybe your fruitful gesture would be better served to the sick and wounded."

His smile is grandfatherly, and although the small man looks much older than any of us, he takes the advice as a child may take a new coin and picks the bags back up and nods his head approvingly.

"Yes, I will do that," the small man answers. "It *would* be a kind and thoughtful gesture."

Ibrahim walks over and pats the man on his shoulder and then takes four apples from off the top of one of the sacks.

"Allah be with you, Haboby," Ibrahim wishes.

"Allah be with you too."

And the small man turns and sways out the door with the weight of the bags hanging heavily from his sides.

When he is gone, Ibrahim tosses one of the apples into Qadro's lap and then hands two over to me. He rubs the last with his thumb and, upon closer inspection, polishes the apple against the fabric of his shirt before bringing it up to his mouth and taking a big bite. I glance at the fruit in each of my hands.

"One for you," Ibrahim says.

"And one for your lady friend," Qadro finishes. "As I understand it, she is staying in the same hospital. I pray she is well."

It then hits me that there is more to this meeting than just a chance introduction. I had originally asked Qadro for a meeting with his friend. But now I am almost certain we would have met anyway regardless of my request. I am reminded of the night we first came to this hospital and Qadro informed me that he knew my room and telephone number by heart. I feel the bond between us suddenly weaken, and I wonder how these two men know about Daniella and why she may be a concern to them.

"What do you know of her?" I demand of them, and Qadro turns to Ibrahim, who simply nods his head in approval. Then Qadro begins to explain it all to me.

"You see, Mikhail, things are never what they appear to be. If you could look past the formalities you'd see that everyone is watching everyone else—not just the president and his inner circle. This has been a country based on suspicion for a long time and many of us have grown tired of it."

Qadro looks back up at his friend and a sadness cuts across his face. He goes on to describe Ibrahim's background, how he was raised in a strict, wealthy family and how it wasn't only the poor and the desperate that opposed the government.

"Everyone has lost something. It is often the people who have had the most—who lose the most—and who feel their hatred like venom pumping though their veins."

I am a bit confused, unsure of the direction of this conversation. Qadro recognizes the lack of comprehension held in my expression.

He continues, "We are not just a painter and a minder"—he points to Ibrahim and then to himself—"at least not anymore."

I stare back and forth between the two men. Nothing has ever made much sense in this part of the world; the truths, the untruths, and the vast differences existing in between. Feinrich, my German colleague, was in Baghdad not even one full day before he was deported out of the country for attempted robbery. The perceptions of right and wrong shift daily like a pendulum. I understand less about this country the more time I spend within its borders.

"You have just been introduced to the new leader of a growing and sophisticated underground movement called the Iraqi Centrist Party, or the ICP, as it has become known on the street."

I look at Ibrahim in this new light. His expression has not changed and he is childishly sucking the remaining juice from the apple and staring back at me.

"There are people who would kill for that information," Qadro says.

When he is finished, Ibrahim tosses the fruit into the garbage. After a few moments of silence he begins to pace around the room as though suddenly energized.

"We seek justice and peace and freedom. Are those not your American ideals?" the tall artist asks with his back to me.

I look over at Qadro. "How long?"

"The group has been in existence for over ten years. In that time it has grown, and it has also shrunk down to nothing and almost disappeared. Now, in the past six months, it has resurfaced and gained a tremendous amount of strength."

It was Ibrahim's father-in-law, a radical shopkeeper, who first introduced him to the group he would eventually lead and help expand. He says the ICP is currently close to six thousand members strong and still growing, spreading as far south as Basra to Al Kut and up through the capital and its surrounding cities and as far north as Samarra.

"There are other groups," Qadro says, "but there are eyes everywhere, and to spread out even further is too dangerous. We can try to unite but then we would have to deal with the intentions of others. What is it you Americans say—too many cooks spoil the broth? This is especially true since there are many objectives we need to accomplish. Our individual tastes are different. They have always been."

When Qadro begins to tell me about Ibrahim's wife, a beautifully shy and ambitious girl educated across the borders in Europe, Ibrahim turns silently toward the window and stares out at the slow-running waters of the Tigris River. The city below us bustles along like it has for hundreds of years, and he seems to look past its history, past his own history, lost in thought. There is a bare space on his finger where one would wear a wedding ring, absent just like on Qadro's hand.

"He, as a lot of others, has lost a lot," Qadro tells me.

"We have come such a long way, my friend," Ibrahim announces to Qadro. "Back in the days of our childhood I only wanted to be a painter. Such naïve and innocent ambitions we possessed."

Ibrahim tells me the story of a barren morning when he stood in line with the other children of his village to meet the vice president while the leader was still a young man. The trip had been a gesture of goodwill to help promote the draft, but to Ibrahim the people of his village seemed to grow dispossessed as the day wore on, especially Hassan Jaffa. It was at that moment, when he stood next to the man who would eventually become known as the Butcher, that Ibrahim could feel the adrenaline pass from one body to the next, and he understood it as though a valve had been forced opened and the current it released in him grew stronger and more forceful over time. Now it also grew stronger with pain. He had sensed the man's electricity but he never feared it. He told the truth at the time, even though something different was expected of him.

"A painter," Ibrahim says pensively. "Even back then I wanted to be a painter."

"And now a revolutionary," Qadro says.

"Call it what you will, but instead of my suffering–I want to see them suffer," he responds coldly, and the clarity and youth-fulness I noticed earlier in his eyes is gone. I can see specks of gray hidden within the hair along his temples.

"When I was a young child," Ibrahim continues, and brings his fingers to the corners of his eyes, "you see, as all children do, with different eyes. But the day comes when you open them to the world as it really is–trying to understand all that happened in the past and still continues to happen. I watched them set fire to my favorite schoolteacher. To this day, I still do not know what became of my father-in-law, but I am not naïve enough to hold out hope for his situation. He was a crazy old fool. They took him before they took my assistant–he is dead, my assistant, that I do know–a man *they* had appointed to me. They have given me so little only to take it all back."

"And your wife," Qadro adds.

"Yes"–Ibrahim pauses–"and my Shalira."

There is another sudden knock on the door, this one louder and more assertive. A scholarly man dressed in khaki slacks and a cardigan sweater enters without waiting for any kind of response or admission.

"Ibrahim, gentlemen, please excuse my interruption," he says, pushing his glasses farther up the bridge of his nose. Then dispensing with his politeness, he moves on to the purpose of his visit and turns toward Ibrahim. "I could not wait. Everything has been pushed up two days."

"It is all right, Savos," Ibrahim tells the man after they both nod toward me. The man, Savos, tries to appear calm but his nerves seem a bit frayed with my presence, and I notice him playing intently with the cuticles of his fingers.

"It must happen tomorrow night," he tells Ibrahim.

Silence sweeps the room and then there is a light thud accompanied by the shuffle of table legs as Qadro tries to rise up. Ibrahim pauses with his hand closed in a fist covering his mouth, and after a few seconds he starts to speak without emotion, as if to justify himself for his future actions.

"They have taken my . . ." He pauses. "They have taken *our* identity. There are good people in this country, hardworking people. They take all of our sacrifices as though they are gods themselves. Well, I can be a god too."

He walks over to Qadro and leans down to hug him, exchanging words in Arabic I am not familiar with, and they embrace like old friends. Before he and the man named Savos leave, Ibrahim turns to me.

"I respect my friend's opinion of you. I only hope we can trust your opinion has not been jaded," he says, and we shake hands before he and Savos turn and leave the room together. I am left alone with Qadro.

The air of professionalism and seriousness that hung in the air exits with the two men. The bond I had felt earlier with Qadro is gone. He is merely a government escort with a stroke of bad luck who had been appointed by his superiors to take me to the war front. We are not friends or even meager acquaintances. A sudden desire to leave this country as soon as possible takes hold of me. My thoughts are cloudy and my judgment suddenly filled with false pride. Whatever affinity I held toward Qadro has evaporated, the connection now broken, if a connection ever really existed. Qadro tries to temper the moment with another glass of vodka. I do not like feeling like I was played or used as a pawn in a dangerous political game, and I tell Qadro as much.

"What do you think, I'm a fool? What gives you the right to use me—we are nothing more than strangers."

"You Americans know nothing of humility. It is nothing like that, Mikhail. I was assigned to *you*, yes, but *you* didn't have to come to the hospital to visit."

"Why speak to me about this? This is extremely dangerous for all of us," I say, my suspicion having turned to curiosity and my curiosity turning to fear. "What do you—what does he—know of Daniella?"

Qadro answers me as though he were simply reading the words from off a newspaper clipping.

"She has been tagged just as you have been tagged. In return for your silence, she is being followed all the way back to London. But before you get angry, she is safe and unaware of her current situation. I made sure of such arrangements myself. She will be in no danger. The rest is up to you."

"You are all crazy," I begin to yell, "this whole thing is crazy. I am going to get her and we'll leave this hosp—"

Qadro leans up, showing extreme agility despite his amputated leg. He forcefully grabs my arm.

"She is already gone," he tells me.

I immediately turn to run from the room, to run back up to where she is sleeping and see her, to make sure she is alright. But something keeps me there. I know he is telling me the truth. I have been in his room for over an hour, and nothing but the truth has been spoken within these four walls.

"You have been down here a long time. She is already en route to the airport." Qadro says. Then he softens, "I am sorry, Mikhail. You as well as anyone should know that what the government says and what they actually do are two separate and distinct actions. It is what Ibrahim wanted. The decision was made without my knowing, and only when I told him your name did he inform me of the situation. She remains unaware of the surveillance and no harm will come to her. It depends on you now; she may never know. Ibrahim wanted to ensure your silence until we were finished, and now we receive word that we'll be finished sooner than we had anticipated. The wheels are already in motion. I figured you weren't a threat to go to the authorities. You understand very well that there is no black and white in my country—it is a gray mass of confused allegiances and beliefs. But Ibrahim wanted to be sure. I told him it may compromise his purpose with regards to you."

I feel the rage grip me like a vise tightening around the muscles of my chest and back. It robs me of clarity, and for a second all I see is red. I feel like I could strangle Qadro, and I am relieved when the impulse quickly escapes me.

"Why tell me at all then?" I yell, and after a tense silence I feel the anxiety take hold of the rest of my muscles. I can't even sit down. I am worried about Daniella. "Who is following her?"

"She will be alright. I am a good judge of character. My position here affords me the opportunity to meet many kinds of people. And my impressions of most have always been accurate. Do not press things, Mikhail. You must trust me on this. You are not in a position to do otherwise. I suggest tomorrow evening that you begin your journey to her as well. Baghdad is extremely dangerous and growing more so every day. Persistent rumors are coming out of the university of a large-scale hostage situation just like the one in Tehran. It is currently being planned."

"But why? Why her, why tell me anything?"

And then Qadro begins to connect the series of events that up until this point have seemed independent and extremely peculiar.

"Ibrahim feels the end is near for him," Qadro tells me. "Several nights ago he had a dream. He told me that in that dream he was lost in a burning building and babies were crying out from everywhere. They were crying throughout every room, every shadow, every corner, locked away somewhere he couldn't reach. Ibrahim opened and looked behind each door, but he couldn't find any of them. He kept running down the halls and into the different rooms and the fires only grew stronger, and still he could not find any of the crying babies. Finally he came to the end of one of the hallways and it grew extremely dark, and the further into the darkness he went, the louder the cries seemed to grow. He ran as fast as he could, and before he could recognize the shadow at the end in front of him, he ran straight into his father. As they picked themselves up off the floor, they both looked at one another, and then the roof of the building was suddenly ripped off by a tremendous wind and the fires were abruptly blown out, ending the inferno, and a tremendous cold descended upon them. They began to shiver uncontrollably, and eventually his father stopped moving and he froze to death. With the cold a large lion with wings across its back began circling its way down from the heavens and suddenly stormed to the ground, stomping on the frozen figure of his father and shattering him into a thousand pieces. Terrified, Ibrahim could only run around in circles, unable to move forward. And as he did so, he cut his feet on the broken pieces on the floor, and then with a brief flash of light the lion dove down once more and devoured Ibrahim without sound or pain and it was all over."

Qadro's voice has gotten lower. The story sends a chill through the room, and although I am not superstitious, the hairs across my forearms have risen.

"You understand, Mikhail, there is an Iraqi legend that to die in one's sleep is a bad omen. Well, Ibrahim woke up the following morning and felt the end coming on closer. Like the setting sun at the end of a clear day, it cannot be stopped."

Qadro has pulled the heavy blanket up to his chest, the coldness of the dream's story also sending goose bumps over his own skin.

"He wants you to write the truth about him, for his father. He believes they will slander his name and his father will live in shame. He worries tremendously about him. He wants you to write that his intentions were noble."

I then understand why I was brought here. I was chosen to learn about a man, this leader of the underground Iraqi Centrist Party, who believed that he would soon be killed and wanted a foreigner to write the obituary to his father. I will lend testament to the love between a father and a son, a bond so strong as to hopefully transcend death.

"This"–Qadro spreads his arms out–"is all for his father." And then with a hint of despair: "I have also died in my dreams."

"Why not choose one of your own?" I ask, trying to sound neutral, and then to clarify say, "A Moslem or an Iraqi. Why me?"

"To do so would be almost impossible. They would be censored or threatened with a punishment of death, and then they too would also worry about their own legacy. Besides, the American press carries the largest following. I also trust you, and before this country can rise again to the heights it once knew, we must rebuild its foundation on trust or else it will fail us once again, even if we must do so with help from the outside. After meeting you it was easy to figure out that you should be chosen to complete this task. I trust you, Mikhail. It is as simple as that."

"Qadro," I ask him, suddenly concerned abut his well-being and what legacy he imagines for himself, "what about your safety?"

"They have taken our meaning in life, Mikhail. Maybe we can find that meaning in death."

With the blanket pulled up to his chest I think of what Ibrahim had said about seeing the world through a child's eyes and the veil of innocence that is lifted off of us too early. Lying on the hospital bed, Qadro can only resemble the child he used to be. I wonder about his wife of twelve years and realize I never asked him if he had any children of his own. He leans himself over onto his side and pushes the counterfeit text of the

Koran over to me. Then he bends down again and slides a large, locked metal case out from underneath the bed.

"You will be happy to know that Daniella has left early and is safe. Tomorrow night," he says, the friendliness and exuberance of his character completely replaced by a voice now filled with sullenness, "they will blow up this hospital."

29

OCTOBER 12, 1984

HASSAN JAFFA IS NOT in his museum office nor is he on the exhibit floors. He is down in the university storage facilities diligently going over an upcoming exhibit of early forms of writing with Savos Adonan, the assistant deputy minister of education and history professor at the university. Earlier that morning Ibrahim had called to double-check Hassan Jaffa's schedule with the museum's secretary, and she confirmed that his father would be gone till late in the afternoon.

Aid Et-Wari, the portly security guard, is sleeping noisily at his station, lounging like a well-to-do stray. Ibrahim heard his restive breathing coming from far down the corridor when he first entered the walkway. He is relieved; his visit is intended to be in secret. He does not want Hassan Jaffa to know he has been here, so he tiptoes carefully around the sleeping man and makes his way past the small sign-in station and empty visitors' log into his father's office. He notices it as soon as he closes the door behind him.

Two weeks had passed since Ibrahim had last visited his

father at work. Hassan Jaffa was kept busy with productions out-side of the museum. Close to the ancient city of Mashkan-shapir an archaeological dig commissioned by the government had uncovered a series of clay tablets marked with cryptic wedge-shaped writings and coded text. The excitement it caused in his father made Ibrahim feel the slightest bit of hope. That hope also increased after the encounter with the American writer.

"He," Ibrahim noted to Savos after leaving the hospital, "had nothing but trust in his eyes."

But Ibrahim also sensed an ominous presence closing in around his father–Hassan Jaffa *had* been in his dreams as well–so he kept himself a safe distance away so as not to fur-ther endanger his father.

He missed the old man and the evenings they used to pass to-gether, sharing sentimental stories about Ibrahim's childhood when their family circle had been complete. One of Ibrahim's favorites, though as a child it used to make him angry, was the time Hassan Jaffa brought home an Egyptian mask modeled af-ter one of the ancient pharaohs. Ibrahim used to play with all the artifacts Hassan Jaffa brought home with him after work. After dinner, Hassan Jaffa would stay up late at night in the basement cataloging the items within his complex journals or studying their compositions under his microscopes. But once Ibrahim learned how to walk, Hassan Jaffa had to be careful and no longer took anything out of the museum for fear his son would "halt history," or worse, put it curiously in his mouth. One evening, when Ibrahim had grown old enough to under-stand the language, Hassan Jaffa relented and brought home a gilded mask striped across the sides with the black, thick lines of a Bengali tiger. He warned Ibrahim that the mask was cursed by the powerful pharaoh Thutmose, and that if anyone touched it, the curse would bring immediate death upon its current owner. Hassan Jaffa's story perplexed Ibrahim, and when the child heard the word *death,* his eyes widened with fear. And it was because he was only a child that his memory was short and he forgot the warning shortly thereafter, only remembering the curse when he brought the mask up to his face for a split second and peered through the feline eyes to watch Hassan Jaffa collapse to the floor. Ibrahim was horrified that he had killed his father and immediately dropped the mask from his hands, shattering the artifact into hundreds of pieces as it crashed to the ground around him.

It took Hassan Jaffa and Fazeera all night to calm Ibrahim down. Hassan Jaffa had rolled about the floor trying to contain his laughter, but the effect of the intended practical joke soon softened his heart as his six-year-old son lay sobbing hysterically over his body. He rose quickly and embraced the boy, careful ever since of his sensitive nature.

Ibrahim grew to like the story because it showed his curiosity even at such a young age. Hassan Jaffa liked the story because it reminded him of better days when the idea of a practical joke was not so uncommon. And both of them liked the story because it showed the undeniable bond between father and son.

Ibrahim hopes that same bond is strong enough to outlast this lifetime. He studies the picture of Fazeera and for a moment wishes he had used more blue in her eyes. But it is too late. Once a painting is seen by someone other than the painter, it is the worst kind of luck to attempt to change it. He followed the same practice with regard to his public work as well. But if he could somehow get away with it, he would ride throughout the entire night changing the murals of Saddam Hussein, painting crimson bullet holes in his starched jacket lapels or adding the horns of the devil atop his bushy, charcoal hair. Those works were something entirely different. They had been bad luck from the start.

By painting Fazeera, it was the closest he could come to bringing her back to life. The immense satisfaction he also felt in doing so was enough to make it worthwhile. Savos often joked that Ibrahim had a "god" complex, and sadly he knew his friend was correct.

He had entered Hassan Jaffa's office wholly expecting the painting to still be wrapped and leaning against the desk where he had placed it months earlier. Ibrahim intended to take the picture back to his studio, where he would open it and rest it upon the easel he kept by the window so Hassan Jaffa wouldn't miss it when he first entered the apartment that night for dinner. But here it was greeting him from behind the desk, hung perfectly straight on the wall facing the door. It was the half-finished painting hanging next to it that disarmed him and caused Ibrahim to fall to his knees and silently begin to cry.

Over Hassan Jaffa's mahogany desk hung the painting of Fazeera Ibrahim had worked continuously and so hard with a heavy heart to finish. He had uncovered memories within himself, some from a place he hadn't known existed, and yet he found his mother had brought him strength rather than sadness. By bringing her back to life on canvas, he could almost smell her presence enter the room. The longer the portrait stayed in its protective covering, the more Ibrahim feared he was disrespecting her. He hadn't expected her to remain covered up. But so much had happened in their lives. It was from an early photo, back when Hassan Jaffa and Fazeera had both worn smiles like birthmarks and their dreams and ambitions for their young family fueled their late-night conversations. He couldn't blame Hassan Jaffa for overlooking the gift of his son; with their most recent struggles, who could possibly be expected to accept any kind of gift? Yet there it was hanging perfectly straight behind his desk. The office was small and the painting was not centered on the wall, placed several feet to the left of Hassan Jaffa's chair, so that instead of staring at the youthful image of his wife every day when he sat down, she stood beside him, just like the partnership they'd shared through almost twenty years of marriage.

But it was the painting of Shalira, smiling elegantly in a black evening gown with her arms outstretched as if to embrace the artist, hanging next to Fazeera that Ibrahim did not expect to see.

◦

The white patch is worn gray, curled at its edges like a well-used map. The number 407 has faded and is only discernible in full light. Nothing else has changed in his days. Other prisoners come and continue to go. He spends some of his time in this world, in a room filled with other men and women he can't see but knows intimately by the smell of their bodies. To him it is not a prison nor is it a personal hell, but rather it is only a transition.

He has come to realize he can achieve a level of peace only when he lifts himself out of this world, out of his sixty-two-year-old, decrepit body held captive like a wild dog, transcending the physical for moments at a time and he feels the rush of youth again. He struggles to push his thoughts into action, and the discipline helps him to get through the hours of the day. In his mind he has already started a revolution. Often he will carry on conversations with people only he can see, speaking of revolt and riotous demonstrations, until the guards come running over and kick at his cage, threatening him back to silence. Even then he only stops the dialogues when he sees the fear etched across their faces. He worries he may be going crazy, but he also understands that the separation of the spirit from the body can be a troubling experience.

He patiently watches the end coming on like the onset of a freight train from off in the distance. And he can hear it rumbling closer. It is only when he talks out loud to the others that the sound is completely gone.

He anxiously nibbles away at the edges of his fingers, alternating between his right and his left hand. The nails are all gone, chewed down to the cuticles. Instead, cracked skin splits open like thick fingerprints and the taste of his own blood enlivens him.

He continues his exercises three times between the rising and setting of the sun, tensing the muscles of his legs for five seconds and then releasing for five seconds. He has continued to do so every day since his confinement, but he isn't sure if the exercise is still working because he lost all the feeling in his lower body almost a month ago, keeping track of the passage of time by the small overhead window that filters daylight through like water to a thirsty animal. Before the final shadow passes by, leaving him in complete darkness, he marks the day across the floor with the bottom lock securing his cage.

"They will not take my mind," he repeats the mantra to himself as though casting a spell over his captors. In the far reaches of his mind he can see the light of the train approaching faster, the sound of its horn growing louder, and if he were able to move, he would stand up and run toward it, greeting it with open arms.

"They will not take my mind," he repeats.

When a loud explosion shakes the foundation of the prison, forcing several of the stacked cages to the floor, a small smile briefly finds its way to his hidden face.

30

OCTOBER 11, 1984

DANIELLA BURKETT WAS DREAMING of a tired, worn-out village when her thoughts shifted into a state of nightmare and the acid rains began to pour down from holes cut deep into the heavens. In the dream she was the only person who did not feel the droplets of water, wrapped instead in a refreshing breeze coming from off a distant ocean. But the caustic water took hold of each villager, burning them from the first touch, and one by one each man, woman, and child began to melt like cubes of ice left out in the sun. Daniella watched the horror, strangely exhilarated by the cool air only she could feel, until the last person, a handsome young man with the face of a statue, finally succumbed to the heat of the final drops, and then she was left standing all alone amidst the stains of the sulfuric puddles.

"Missus, missus." The minder tenderly shook her awake. "New orders have been issued from my superiors and we must leave for the airport right away."

The man closely resembled the one in Daniella's dreams except he was younger and fresher in his appearance. Daniella stared back at him quizzically, caught within the power of her previous thoughts and unsure of the fabric of her current situation.

Alright, she thought to herself, this must still be a dream. Why am I here and why is this strange man waking me?

But she knew she wasn't dreaming anymore when the young man's superior, a retired general dressed in a starched army uniform, marched straight into the room and began to scold the young minder for what appeared to be his lack of progress toward his subject, Daniella. Then he noticed Daniella was awake and he quickly readjusted his manner.

"I am so sorry for the inconvenience, madam."

He bent slightly forward at the waist and smiled with the blandness that comes from someone used to giving orders. The contrast of the man's thick and wiry gray hair matched against the tufts of his charcoal eyebrows gave him a sinister and almost devilish appearance. Upon closer inspection, he seemed to be off center—literally tilted to one side just as the earth leans over favorably upon its axis. Daniella noticed he limped when he moved, and when she looked down at his feet, she saw the thin, compact detachment of wood supporting the left side of his upper body. The man maneuvered quite easily considering the artificial leg, and he waltzed over to where the young minder had abruptly begun to gather Daniella's papers and credentials from off the dresser.

"Orders are to be obeyed," he boomed with authority. "Those who do not follow the orders of their superiors will in turn die by the sword of their superiors. It is the law of our great Saddam. Do you not understand?"

The general pressed himself up in the face of the minder, who held close to a foot, not to mention a solid foundation, over him. But the young man backed himself up against the wall meekly, trying to get away from his superior's indignation while doing his best not to cower too visibly within the shadow next to Daniella's bed.

"Yes, I understand," he replied, shamefaced.

"It is my fault." Daniella stood up and tried to come to his aid. "I would not wake from my sleep. What is the meaning of this sudden change in plans?"

The general looked over at the minder with disgust and would have spat upon the ground in front of him if not for the presence of the woman. He retained the decorum of his upbringing and instructed the escort to wait outside in the hallway. When the young man made his way past, for the general did not move out of the way to accommodate him, he stumbled over the metal-framed partition covered by a hanging white sheet and rolled clumsily out of the room, closing the door dejectedly behind him. The veneer of steel and tempestuousness the general had maintained lifted itself, and although his officious manner remained behind, it was now without threat or intimidation.

"Madam, the order comes directly from the Ministry of Information and it is to be executed immediately. I formally apologize but there is nothing to discuss."

With the word *executed* Daniella suddenly gasped, and the general understood her reaction because in his years of experience he had seen the exact same look more times than he cared to count. He offered his placid smile once again.

"Forgive me. It is not so severe. Rather, an *execution* of only the orders for transport. You are to be escorted to the airport for your trip back to London ASAP," he instructed and then directed his head toward the young man in the hallway. "I hope he has your bags packed and ready."

The general walked over to where Daniella's suitcase sat on the floor next to the door. The large bag was buckled shut. He leaned down and lifted it up from his side, allowing for the limits of his artificial limb. Its weight hung heavy in his hand.

"It appears he is not a complete waste after all. Ma'am, you are packed and ready to go. A car is waiting for you downstairs and it will take us directly to the International Airport. I will wait outside this room for exactly five minutes as a courtesy to you so you can rise out of bed and gather yourself in private. I will knock after five minutes have passed for you to come out. And I will knock only once."

"This can't be happening," Daniella began. "We were told tomorrow."

She thought of the telephone numbers for the British embassy, the number for the London *Times,* for the other foreign newspapers, and for the press watch groups located in Baghdad. She wanted to speak to someone in a position to help, but also understood the process of the country and that it would be impossible; no attempt or offer of any type of alternative would be given her. The telephone in her room was gone, removed while she had been asleep, and the numbers she could remember only got jumbled with her thoughts and the countless other telephone numbers she was faintly able to recall. She worried about Michael and immediately felt her head lighten and had difficulty gasping even the shortest of breaths.

"My God," she cried, "what is going on?"

The general walked over to the bed and stood next to her. He maintained his eyes level with hers so as to appear the proper gentleman.

"All your passes and visas have been revoked. The Revolutionary Command Council has also authorized your removal. But you are safe. You are in the custody of the government of Iraq, under control and jurisdiction of the Baathist regime, who fully guarantees your safety out of the country. Please, we must go, the plane will be waiting. I grant you your five minutes as of right now."

Daniella kept silent on the ride to the airport. She didn't have the strength to watch the changing scenery let alone argue with the Ministry of Information. She had known her time in Iraq was winding down, she just didn't expect it to be so sudden and twelve hours earlier than she had recently been told. She knew how the government operated. Her father had warned her many times about the intricacies of foreign countries and their ruling governments, especially the country he had learned to love. She also knew she had crossed an imaginary line. "Tell them we have come to see the horses," she'd instructed Atheer, and he had obediently turned the car into the hedged pathway. Then she wondered to herself what her father or Michael would do if they determined her to be missing. A large number of stories concerning the beheading and execution of foreign journalists were being reported. More often than not, the stories were complete fabrications used to sway public opinion. But it was enough to instill the idea and the fear that accompanies such possibilities into one's mind. She did not take the general for a liar. She was part Iraqi herself, 50 percent to be exact, and she had understood the authority and command in his unwavering voice. And she also understood the world of absolutes the man lived in that was necessary for his own sanity. The only gray area associated with him sat atop his head like a colorless bird's nest. She felt reassured by his calm demeanor and the firmness of his gaze when he claimed she would be safe. She had recognized the same trait in her uncles before their farms were unceremoniously taken away from them.

She had trouble focusing on the car ride and struggled to keep her eyes open. She felt slightly drugged and had difficulty fighting off a persistent weariness. Her strength had left her once again and she tried to concentrate on the passing buildings, only to have the structures turn into vague and indecipherable monuments, the passing silhouette of a strange city.

When the car pulled up into the airport drop-off lane, she

was quickly shuffled out and then passed through the security check-in station without hesitation. Her belongings were stamped and tagged and then carted away by a security officer. The general confiscated her passports and press badges before finally leading her onto the plane and directly to her seat. By the time Daniella secured the seat belt around her waist, he was already back inside the terminal, and the engines quickly roared to life with energy and the plane pulled out onto the tarmac. Within seconds the wheels lost touch with the ground, and when she peered out the side window, she could make out the fading lights of Baghdad being devoured behind her by the overwhelming darkness of the desert flatlands.

31

OCTOBER 12, 1984

ONE NIGHT LATER ON Friday, October 12, at eight forty-five in the evening, an ambulance routinely passes through the raised entrance gates and into the basement garage of the Say ad Manood Hospital. The driver waves casually to the attendant sitting in the security booth as he rides by, both of the men familiar with the procedure they have repeated for close to three years while working the same graveyard shift. After exchanging pleasantries the attendant presses a lever and the orange gate lifts up, granting the driver access to the lower levels. Another ambulance follows shortly thereafter with its lights flashing but its siren remaining off, a courtesy granted the attendants because the lights are enough—they are almost impossible to miss. The noise of the siren is known to echo painfully off the cement walls and reverberate against the booth, rattling the glass in its casement. Its piercing sound is not only unpleasant but also not good for the hearing.

The gate lifts up once again and the ambulance speeds through with its circling red and white lights flashing until they disappear around the cement pillars and the vehicle turns down the corner and heads underground. The same process continues for the next three hours until a total of seven ambulances are parked in the two levels directly below the heart of the building. The drivers cautiously check their watches, synchronized earlier in the basement of the Papous Bake Shop, where they had gathered to go over the details of their assignments one final time. Travel routes were updated based on police activity reports received earlier that afternoon. The predetermined pickup stations were mapped out again, and in the unlikely event any of the drivers were uncovered, alternative plans were defined and individual exit strategies arranged.

The aroma of freshly baked biscuits hung in the air while the men ate pieces of warm pita bread spread lightly with heavily flavored goat cheese, although most of them were not able to enjoy the richness of the food due to their nervousness. Some of the men laughed and joked with one another–kidding themselves by making plans to meet and play dominoes later in the outdoor cafés when the job was complete–to ease the tension. But as they got ready to depart, a grim silence fell over them.

Each man needed to remain inside his designated truck. The radar devices were not strong enough to allow the signals to penetrate through the foundation and underground barrier walls and into the basement from an area outside the hospital. The group leadership had been efficient in their planning except for one fatal oversight. Each driver would have to remain seated in his ambulance to ensure the accurate transmittal of the electronic triggers. Some of the other man had called them martyrs. But most of them readily admitted to themselves that they had simply given up hope a long time ago.

After the explosions their bodies would be burnt beyond recognition and their remains would be unidentifiable. With help from the deputy minister of information, each man received a guarantee that he would instead be officially reported as killed during battle against the Iranians on the southern front days later. The promise ensured an honorary war payment of $10,000 from the Iraqi government to their respective families in recognition of their ultimate sacrifice during a time of war.

As soon as the group realized that the radio signals were too weak to pass over a distance of more than one hundred yards, let alone through the massive cement embankments surrounding the hospital's perimeter, Ibrahim had been the first to volunteer his life to the cause.

Each driver waited half an hour after the previous truck's scheduled departure time before driving to his own respective pickup point located at different sites throughout the capital. It was at these secret locations–hidden alleyways or abandoned garages–where the curtains on the back doors of the ambulances were drawn tightly shut and the entire cavities of the automobiles filled up with C-4 explosives.

The last ambulance finally joins the others and a collective calm descends over the men as they sit by themselves and pray and begin to count down the seconds. When the watch of the first driver beeps 11:45, a sudden flash of light illuminates the underground corridor, sending a shock wave of heat strong enough to burn through the metal support beams, and the main floor of the Say ad Manood Hospital falls through the ceiling.

32

OCTOBER 13–14, 1984

THERE HAD BEEN ENOUGH explosives to take down five hospitals. The ambulances had parked close enough together and in similar positions on each of the lower levels. The plan called for them to form a circle in order to concentrate the force of the blast. When the C-4 collectively went off, a fireball tore straight up and through the three upper floors of the building all the way through the roof, sending cement chucks and debris scattering up to a quarter mile away.

I know this because I am listening to the reports coming over a transistor radio as we make the drive back west toward Amman, Jordan. I had left Baghdad as soon as possible, and am in a small caravan with two deserting soldiers, an official from Iraq's Atomic Energy Commission, a French journalist, and two Syrian businessmen suspected of illegally transporting goods into the country. We are all packed tightly into an unmarked cargo van with no windows. I held a small splinter of gratitude toward Qadro's group for their prompt arrangements to get

Daniella out of the country, but I was also angry over the fact that she was involved in this madness at all.

After my meeting with Qadro and Ibrahim, my conscience got the better of me as I thought about their plans to blow up the hospital. I immediately went to Daniella's room, hoping their story about her departure wasn't true, yet also hoping that she was on her way home and back to the safety of London. When I entered, I was greeted by a disheveled elderly man who cursed out at me in Arabic from the same bed I had left Daniella sleeping on hours earlier. All her belongings were gone. She had been checked out of the hospital almost an hour earlier, according to patient records at the admittance station.

I thought about going to the authorities, but then I wasn't sure who the proper authority might be. My mind was made up for me when I found the deputy minister of culture and information, a man named Jazeri, waiting for me in the lobby of my hotel, the al-Rashid. I was not surprised to see him.

"You must leave this country immediately. Do you understand?" the minister implored after whisking me over to the solitude of the maid's supply chamber. "You do not know the extent of such things. There are arrangements that must be met."

He offered no information when I asked him about Daniella's safety or the ICP, and he grew irritated when I questioned his affiliations. I was not able to obtain any concrete answers and he abruptly cut me off in midsentence.

"I am an employee of the Ministry of Culture and Information," he explained, "that is all. I work under the will of our great leader Saddam. Now I recommend you go before you are imprisoned. We do not wish to proceed with such an incident. Go back to where it is you are from and leave this country to those who have tasted the blood running through its soil."

Jazeri pulled a business card out of his wallet, and after writing down an address, he pressed the card into the palm of my hand. Then he quickly departed without uttering another word, and I left the lobby and caught the first elevator up to my room. Once inside I read the blue lettering off the front of the card: LAFEVRE, a French energy firm, written in boldface, and underneath it was the phrase *LIGHTING THE WAY FOR ALTERNATIVE ENERGY SOURCES*. The address Jazeri had written on the back of the card was to a warehouse located somewhere out beyond the western section of Baghdad.

I couldn't call anyone at the *Times* because every telephone call in Iraq was being monitored or bugged by the regime. I desperately wanted to hear Daniella's voice, to hear her tell me she was alright and home safely in London. The telephone in my room still did not work. I had ripped the cords out of the wall about a week ago and they had not been replaced. Daniella would not be home yet anyway, and I hoped she was sound asleep somewhere high above the waters of the Mediterranean Sea.

I fingered the card Jazeri had given me and studied the address he had written on the back. With no alternative, it took me twenty minutes to pack my bags and then I headed back downstairs to the lobby. I didn't bother to check out of the hotel. I knew I was probably being followed, but I wanted to make things appear as normal as possible and to buy a little time. Outside the al-Rashid I hailed a gypsy cab and offered the driver $100 for a ride to the address written on the back of the card and for his silence afterward. He drove me out to the small district of Batrah, west of the capital, and after some intense haggling and ultimately lighter by $500 and my silver watch, I entered an old structure resembling a vacant airplane hangar where I was led by another man into the back of a van. I nodded to the other passengers already seated inside and after a short delay began my journey out of Iraq, following eerily along the same passage I had taken a week earlier when I had first arrived in the country. Only this time it felt more like a retreat.

I am happy to leave Baghdad and Iraq behind for good. If history is to repeat itself as it seems to do here so often, let another person have the opportunity to report on its cycles. From the Assyrian rulers to the reign of Cyrus, from the empire of Alexander the Great through the conquests of the Persian army, and from the Mongol invaders past the not-so-distant control of the Ottoman Empire—the former British mandate has achieved its independence only to become a violent and fragile state overcome with fear and suspicion. It is a country that runs in circles. In Amman I will catch a flight to London, where I will be reunited with Daniella.

The reports from the radio claim the Say ad Manood Hospital housed 900 official patients, and close to 150 more unofficially, for medical treatment. Most of the patients were military personnel or government officials and administrators. Three hundred regular army soldiers, 125 members of the Republican Guard, the elite fighting force of the regime, 5 generals and 200 various governmental officials consisting of minders, administrative office workers, and internal managers, as well as 5 members of the family of the president, had all been killed. The Associated Press is reporting that an underground movement known as the Iraqi Centrist Party, or the ICP, is behind the attack. The ICP, the report claims, consists of over six thousand citizens from throughout the region and has ties to the Iranian and Syrian governments as well as the Russian underground. Authorities had recovered several cartons of nonfunctioning explosives that did not detonate from inside a commercial van parked within the vicinity of the hospital. The name of a Russian manufacturer—Peshuska—was labeled in red across the side. Authorities were also hunting down an Iranian arms dealer named Mossan Behradi, who is said to have financial ties to the religious scholars at the university. Due to the destruction of the facility, the sick and wounded are being rerouted to all other area hospitals, but many of the medical centers are so overcrowded that patients are being turned away and left without treatment in the streets. The administration is waiting for more ambulances and transport vehicles to be delivered to the capital after an emergency order was submitted to French and German automakers.

The news will all soon be behind me, but I know my part of the deal is not yet done. The large envelope Qadro handed me before I left him is secured to my lower back. I fake a scratch to periodically check that it is still in place and then lean back against the inside of the van and close my eyes as the news reports come in static spurts over the transistor.

It is an easy ride. After a few stops, the van picks up speed and we cruise forward in silence. I look at all the others who are seeking an escape from Baghdad, but I am too tired to wonder about their individual circumstances or reasons for leaving. We take the reverse cannonball run back to Jordan in stride. I can only assume it is not the first time for any of the others as well. There are no windows in the cargo space of the van, and since I was the last passenger on board, I am seated against the back doors and facing toward the front of the road. I am able to see bits of the country as it passes by.

Traipsing across stretches of marsh and desert lands that a week ago held so much promise, we pass the same plastic park benches outside Habbaniya, which remain unchanged and unused. But the green umbrellas are now scorched, frozen in a state of molten plastic suspension. Naked wires hang sadly over seats charred from explosives and riddled with bullets. The caviar plant is still open, but no caviar has been produced for weeks. Instead, rumor suggests the plant is manufacturing ricin and other chemicals to ship off to the war front in the south or to the Kurdish territory in the north.

The news report begins to come and go and I know it isn't the radio's fault but my own consciousness slipping. I catch a glimpse of light off the glasses of the Iraqi scientist while he dozes, and then I also succumb to the calming motion of the van.

In my dream, the lines of Iranian children come toward me, but they are not bound by ropes. Instead, there is a radiance emanating from inside them and I can make out the majestic wings of angels fanning across their backs. With the brilliant light I am able to see their young faces even from this far distance, and I can recognize their steely determination as one by one they evaporate like glowing smoke into the air.

I awake hours later. The van has stopped and the driver is talking to someone outside his window. The back door suddenly opens and I almost fall out but am caught by the arms of the man who had earlier led me into the warehouse hangar. The darkness of the desert flows like a silk cape trailing away behind us. Some of the others remain asleep. I make my way out of the car to stretch my legs and notice plumes of smoke rising from up ahead. A small man is standing on a milk crate, his dark head invisible underneath the raised hood. His motions are exaggerated as he works over the engine. His shoulders press back, inviting his elbows to do the same. He jerks his right hand forward and the van emits a hiss. I hear the rhythmic beat of a ratchet wrench. He steps back off the milk crate and is even shorter than I would have guessed. Off to the side of the road is an outpost looking like the many others I had driven past on the road connecting Baghdad to Basra.

"Oil," the man says with a high nasally pitch, and I recognize him almost immediately.

"Mahwi," I exclaim, and his face almost softens at the recognition.

"You made it back," he deadpans in perfect English.

We eat around a campfire while we wait for the van to be fixed; a leak in the oil reserve that needs to be plugged. Small pieces of sliced fish and another stringy meat I am told is camel sizzle over the flame. The others are anxious to get moving. I look around the site and everything seems the same. There is the same kitchen station surrounded by a group of tents, the same propane gas hookups and washing station. A shelved partition houses tools and gallons of machine oil. Sabawi sits on the back floor listening intently to the news flashes coming from an intercepted feed, and he follows the flashes of a red light across the machine with the tip of his index finger. Mahwi's bamboo spice rack hangs like a wind chime from off a chain linked to an overhead lamp. There are fewer animals than before when they had to be gathered and tied up behind the tarps to protect them from the sandstorms. I glance at the fire and hope this meal is not the reason why.

Mahwi doesn't ask me about my stay in Baghdad, keeping in line with the silence that has served him well. He invites no opening for conversation, and considering the circumstances, I can only respect his distance. As soon as we finish eating, we are told that the van is fixed and we gather up to say good-bye. I take Mahwi aside and offer him $400, leaving me with the same amount to get home, but he politely declines.

"There is no need for money out here," he says, looking out past the darkness as though the answer to life's riches lay somewhere within its depths.

But before we leave I fold the bills into a tin can anyway and leave it over the small tub in his kitchen when he is out taking one last look at the van.

As I get back in the cargo space, the stars illuminate the sky to the west ahead of us, but to the east there is a vacuous blackness stretching to infinity, unhealthy like an oil slick upon the ocean. If the Middle Eastern night sky is filled with the stars of the fallen, it is said to be the eyes of their loved ones that have closed to create such darkness. We leave the last outpost of civilization behind us, about to leave a storied land whose history overflows with violence and conquest but also with the lingering spirit of family and the feelings of hope we somehow find in each other. I am excited to be closer to the end; Amman is less than four hours away. I turn the radio on; no one else in the van seems to mind, and in fact the noise is welcomed instead of the silence. Seeing Mahwi and Sabawi has reenergized me. As we pull away, I can hear the small pebbles from the motion of our tires flung out against the road. I can't wait to touch down in London.

A new day rises behind us. In this ever-shrinking world there are corners that contain no new beginnings, areas with no fresh starts, just a series of concentric circles of light breaking and receding over time. These fractured arcs dim slightly until they eventually become darkened spaces, falling as shadows upon those we have known like the headlamps of an approaching train quickly speeding to catch up and then passing us by in the flash of a second, those shadows becoming memory and memory becoming stone.

An hour passes and everyone in the cargo space is asleep. The constant drone of the engine is almost hypnotic, and I find my eyelids are getting heavy again. I think of the outpost we have just passed and of Mahwi and how he lives outside of it all, in the darkened spaces. The van sounds fine as we pass stretches of land that haven't visibly changed since we left the outskirts of Baghdad the night before. Over the radio comes a report that the Iraqi government has recovered the remains of one of the suspected leaders of the Say ad Manood explosion. Officials are trying to identify the body and appear to have found a match with records obtained from the Ministry of Information's internal employee files. I listen intently but the report soon shifts to the overflow of patients and wounded soldiers arriving into Kut, a city southeast of the capital. I begin to doze, slipping into that void of unconsciousness once again, when a man's voice comes on the radio to proclaim, "Ibrahim Galeb al-Mansur is dead," and I can only wonder to myself who will be the next to follow in his footsteps.

Hassan Jaffa received the two packages in the mail around the same time. He would open neither of them. The thin envelope stamped with the red-and-black military crest of the Iraqi army along with the words *Allahu Akbar,* Arabic for "God is great," he knows to contain the standard government-issued death letter and its accompanying payment. His son had been the only member of the ICP identifiable after the attack. Some even called him the group's leader. Yet the government went ahead anyway and issued a check for $15,000, despite the fact his death did not come during battle nor was he a member of the republic's military. Hassan Jaffa understood his son had been killed in the capital while carrying out a terrorist attack against his own country. The letter would never be opened and the check never cashed. Jazeri, the deputy minister of information, did not have to lose as much sleep as he did during those first few months after privately erasing the transaction from all official records held in the treasury office. The check could be traced only upon its clearance. Jazeri had sent the payment despite his better judgment but in keeping in line with his promise.

The other package is a small box, thick and heavier than a ball-peen hammer, bearing a postmark from London, England. In another time, perhaps in another place, his curiosity would have gotten the better of him and he would have ripped open the package and anxiously gone through its contents. He noted the postmark as one might recognize a slight change in temperature and then forget about it as soon as his eyes passed it over. Not once did he wonder how the item had successfully made it through customs.

One night after the power in his home had been out for three days, for Hassan Jaffa forgot to not only pay his bills but also all basic tasks except those most primal, he broke out in a dizzying fever, the sweat draping down from his forehead, and thoughts of blood began to unravel within his head.

He took the two packages, tucking the thin one within the back of his pants and using both arms to carry the heavier box, out into the solitude of his courtyard. He no longer hears the sirens or the air raids, the emphasis of the war having shifted farther south with the death of his son. He kneels down and places both of the items on the ground in front of him. After a few moments of silence he rises and pulls a small container of kerosene he keeps to light the lanterns in his basement office from out of his jacket. It seems like more than a lifetime ago when Fazeera had pleaded with him that the fumes and the gas were too dangerous a combination to keep in their house, especially with a child. He patiently explained to her that their lighting provided better clarity and focus under which to examine his exhibits, much better than the scant illumination of the electric lights, whose ceaseless humming always seemed to break his concentration. She soon succumbed to his pleadings after two nights when he came to their bed with eyes as red and as bloodshot as a drunken mule's.

He pours the remaining kerosene left in the bottle over the top of the small pile, baptizing it with the thrust of negative energy he had fought for so many years to keep from their home. He stands up straight and strikes a match, and when the aroma of sulfur hits his nose, the smell almost makes him nauseous. He drops the match onto the mound and immediately the fluid catches. Before the first flame can rise up to meet him, the tears have already begun to flow freely down his cheeks.

⌄

Ibrahim Galeb al-Mansur counted the ambulances in his head and immediately he knew he was short by one. The gates had not risen within the last fifteen minutes because one of his men was missing. He drove back up the ramp to the ground-level security booth thinking of a reason to give the attendants for leaving the gates up. They would save valuable time if the last ambulance was able to drive through without having to stop. It was Omadan's vehicle—the last one to leave the bake shop—and Ibrahim glanced at his watch and knew he would not make it in time. All was quiet outside and there was no sign of the street sweeper nor anyone else coming down the road. For a spilt second he looked up past the roof of the building across the way, and Ibrahim could make out the light of the moon shining full over the horizon. Then the blast sent him suddenly catapulting against that same building, the force of the impact crushing the weight of his body and the frame of the windshield violently detaching from the vehicle and severing his head from below the neck. The explosives that were earlier loaded into the back cargo space somehow never went off.

⌄

Later the same night and several hours after the attack on the Say ad Manood Hospital, Yusuf al-Mahoudi no longer felt the need to perform his exercises. A welcoming calmness took hold of his soul, and he no longer felt the need for such discipline he had once thought served him so well. He was past such acts of self-control. When the overhead lights went on in the basement of the Sijn Al-Tarbut prison, the idea framing a sun had slowly begun its ascent from behind a clear purplish sky. He accepted the guards' entrance as one might accept an expired raffle ticket and did not struggle when they pulled him forcibly out of his cage. A group of six men led him outside and into the small, vacant playground, an area close enough to the facility so that the other prisoners would be able to hear the shots. Yusuf breathed in the coolness of the fresh air, the freshest air he ever recalled breathing, and smiled at the men as they lowered their rifles and fired until their weapons were empty.

On May 15, 1985, Daniella Burkett was awarded the Pulitzer Prize in journalism for her work detailing the chemical attack on the small village of Shiek Wiha Aan in northern Iraq. For two weeks her articles had concurrently run in both the London *Times* and *The New York Times* and helped bring to light the human rights and Geneva Convention violations committed by both the Iraqi and Iranian governments.

She would be unable to accept the award in person, recuperating from the birth of her first child, Johnathon Michael Young, who had been born in Airedale Hospital in London less than one month earlier. Her husband, Michael, would accept the award on her behalf. It was the last article she would ever write.

The Iran-Iraq War lasted almost eight years and is the longest conventional war of the twentieth century. More than 350,000 people were killed and over 650,000 people wounded. The economic cost to both sides was tremendous. A cease-fire was reached on August 20, 1988, ending the war in a stalemate.

ACKNOWLEDGMENTS

I would especially like to thank the following individuals: Sidney Offit, for his generosity, encouragement, and support and without whose influence this story would not have been possible; Peter Joseph, for his patience and dedication and for helping me along this journey; Thomas Dunne, for the opportunity; and to Marilyn, for being the calm within the storm and for always providing a smile.